The Cuckoo is
a Pretty Bird

The Cuckoo is a Pretty Bird

Ted Darling crime series

'Murderer? Or victim?'

LIVRES
LEMAS

L M Krier

Published by LEMAS LIVRES
www.tottielimejuice.com

© Copyright L.M.K. Tither 2020
Cover design DMR Creative
Cover photo Neil Smith

THE CUCKOO IS A PRETTY BIRD

ISBN 978-2901773-46-7

Contents

About the Author

L M Krier is the pen name of former journalist (court reporter) and freelance copywriter, Lesley Tither, who also writes travel memoirs under the name Tottie Limejuice. Lesley also worked as a case tracker for the Crown Prosecution Service.

The Ted Darling series of crime novels comprises: *The First Time Ever, Baby's Got Blue Eyes, Two Little Boys, When I'm Old and Grey, Shut Up and Drive, Only the Lonely, Wild Thing, Walk on By, Preacher Man, Cry for the Bad Man, Every Game You Play, Where the Girls Are, Down Down Down*

All books in the series are available in Kindle and paperback format and are also available to read free with Kindle Unlimited.

Contact Details

If you would like to get in touch, please do so at:

https://www.teddarlingcrimeseries.uk/

tottielimejuice@gmail.com

facebook.com/LMKrier

facebook.com/groups/1450797141836111/

twitter.com/tottielimejuice

For a lighter look at Ted and Trev, why not join the fun in the We Love Ted Darling group?

FREE 'Ted Darling is billirant' badge for each member.

Discover the
DI Ted Darling series

If you've enjoyed meeting Ted Darling you may like to discover the other books in the series. All books are available as ebooks and in paperback format. Watch out for audio-book versions, coming soon:

The First Time Ever
Baby's Got Blue Eyes
Two Little Boys
When I'm Old and Grey
Shut Up and Drive
Only the Lonely
Wild Thing
Walk on By
Preacher Man
Cry for the Bad Man
Every Game You Play
Where the Girls Are
Down Down Down
The Cuckoo is a Pretty Bird

Acknowledgements

I would just like to thank the people who have helped me bring Ted Darling to life.

Beta readers: Jill Pennington, Kate Pill, Karen Corcoran, Jill Evans, Alison Sabedoria, Emma Heath, Alan Wood, Hilary Battersby, and The Dalek, for editing assistance.

Police consultants – The Three Karens.

Police dog information – Police Dog Quest and his handler.

Colourful language consultant – @Menarms1 on Twitter

Medical advisor – Jo Baines

Makaton advisor – Chris Flounders

And a very special thanks to all Ted's loyal friends in the We Love Ted Darling Facebook group. Always so supportive and full of great ideas to be incorporated into the next Ted book. FREE 'Ted Darling is billirant' badge for all members.

To Hilary

who has helped me so much in so many ways
with the Ted books

Author's Note

Thank you for reading the Ted Darling crime series. The books are set in Stockport and Greater Manchester in general, and the characters use local dialect and sayings.

Seemingly incorrect grammar within quotes reflects common speech patterns. For example, 'I'll do it if I get chance', without an article or determiner, is common parlance.

Ted and Trev also have an in-joke between them - 'billirant' - which is a deliberate 'typo'.

If you have any queries about words or phrases used, do please feel free to get in touch, using the contact details in the book. I always try to reply promptly to any emails or Facebook messages.

Thank you.

Chapter One

'Nuh nuh nuh? What's that supposed to mean, you fat retarded slag? Shut yer gob and get me another beer before I slap you one.'

The youth, lounging in a tilted wooden kitchen chair, his booted feet up on the table, shouted the words. His tone was harsh, aggressive.

The young woman tried again to articulate something in reply. It was sounds, rather than words. Her efforts served only to enrage the boy. He sprang to his feet with enough force to send the chair crashing backwards onto the kitchen tiles.

The woman didn't react to the loud sound but her face screwed up in fearful anticipation as he took the couple of strides which brought him close to her. He put his face so near to her ear that she could feel the heat of his breath on her cheek. Smell the rancid mix of beer and tobacco.

His mouth was right up against one of the powerful hearing aids she wore. She tried to recoil from the touch of his lips against her earlobe but there was nowhere for her to move to.

His voice was staccato now. Excruciatingly painful through the amplification.

'Get. Me. A. Beer. You. Fucking. Stupid. Bitch.'

Burning tears sprang to her eyes. She cringed as she turned, one hand going to the fridge door, the other to the nearby drawer for the bottle opener.

When she whirled back to face him, with surprising speed, it was with a different implement in her hand. A long steel kitchen knife. Which she plunged with little effort into his scrawny chest. In between two ribs. Right up to the hilt.

The expression on his face slid from anger to bewildered surprise. He looked from her to his hands, cupped instinctively to the front of his T-shirt, either side of the protruding weapon. Blood was seeping freely through his fingers.

He opened his mouth to speak but blood was already filling it, leaking out between his lips and down his nose, dripping steadily to the floor.

His eyes were already becoming unfocused as his legs slowly buckled. He sank first to his knees then into an untidy heap, face down.

He didn't move again.

The young woman looked at him for a moment. Mild curiosity on her face. No more than that.

Then she shut the drawer and went to put the kettle on.

'Hello, Abigail, my darling. Daddy and I are just going out to dinner with one of his boring friends so I thought I'd call my precious girl first to see how you are. Are you all right, sweetie?'

'Nuh, nuh ...'

Abigail looked at Mummy's smiling face on her phone and tried to make the right words come.

'Fabulous, darling, I'm so pleased you're managing. Daddy and I are very proud of how independent you are. Now, have you had something to eat today?'

'Tuh, tuh ... ee.'

'You've had your tea? Clever girl. Well done. Just remember not to eat too much. You know you have to be careful with your weight, poppet.'

Mummy suddenly turned away from the camera, so it was harder for Abigail to make out what she was saying. But she could tell that she was shouting, and she looked cross. Even from the side view she could see that her face looked scrunched up and not smiley any more.

'Oh, for god's sake, Frank, I'm coming. I'm talking to our daughter. Remember her? She's yours, as well as mine, although you'd never think it. Go and get the bloody car out and I'll be right there.'

Mummy was looking back at her now, all smiles again. Abigail was pleased. She didn't like it when Mummy shouted. It made her think she'd done something wrong.

'Sorry about that, darling. You know what a fuss silly Daddy makes about being on time. Sweetie, your hair looks a mess. Have you not washed it recently? Make sure you take proper care of yourself. Mummy's a bit busy at the moment but as soon as she can she'll take you into Wilmslow to that nice hairdresser and get it properly cut and styled for you, if you'd like that. Perhaps a facial and a manicure somewhere, too? And some new clothes? Anyway, I must dash now, sweetie. Love you.'

Abigail was still trying to articulate a response, 'Luh, luh ...' when Mummy disappeared.

She put her phone down on the table and stepped carefully past the figure on the floor. There was nasty sticky stuff round it now that she'd nearly slipped in a couple of times. It hadn't been there before. Not at first. The smell was bad, too, but she didn't know what to do about it.

She went to look in the cupboard under the sink. Mummy did most of her shopping for her online, although Abigail also had a generous allowance from her parents. The purchases were delivered to her door. It took her some time but she managed to read most of the words on the labels, except the very big ones, so she knew where to put most things. She found the bottle she was looking for. It had pictures of flowers on the front. Mummy had told her to put some down the plughole in the kitchen sink to make it smell nice.

It was hard to get the top off it but she was pleased with herself when she managed it. She poured out about half of the bottle, round and round where the boy was lying. That made the smell much better and she was pleased with herself again because she'd had a clever idea. Mummy would tell her what to do next when she saw her. She never came to the flat, but Abigail would try to make her understand what the problem was and Mummy would make it all better.

Abigail was smiling as she went to put the kettle on, stepping wider now to avoid the nice smelly stuff she'd just put down.

Detective Chief Inspector Ted Darling put a pint and a glass of whisky in front of Inspector Kevin Turner, as requested, then sat down opposite him with his Gunner.

'Not like you, that,' he told him, nodding to the Scotch which Kevin was knocking back as if he'd been waiting all day for the opportunity. 'Work problems or home stuff?'

Kevin put his now empty glass down on the table and smacked his lips in appreciation. He and Ted were having a quiet moment together at the end of another busy day for both of them.

'Both. First off, the missus and me have a special anniversary coming up and she's got some daft idea in her head she wants to go on a cruise round the Med. A bloody cruise! I ask you. Do I look like the cruising type?'

'Can't you appeal to her inner green? Tell her how environmentally unfriendly it is? Especially now you have a little granddaughter and you need to think about the planet's future, for her,' Ted suggested. 'Those big ships do a lot of polluting of the seas and oceans.'

Kevin scoffed. 'She doesn't care about any of that sort of stuff. Not her thing at all. She wants to do the damn cruise because one of her friends has been on one and not stopped raving about it ever since she got back.'

'And what do you want to do?'

'I'm not much good at holidays. I'd be happy with a week

in a guest house in Rhyl. Something like that. Or maybe even on the south coast, if she wanted to try somewhere new. But she won't hear of it. It's got to be the high seas or nothing. And apparently we have to dress up like a dog's dinner for evening meals. Black tie and all that shit. I spend my working life in uniform. I want to wear what the bloody hell I choose on my holidays.'

He pushed his empty whisky glass to the other side of the table and pulled the pint nearer to him before he spoke again.

'What about you and your Trev? What have you got planned in the way of holidays this year?'

Ted looked smug. Still pleased with his inspired idea of a surprise holiday for his partner.

'Trail-riding in Corsica.'

Kevin looked surprised. 'What, motorbikes? And where the bloody hell is Corsica, anyway? Is it somewhere in Italy?'

'Horses, believe it or not. That's Trev's other thing, and I can do it a bit, as long as it's on something safe and steady, with good brakes. And it's an island. Near to Italy, but I think it's French. They certainly speak French there.'

Kevin looked impressed. He picked up his pint for a long swallow.

'Anyway, I need to run something past you which you might not like, so I needed the Scotch to fortify me in case you decide to karate kick me round the room,' Kev went on when he'd had a drink.

Ted took a mouthful of his own drink then smiled at him. 'You know I'm very mild-mannered most of the time, Kev – until crossed.'

'Well, I just want to stress this wasn't my idea. You might have heard the rumours already. We both know we're ridiculously short of officers. One idea being mooted is sharing resources. Like we help you out when needed. So when Uniform has something big on, like these bloody "British jobs for British workers" rallies, which take up so much manpower,

I should ask for some of your CID officers to put uniforms back on and come and join us on the front line.'

He picked up his beer and took another gulp, watching Ted anxiously for his reaction.

'I had heard the suggestion. I don't see anything against it in principle,' Ted told him levelly. 'You know me. I think all police officers are equal, Uniform, CID and everyone else. I'd be up for it, as long as we weren't busier than you were.'

He sipped his Gunner again then grinned. 'Mind you, I think some of the team might need to get new uniforms issued. Virgil has bulked out so much with all the weight training I doubt he'd even fit in his now.'

Kevin gave an exaggerated 'Phew' and took another mouthful of his pint. 'I should have known you'd be reasonable about it. And your Jezza in her battledress would be worth two of any other officers. I don't know what she does to the enemy but there are times when she frightens me.'

Ted laughed his agreement. DC Jessica 'Jezza' Vine had joined his team on a last chance basis. She'd proved a challenge but was now a valued member of the unit. Even so, Ted understood what Kevin meant. There were times when she was definitely scary.

He was about to reply when both men's mobile phones went off at the same time. As they reached for them, looking at the screens then exchanging glances, Kevin said, 'If the nick is calling us both at once about something, it's not likely to be good news. And I'm bloody off duty. I handed over to Irene, so it must be something big if they're calling me as well.'

'Off duty. I remember those days,' Ted told him, as he picked up his own call.

'Eric Morgan here, guv,' the Uniform sergeant told him. 'I know it's already been called in but I'm here on a case as a first responder. I've got a young probationer with me who's not stopped puking since we got here and this is clearly going to be a kid glove job for so many reasons, so I thought I'd call you direct, if that's ok?'

'Yes, go ahead, Eric. What have you got?'

'Neighbours phoned in reporting a bad smell coming from a flat. The resident opened the door to us with no problem, after a couple of rings of the doorbell. That's when it started to get a bit complicated.

'The flat occupant is a young woman, early to mid-twenties, I'd say. But she seems to be non-verbal, apart from a few sounds. She's also very deaf, even with hearing aids, and at a guess, she's learning disabled.

'All of that's tricky enough. Then we come to the source of the smell. One very dead body. Several days, at least, I would say. We haven't touched it to check for cause of death but there's a lot of blood. And, get this, the place reeks of that very flowery disinfectant stuff. It looks like it's been poured all round the floor in an attempt to hide the smell, but the body's just been left there.'

'Do we have an ID on the young woman?'

'You know when you think a case can't possibly get any worse? I may be wrong on this, Ted,' Sergeant Morgan slipping into informality let Ted know he was on his own and couldn't be overheard, 'but I've found documents which suggest the young woman is Abigail Buller. And if I'm right, she's the daughter of a Cheshire County Councillor. One of those "the police have plenty of resources, it's just bad management if they can't use them efficiently" types.

'If that is who she is, I happen to know that she was left disabled after some preventable childhood illness or another because the parents were trendy campaigners against vaccines with the supposed dangers of them. She's at least early twenties now, I'm pretty sure, but not functioning at that level. So anything to do with the councillor's daughter is going to be one big prickly hot potato. Especially as, at the moment, she looks like being your prime suspect for a possible murder.'

Ted let out a low groan and looked longingly at Kevin's

empty whisky glass. He'd never been a whisky drinker but right now he could really fancy something a bit stronger than his habitual Gunner. The job was hard enough these days, without politics coming into it.

Eric Morgan was still talking. 'Now, I know us humble Woodentops are supposed to do all the initial legwork and only call on the mighty CID to ride to the rescue on their white chargers if we get out of our depth. But I'm telling you now, Ted. This is way above my pay-grade. As soon as there's any hint of politics, I'm passing the buck. And I've not even told you all of the bad news yet.'

He paused, while Ted inwardly groaned once more.

'I happen to know Doug's gone off on sick leave. So you won't have him as Crime Scene Manager. So all in all, I can't wait to hand this one over.' He paused, then added an ironic, 'Guv.'

Kevin was just finishing up his call, making a rueful face at Ted, who guessed he had probably been told most of the same facts.

'I'll come over myself, Eric. At least to do an initial assessment. Do we know if this Abigail signs, if she's deaf? Do I need to arrange a sign language interpreter?'

'I have tried to engage with her but I'm not getting very far. I've requested a female officer and Susan Heap's on her way, in case Abigail relates better to a woman. I'll hold the fort until you get here but seriously, this is definitely one for you.'

'Thanks, Eric, I'll be there as soon as I can.'

'Right you are, Ted. At least you know I won't puke on your crime scene while I'm waiting for you to turn up.'

'Well, that all sounds like a lot of fun,' Kev commented as Ted ended his call. 'That was Irene, just giving me the heads-up on what was going on as I'm back in tomorrow. Who are you sending?'

'I think I'd better go myself, initially. Maybe a bit of rank might pacify Councillor Buller, at least. I take it Irene mentioned that's who seems to be the father of our presumed suspect?'

'Does that mean you'll owe your Trev another holiday? Picking up something like this just before the weekend?'

'I'll get away with it this evening. He's gone out on a social night with some of his English students. He'll be late back himself. And feeling mellow, with any luck.'

Kev drained his pint then stood up.

'I'm going to escape while I can. Good luck with it all.'

Ted's phone rang again. DC Jezza Vine calling him.

'Boss, you've heard, I take it? There's just me left in, so do you want me to go straight round?'

'I'm going to go myself, Jezza, given the political sensitivity around who the potential suspect seems to be. I'm round at The Grapes at the moment, but if you get my service car, you can pick me up on the way.'

'Well, from the few details I've heard so far, it looks like this one is going to be a barrel of laughs. A several days old corpse could turn out to be the least of our worries. I'll see you in five minutes, boss.'

Chapter Two

'You've got the address?' Ted asked, as he slid into the passenger seat of his service vehicle next to Jezza, at the wheel.

She turned to him and rolled her eyes theatrically.

'No, boss, I'm going to do it all telepathically, reading your thought processes as I drive.'

Ted suppressed a smile. He was used to Jezza by now, but he could see why some senior officers in the past had found her hard to manage.

'I walked right into that one,' he conceded. 'Have you got cover for Tommy? Or I suppose you're going to tell me you just let him roam the streets alone at night when you're on a shout?'

It was Jezza's turn to smile at the boss's humour. Her autistic younger brother, who had lived with her since they were both orphaned, could present her with problems from time to time.

'Nat's taken him to a quiz night,' she told him. 'He'll no doubt be the youngest team member there and I wouldn't be surprised to hear he's thrashed everyone. Nat's a great influence on him. They've really hit it off. It's even working out now Nat's moved in and I was worried it might not.'

Ted was looking at her shrewdly.

'And are you all right, though, Jezza? Is everything all right with you? Only, I don't mean to sound personal or intrude on your private life, but you're looking a bit tired.'

Jezza shrugged. 'You know what Tom can be like with his

endless questions. Usually in the middle of the night. You perhaps can't imagine how much worse that's been with a quiz coming up and him wanting to be perfect. But I'm fine, thank you. Thanks for asking, boss.'

They drove the rest of the short distance in companionable silence. Their destination was a converted former mill, red brick, now containing expensive private apartments. As Ted and Jezza both knew, violent crime, if that was what this case turned out to be, was no respecter of wealth or of status.

There was a marked police vehicle in front of the building, plus vehicles from the Crime Scene Investigation team, who were just setting up. The young probationer had been relegated to the main entrance, checking the identity of anyone arriving, turning away all but verified residents. He still looked pale. Ted knew him by sight, had seen him around the station a time or two, although he was new. He clearly knew exactly who Ted was and snapped to attention at the sight of a senior officer arriving.

Ted produced his identity, for form's sake, and spoke quietly to him.

'Stuart, isn't it? No need for that, but thank you. Are you all right now?'

'Yes, sir, thank you, sir. I'm sorry I threw up on the scene, sir.'

'You're not the first, and you won't be the last.'

The flat was on the first floor. Ted and Jezza opted for the stairs rather than the lift. As they fell into step side by side, Ted asked, 'Does it make me sound ancient if I say I wonder if his mam knows he's going to be out late tonight?'

'Positively antediluvian, boss.'

They'd reached the first floor landing. In the hallway to their left, they could see PC Jack Hargreaves standing guard over a front door. Clearly their potential crime scene.

'Guv, Jezza,' he greeted them. 'CSI have just arrived and are setting up. I should warn you, it smells bad. I mean really

L M KRIER

bad. You can probably get a whiff from here but it's much worse inside. Susan's with the young lady. She's taken her into the lounge, but that's about all I can tell you for now. Oh, and Sergeant Morgan has left. He got called away on an urgent shout. He left Stuart behind, but outside so he shouldn't throw up any more.'

Ted signed them both in, then reached for his Fisherman's Friends. Jack hadn't been wrong about the smell. No wonder neighbours had reported the incident. He offered Jezza a lozenge but she shook her head, a hint of scorn at the mere suggestion she would need one.

They both put on gloves and shoe covers from the box outside the apartment. Ted paused before going in to have a close look at the front door from both sides. He'd noticed the glass spy hole in the wood which would give a clear view of anyone outside. There were solid security bolts and a safety chain on the inside.

He pulled the door towards him with a gloved hand to check the angle of coverage from the viewer. A voice, female, which he didn't recognise, bellowed from the interior, 'Don't touch anything on my crime scene!'

Jezza, like all of Ted's team members, knew of his fondness for the film *Blazing Saddles*. She'd watched it a couple of times, to analyse his fascination with it. She paraphrased a line from it now, under her breath, so only the boss could hear her.

'Boy, is she strict.'

Ted once again had to hide his amusement as he weighed up the woman walking towards them. He couldn't see much of her behind the coveralls and mask, just intensely dark eyes, which looked angry. Ted was short, but she was smaller. He put her at about five feet two.

'I'm Priya Chowdhury, the Crime Scene Manager. And you are?'

'DCI Ted Darling, from Stockport. I'm here to find out if

12

this is a case for us.'

'Well, you should know better than to come trampling in without liaising with me first. One of your Woodentops has already thrown up all over everywhere, which only goes to make our job harder.'

Ted's voice was even quieter than usual when he replied to her. Jezza was looking from one to another. Like a spectator at a tennis match. Waiting for the boss's next volley.

'I'm sorry if one of our officers made your job more difficult. He's young, on his first sudden death, and this is clearly a gruesome one to start on. But perhaps you would please refer to Uniform officers in a more respectful manner. Especially as, if this does turn out to be a case for us, I'm likely to be the SIO on it, so we may well have to work together. A bit of mutual courtesy would help, in that case, Ms Chowdhury.

'So what can you tell me about it so far, please?'

She was quiet for a moment, eyeing him up, still bristling and hostile. Then she went on, 'Not a lot at this stage. An as yet unidentified male person dead in the kitchen. Face down. No visible wounds to the rear. The body has been there for a few days at least and we haven't yet touched it at all. The coroner's office are sending out a pathologist to view the body in situ, then we might be able to give you a better idea of whether or not we're dealing with a homicide here.

'The only other person present is a young woman who appears to be the main occupant of the flat. She's in that room there with another of your officers.'

'Thank you, Ms Chowdhury. We'll go and talk to them shortly. First I would just like to view the body, even if only from a distance. I imagine you have stepping plates out already. If not, just tell me where it's safe to stand, please.'

His polite manner seemed to unsettle her. He wondered if her brittle exterior was born of having to deal with too many old-school macho types who no doubt had made jibes about her gender, her height and her ethnicity, when they thought they could get away with it.

He followed her to just inside the kitchen, Jezza at his heels, stepping where they were told to. The smell became overpowering the nearer they got to where the body lay. Ted heard Jezza give a groan and a retch as she pivoted on her feet and bolted for the open front door. He was glad of the strong menthol smell and taste of his lozenge. It helped a bit.

'Based on your experience, Ms Chowdhury, could you please give me at least an estimate of how long the body's been here?'

'You'll need to ask the pathologist that,' she said stiffly, then, seemingly mollified somewhat by his manners, if nothing else, she said grudgingly, 'but if I have to take a guess, I would say between five and seven days.'

Ted went first to find Jezza, who was taking deep breaths of the cleaner air outside the front door. Wordlessly, he offered her a lozenge, which this time, she accepted gratefully.

'Sorry, boss, but the smell was something else in there. Especially with that flowery smell on top of it. How could someone just leave the body lying there in that state?'

'That's what we need to try to establish. So if you're up to going back in, we should go and talk to the occupant.'

Ted stood aside to let her go in first. They both headed to the open door which revealed a bright living room which should have been airy and pleasant. Instead it was in a state of dirty disarray. PC Susan Heap was standing near the door. A young woman was sitting on the sofa, her face placid, expressionless. Ted greeted them both, but only Susan replied to him.

'Boss, this is the occupant of the flat. I think it's Abigail Buller, but I'm not having much luck communicating with her.'

'Sign language?'

'I only know "hello, my name is Susan", but that didn't get

all that much of a reaction and I didn't understand what she was trying to say in reply. I think there may be some comprehension issues, not just the hearing difficulties. It's just possible my uniform intimidated her, of course.'

Jezza stepped forward, walked over to where the young woman was sitting. She made a gesture like a brief sideways wave, then three more rapid hand movements as she said distinctly, 'Hello, my name is Jezza,' drawing a letter J on the palm of her hand with one finger as she said it.

The young woman's face broke into a beaming smile as she returned the wave and repeated the hand movements, speaking indistinctly as she replied, 'A-a-a-b-b-b-i,' touching her thumb as she made the A sound.

'Do you need some help?' Jezza asked her, putting one hand under her other one which was closed into a fist, lifting it and moving both towards Abi.

Again the broad smile, this time with an enthusiastic nod of the head, a closed fist held up and tipped forward as she did so. She repeated Jezza's hand-lifting gesture, then put her flat hand to her chin and moved it forward and down, at the same time saying what sounded like 'ep, ease.' Then she moved her right hand to her left shoulder and made a brushing gesture with her middle finger.

'You need the toilet? Okay, we can arrange that for you.'

She looked to Ted for instruction.

'Susan, please could you take Abi to the bathroom, and stay with her?'

Once they were alone, Ted turned to Jezza.

'I didn't know you knew sign language.'

'That was Makaton, boss. A simplified form. And as that's about the sum total of what I do know, it's not going to get us very far in a potential suspect interview.

'Long story short, Tommy wanted to try riding. But because of his special needs and tendency to meltdowns when things don't go how he expects, only the local Riding for the

Disabled group would take him. I went with him a few times, hence learning the Makaton basics, which some of the riders and helpers use. Tommy soon got bored. Being Tom, he thought he'd be galloping and jumping in the first lesson and when he wasn't, he quickly lost interest. But I kept going for a bit, as a helper.'

'Well, it's helped us already. At least she got to go to the bathroom when she needed to. I'll give the station a quick ring, see if they can find us someone who knows more Makaton. We're going to have to jump through hoops to do any kind of PACE-compliant interview with her in the circumstances. I don't suppose your horsey Makaton runs to issuing a caution, should we need to.

'I'm also going to phone one or other of the bosses for some guidance on this. Can you please see if there's anything else at all you can get out of her, but carefully, of course. In the meantime, get Susan to film anything she might say on her body-cam, please. But Jezza, if she happens to say anything incriminatory, stop straight away.'

Jezza looked uncertain. 'Boss, I'm a bit uncomfortable with the whole idea of that. I really don't know enough Makaton to understand if she suddenly confesses to a murder. It's not something which came up in RDA sessions, funnily enough. And her speech is so indistinct I'm not sure I'd know from that. Are you sure we shouldn't just take her straight to the nick, then wait for a proper Makaton person? And while we're on that subject, should we not get her checked out by the doctor before we ask her anything? We really don't want to get this one wrong.'

'We, or more precisely, you, Jezza, are still going to have to try to explain to her that we need to take her to the station, though.'

Jezza sighed.

'I know the sign for home, which is the same as house. So I should be able to check that this is her home. And then I suppose if I point to Susan's uniform and say we need to take her to the police house she should understand. I can look online for some more signs which might help. I just don't want to find myself deep in the shit if I get it wrong.'

'You won't, Jezza, I promise you that. I'm the senior officer, so it's my neck on the block if I've got it wrong. I'll go and make the calls. Just do whatever you can, please.'

Ted stood aside in the hallway to allow Susan and Abigail to return to the living room. Susan spoke quietly to him as they passed.

'Sir, we need to be so careful here. She's not functioning at adult level at all.'

'I know, Susan, thank you. I'm on it.'

He stepped out onto the landing and found a quiet corner. Luckily there was no one around. Not even curious faces looking out of the doors of their own flats. Hopefully at this time on a Friday evening, the people likely to occupy apartments in the price-range of the building were probably all out enjoying end of the week drinks and meals with friends and colleagues.

He phoned Superintendent Jim Baker first. He had plenty of experience in murder cases, and if this was one, it would come under his remit as Head of Serious Crime.

Big Jim listened in silence as Ted outlined what he knew, as succinctly as he could. Then he growled, 'Bloody hell, Ted. That's all we need. I know that twat Buller. I've seen him in action on a few committees and he's a nasty piece of work. It would have to be his bloody daughter. For god's sake be careful how you handle it.'

'That's why I'm phoning you first, boss,' Ted told him dryly. 'At the moment we're a bit stuck as we have no clue as to the cause of death or identity of the victim. Jezza's made some sort of connection, but I favour taking Abigail to the nick as soon as we can, if we can get her to understand what we're doing and why. Jezza's just seeing if she can get anything from her to help us ID the victim.'

'Have her parents been informed?'

'That's tricky, Jim. She's clearly of age, she apparently lives independently, so is there any reason why we would inform them?'

'Stop right there, Ted. Don't start with the positive discrimination shit on top of everything else. You're just making a rod that's going to come back and beat you at some point. With all the comings and goings there, they'll probably get to hear of it soon anyway. It might be politically expedient to let them know first. As a courtesy, if nothing else.'

'Since when have you known me to be politically expedient, Jim?' then, before the Big Boss could cut in, Ted went on, 'Can we compromise on this? She clearly can't stay here, with CSI all over the place. The smell is dire, for one thing. There's a pathologist on the way because with the position the body's in, we can't get any idea of a cause of death so we really don't know what we're dealing with. Failing to report a death, clearly, but that might be the extent of it.

'Let's get her to the station as soon as we can, then once we've got someone to communicate properly with her, we'll sort her out a solicitor and inform the parents. Are you happy with that?'

'I'm not happy with anything involving Buller. Watch yourself, Ted. He's a seriously nasty piece of work. He'll be gunning for you from the start. And you know as well as I do there have been SIOs who've been thrown to the wolves by the top brass for the slightest mistake, to avoid any shit flying their way. We wouldn't want to lose you. God knows you can be a bolshie little sod, but you're bloody good at your job.'

Ted chuckled. 'Thanks, Jim. I love you too.'

Chapter Three

Jack Hargreaves was finishing a call on his radio when Ted went back into the flat.

'Sorry, sir, we're going to have to leave you to it. All three of us. It's all kicking off in the town centre and they need all available units.'

For a fleeting moment, Ted hoped Trev's social night out hadn't got out of hand, then pulled himself up short for even thinking it.

'It's fine, Jack. There really isn't a lot we can do here until we at least have a clue as to the cause of death.'

Jack called for Susan and the two of them hurried away down the stairs. Ted went to see how Jezza was getting on with Abigail, who was still sitting smiling serenely.

Jezza turned her face towards him so Abigail wouldn't be able to follow what she said.
'I didn't want to carry on until you were back in the room, boss. I know you said to record it, but I'm so worried about getting it wrong on this one.'

'That's fine, Jezza. We can't really make much progress for the moment. Can you at least try to find out a name for the victim? That would be a helpful starting point.'

Jezza had put the waiting time to good use, searching on her mobile for any words and signs which might help her to at least try to communicate with their only witness so far to what had happened in the apartment.

'Abi,' she began, facing her and speaking clearly, 'Who,'

holding up an index finger and making a circle with it, then she went on, miming stroking a beard, 'Who man in there?' pointing towards the kitchen.

Abigail laughed delightedly and clapped her hands in evident amusement. She shook her head, made a negative gesture with her hand, then used one finger to stroke her chin as she stuttered, 'Nuh-nuh-nuh man. Buh-boy.'

Jezza glanced at Ted again. 'She has some cognitive skills then, if she's aware of the difference.' Then she turned back to Abigail, made a circling motion with her fist to her chest and said, 'Sorry. Who boy?'

Once more, Abigail signed as she tried to speak. 'Ah-ah-tti.'

Jezza looked puzzled and asked her to repeat it. Once she had, with a different hand gesture, Jezza spoke to Ted, with Abigail's gaze glued to her face.

'Well, she has me stumped there. She's signing the word for coffee, so I don't know what "atty" can be.'

Abigail made a small sound of frustration, sensing she hadn't been understood, then repeated the sound, but said, 'Luh-luh-luh ...' in front of it, distinctly, this time.

'Latte,' Ted and Jezza said in unison.

Abigail smiled from one to another, pleased that she'd made them understand. Happy that she'd been able to help the nice lady who was being kind to her.

'Is that a name or a nickname?' Ted asked Jezza.

'Boss, seriously? I'm already at the limit of what I can ask her. Can we please think about getting her to the station now and me handing over to someone who does know what they're doing? Sorry to keep repeating myself, but I really am so worried I'm going to convey the wrong meaning to her.'

'Yes, sorry, Jezza. You're doing a great job. And please don't worry. You know I'm here to head off any flak which might come your way. Show me how to thank her, can you, please.'

Jezza made the gesture and Ted copied it, speaking directly to the young woman. 'Thank you, Abigail.'

Abi signed and stuttered. Jezza interpreted.

'She said she likes you, boss. But she's already told me she loves me. I get two hands over the heart. You only got one.'

'Right, well, if you can explain to her that we want to take her to the station, I'll just go and have a word with the CSM before we leave. Whatever happens, and whatever the cause of death turns out to be, we can't leave Abigail here, with the state this place is in. She's going to need a place of safety, and that might well involve the parents. And I really only want to involve them if it becomes essential.'

'Mind she doesn't bite you, boss,' Jezza said to his retreating back, as Ted went to find the Crime Scene Manager. Then she concentrated her efforts on telling Abigail they needed to take her to the station. Although after her declaration of love, she had a feeling Abi would be quite happy to go anywhere with her.

Ted stood just outside the open door to the kitchen, where the CSI team were concentrating their efforts. No attempt had been made to move the body or reposition it until the arrival of the pathologist. Ted hoped it was going to be Professor Bizzie Nelson, but suspected one of her assistants might be sent, at least in the first instance, until it became clear if the death was suspicious.

'Ms Chowdhury, we're going to get out of your way now. Thank you for your help.'

She glared at him, clearly suspecting he was being sarcastic. She saw no trace of it in his expression, but she didn't respond.

'Perhaps if you come across anything at all which might help us, you'd be kind enough to let me know. I'll leave you my direct number, just in case.'

'I don't know how you're used to working with your usual CSM – Doug, isn't it? – but I don't do guesswork. I do science.

I've made a concession in giving you a very approximate timeline for how long the body has been in place, but that's as far as it goes. And since Doug seems to have been careless enough to put his back out tripping over a cat, I personally wouldn't set much store by his powers of observation.'

'Ms Chowdhury, have I done something to offend you? Apart from not introducing myself right at the beginning, for which I have already apologised. Doug is an excellent CSM and we get on well. I also have cats, including one which he gave me. As I said before, if you and I are going to be working together, it would help if we could at least be civil.'

She finally pulled down her mask so he could see more of her face. There was a flash of something different in her eyes now. The slightest twitch at the corner of her mouth.

'This is me being civil. You should avoid me on a bad day. Look, I'm sorry if I was a bit sharp. Call it an automatic defence weapon. You'd be surprised, in this day and age, how many cavemen SIOs I encounter who insist on calling me "love" or "darling" and talking to me as if I were still at school.'

Ted gave her his most disarming grin. 'Imagine what it's like for me actually being called Darling. Not to mention being a skinny little runt and living with another man. And seven cats.'

'Seven?' she almost smiled at that. 'Well, since you've at least been polite, I will say that if I do happen to find anything useful, I'll give you a call.'

As Ted reached the still-open front door, she called after him.

'Carnivorous plants.'

Ted turned and looked back at her as she stood framed in the kitchen doorway, still with her mask pulled down.

'Sorry?'

'It's what I keep. No cats. No domestic animals. But I have a collection of carnivorous plants. Whenever I feed them, I think of whichever misogynist I've had a run-in with most recently. You can join up the dots about my thinking for yourself.'

Despite the grim circumstances surrounding them, Ted chuckled.

'I can understand that.'

Then as he turned again to go, she added, 'And a knife wound from the front. If I had to make any kind of an educated guess, based on my observations of the scene, that would be it. It would fit with the large quantity of blood. And also with a drawer standing open. One which contained various utensils, including some good quality kitchen knives.'

Jezza was standing outside the car, Abigail safely installed in the back seat, when Ted came out of the building.

'Sorry, boss, I thought the smell was bad enough in the flat, but it's clinging to Abi, too. To her clothes, at least. I didn't fancy it at close quarters until I had to. How can she be on her own like that, when she clearly can't manage?'

'I'm trying not to jump to any conclusions until we have all the facts. Perhaps if I drive and you sit in the front passenger seat it might not be too bad. As long as you can turn round so she can see your face and your hands if you have to communicate with her on the way. Does she understand where we're taking her, do you think?'

'I did my best, boss. I think she understands we're taking her to the station, although I'm not sure she has any idea of what's going on, really. I just hope they've found us a proper interpreter for her.'

'Ms Chowdhury thawed enough to tell me there's a possibility that the victim died as a result of a knife wound to the front. Do you think Abigail understands that this Latte, whoever he is, is dead?'

'I honestly don't know. Sometimes I think she doesn't understand much at all. Yet she differentiated between man and boy, so there's clearly some comprehension there.

'Boss, speculating here, which I know you don't like, but if he died from a knife wound, and if it was Abi who stabbed him, should we at least consider the possibility that she's another victim in this? That she might have been assaulted by him? Raped, even? So should we arrange a medical examination to cover that possibility?'

'I think the only answer with this one is to cover all bases from the beginning. But I can't see how we can proceed to anything like that if we can't find a proper interpreter for her.

'One thing which did strike me at the scene was that spyhole in the door. Sergeant Morgan said she opened up to them reasonably quickly. She must have been able to see that it was the police outside her door, yet she let them in willingly enough. Not the normal reaction of a guilty person at a murder scene, but that could just be her limited comprehension.

'Then again, she seemed reluctant to talk to Susan, in her uniform, but you made a connection with her instantly. There's clearly a lot about her we don't yet fully understand.'

'If the body has been there long enough to be in that state, that must surely mean that no one has been to the flat in all that time. Is she just there by herself, expected to manage?'

'If the case is one for us, we'll need to look into all aspects of it. For now, we should get her to the station, at least.'

A man with a dog was walking past. The dog went to sniff at something and the man jerked it back to heel with a savage yank of the lead. He snapped something at it in a language which wasn't English.

He turned into a side street and took out his phone to make a call. This time he spoke in English which was heavily accented.

'The police are here. And I can't see any of our friends.'

'Damn!' a man's voice replied. 'This is a disaster waiting to happen. Find them, Ivan. Find me an expendable one who'll talk. Above all, find me the Chosen One. I don't want to lose

that one.

'Yes, Mr Beeg.'

Ted drove while Jezza sat in the front, turning occasionally to reassure Abi and try to keep her informed of what was happening, as best she could, with help from gestures she researched on her mobile phone.

'Did you manage to make her understand that she's not under arrest?'

'Boss, at the risk of repeating myself, the vocabulary for that wasn't something which tended to come up, leading children round an indoor school on hairy ponies. I've tried my best, but the sign for police did strike me as looking a bit like putting the first handcuff on.'

'Sorry, Jezza, I'm asking a lot of you and I appreciate your efforts. As long as we do our best ...'

He was interrupted by his mobile phone ringing. He put it on speaker, hoping Abigail really couldn't hear much. The frosty tones of Superintendent Debra Caldwell, the Ice Queen.

'Chief Inspector. I imagine that at some point you were going to inform me personally that you were bringing in Councillor Buller's daughter.'

'Ahh. Ma'am, sorry, I can't talk now. I'm driving and I have the person in question in the car.'

Ted opted for the formality in response to her opener.

It was an excuse and a lame one, but he wanted to buy himself some time.

'I see. Well, I'm also driving. On my way to the station. So we'll talk there shortly.'

'Ouch,' Jezza said, half under her breath. 'Now you know why I'm not interested in climbing the ranks and having to deal with cases like this.'

Wherever the incident which had taken the Uniform officers away was happening, there was nothing on Ted's drive back to the station to delay them. If anything, the streets were quieter than normal for a Friday evening.

Once they'd arrived and parked, Jezza opened the door to let Abigail out and started to explain to her, her hands working to put in the words she knew.

'Abi, this is the police house. We work here. We want to talk to you in there. Give you a cup of tea or coffee. Would you like that?'

Abigail signed and spoke. 'Es p'ease,' then made another gesture.

'Toilet? You need the loo again? Okay, we can do that too.'

'Jezza, can you please take Abi to the ladies then take her to the vulnerable witness room. I'll go and report in. See where we're up to on that interpreter, and a doctor.'

He turned to Abigail so she could clearly see his lips and did his best with some accompanying gestures, which he hoped would make sense. 'Abigail, can you go in there with Jezza? Thank you.'

The main entrance was closed by this time on a Friday evening. The days of a front-desk presence round the clock were long gone. Another visible face of the cuts. Ted used his pass card to let them in at the side entrance then left Jezza to see to Abigail while he went in search of Irene, the Duty Inspector, and to find where the Ice Queen was.

He found them both in a buzzing Control room, carefully monitoring a lively situation in the town centre. CCTV screens showed two groups of largely middle-aged men engaged in violent confrontation, hurling any missiles they could lay hands on at one another.

'What's kicked it off this time?' Ted asked them.

'Who knows,' Irene replied. 'Football? Religion? Politics? One half of the town seems to permanently hate the other at the moment. It's just the reason why that varies, and sometimes old adversaries become allies. All I know is it's stretching our available officers to the limit, which is why I had to pull three back off your case, Ted.

'And before you bloody ask, your Macaroon interpreter, or whatever it's called, has been the last thing on my mind, funnily enough, but I have tried. The best I've found you to date is a young lass from a local care home who's got some Brownie badge in it or something. But it's better than bugger all and she's on her way. Plus the doc should be here in,' she glanced at the time, 'ten minutes or so. But as you can see, we've been a bit busy in here.'

'Makaton. And thank you. Any officers injured?'

'I've got one young PC at Stepping Hill having his scalp stitched back to his head. Lots of blood, but I'm told it's not serious. Not one of our brightest, so it might even improve him. If I had water cannon at my disposal, I'd be giving the order to use them right about now. Only joking, ma'am,' Irene added hastily in the Ice Queen's direction, knowing how formal she could be.

The Superintendent surprised both Irene and Ted by a brief smile and a quiet, 'I might even sign off on it, Inspector.'

Then she looked at Ted and said, 'I think perhaps we should find somewhere quiet while you fill me in on the potential case involving Councillor Buller's daughter.'

She led the way to her office, nodded for Ted to sit down and went to her coffee machine. It always seemed to be on. Her first reflex action on entering the room must have been to set it in motion. Ted would normally avoid coffee in the evening but he had a feeling it could be a long night and he might well be glad of it.

'Tell me what we're facing so far,' she instructed, as she put delicate floral mugs in front of both of them.

Ted did so, succinctly. As he was finishing up on the sparse details to date, his mobile phone buzzed in his pocket. He took it out to check the screen.

'It's Professor Nelson calling. She might hopefully have an update for me.'

The Super nodded to him to take the call.

'Just a very quick call, Edwin, to give you the heads-up on what I know so far, as I imagine you need all the info you can get. None of this is confirmed, of course, until I do a full post-mortem. I understand that the flat occupant is the daughter of the utterly loathsome Councillor Buller. Is that right?'

'You know him?'

'I've encountered him several times in various settings. Suffice it to say that I would be delighted were I to be in the position of autopsying his body before too much longer.

'But back to our current body. I believe young Ms Chowdhury has already speculated on a frontal knife wound. We've now turned the body and I can confirm that that is in fact the case. A really rather nice French kitchen knife, all one piece, blade and handle, pushed in as far as it would go. It's highly unlikely your victim would have survived very long at all, in the circumstances.

'I can't, of course, speculate whether or not this was a murder. Not until I carry out a full post-mortem. However, I would just say that, even with the level of decomposition making it rather tricky, I can't immediately see any defensive wounds. On the contrary, from a postural point of view, it looks rather as if the hands were clasped to the wound area after the knife entered, if that's helpful. And it's certainly not self-inflicted, I would say with a degree of confidence.'

'Now to our victim. As ever, this is all very guarded until the PM. All I can tell you so far, since I know you'll be keen to get an early ID, is that the body is male, young – late teens at a rough guess – and rather on the tall and lanky side, if that helps.'

'Skinny Latte!' Ted exclaimed, then explained to Bizzie, 'The flat occupant gave us his name as Latte. We thought it might be a nickname, so that makes sense now. Thanks so much, Bizzie, you've been a great help. Any idea when you can do me a full PM?'

'The impossible I do today, Edwin. Miracles will have to wait until late Monday morning, if that suits you?'

'Marvellous, thank you.'

He ended the call and looked at the Ice Queen.

'Early days but she wanted to let me know that it's looking as if he was stabbed by someone and he wasn't expecting the blow.'

'So now we have to contend with the possibility of Buller's daughter being a prime suspect for a murder case. It just gets better.'

There was the briefest of knocks on the door and Irene's head appeared round it.

'Ma'am, sorry, but this is definitely one for you. There was a commotion at the front door. It sounded like someone trying to kick it down. I sent officers to check and they found a very angry Councillor Buller ranting that we've wrongfully arrested his daughter. He's with his wife. I've parked them in reception with an officer to watch them, but I can't really spare a babysitter. Can I safely leave this one to you and the DCI?'

Chapter Four

'Are you happy to handle the delightful Councillor Buller, Ted? Only I should be here overseeing. But call me if you think a bit more rank is needed, even if I'm not in uniform and sporting my shiny crown.'

She was casually dressed and looked as if she might have been called away from a relaxed meal out somewhere with her long-suffering husband, an inspector in Traffic. Out of uniform she looked younger but still formidable.

'If it helps, I can liaise from here with the doctor when she arrives. I believe there was a specific request for a female doctor. And with the Makaton interpreter when they get here.

'Thank you. Yes, DC Vine raised the possibility that Abigail may have acted in self-defence in the face of abuse of some sort. Possibly sexual. I'll go and see what I can do to placate the councillor, but as Abigail is of age, I'm not sure he has any right to see her at this stage.'

'I'll trust your judgement on this Ted, as in all things. But I'm here should you need me.'

He was encouraged and somewhat surprised by her words. He hoped her faith in him was justified in what was likely to be a tricky encounter.

There was a PC from Uniform in the dimly lit reception area. Councillor Buller was striding up and down. A big man, bulky, with a florid complexion, who looked dangerously close to exploding.

The person Ted took to be his wife was the polar opposite.

A tiny, thin figure, she sat demurely on a chair, knees together, feet to the side, her eyes following every movement her husband made with nervous anticipation.

Ted could smell her expensive perfume from yards away. Everything about her reeked of money, from the clothes she was wearing to the exquisitely cut and styled platinum blonde hair. Not to mention the flawless complexion, devoid of even the hint of a wrinkle. A face totally immobile and lacking in any expression, apart from the eyes. Deep violet-blue, showcased by tautly-stretched surrounding skin which made her look permanently startled.

'Thank you, PC Grover, I'll take over from here,' Ted told the waiting constable, who looked glad of the chance to slip away. Then he turned to the pacing man and said, 'Councillor Buller? I'm DCI Darling ...'

Before he could go any further, Buller bellowed, 'Are you the cretin who's arrested my daughter? Where is she? I demand to see her.'

'Perhaps if you'd both come with me, we can sit down and I'll explain everything to you. I can start by assuring you that Abigail is not under arrest. We merely want to talk to her at this stage and that wasn't possible at her flat.'

'I demand to see her. Before we go any further.'

Ted ignored his bluster and turned instead to the seated woman.

'Mrs Buller? Would you please come with me and I'll give you all the details I can at this stage.'

Ted led the way to the nearest interview room, reached in to put the lights on and stood aside to let the woman go in first. Councillor Buller barged in front of her. As soon as they were all inside and Ted had shut the door, he rounded on him again.

'I don't like your attitude. We want to see Abigail. Now. You shouldn't be speaking to her without us there. She can't cope. She's retarded.'

His wife put out a timid hand to restrain him.

'Frank, you mustn't say that. She's learning disabled. Abigail has learning difficulties, inspector.'

'Please sit down, both of you, then we can talk properly.'

'She needs a solicitor. Before anyone talks to her.'

Buller was still standing, looking belligerent, but his wife sat down as instructed, looking anxiously from him to Ted as she did so.

Ted didn't raise his voice but his tone was firm. He wanted to be in control of this situation right from the start.

'Councillor Buller, please sit down.'

He did so. Not with good grace.

'First let me assure you both that Abigail seems to be uninjured. But we are, as a precaution, getting a doctor to examine her and assess her fitness for interview.'

'She has the right to a solicitor. I'll call mine.' Buller was already pulling out his mobile phone when Ted cut in.

'If you'd perhaps first allow me to fill you in on what we know for now. Abigail is, of course, entitled to a solicitor, but at present the only people having contact with her will be the doctor, one of my female officers, with whom she's already formed a bond and a Makaton interpreter who is on her way.

'We were called to Abigail's flat following complaints from neighbours about a smell ...'

Once again Buller interrupted.

'Bloody nosy people. That's easily sorted. I'll get a cleaner, if Abi has been letting things slide.'

'Perhaps you would allow me to finish? It's not, unfortunately, a cleaning issue, but rather a suspicious death. We found a body in Abigail's kitchen.'

Mrs Buller's hand flew to her mouth in a gesture of surprise. Her frozen face showed little reaction.

'Abigail lives alone, as I understand it. Could you tell me, please, when was the last time either of you visited her at the flat?'

Buller's colour darkened further. 'What are you insinuating? We're in regular touch with Abigail. But she has her own life, her own friends.'

'And do you know the names of these friends? Would the name Latte mean anything to either of you? Perhaps as someone Abigail is friends with?'

'Latte? Never heard of such a name. Have you, Harriet? It sounds foreign.' He said it with an expression of distaste.

'Oh, poor darling Abigail. Somebody died in her flat? How horrible for her. I FaceTimed her a couple of evenings ago and she was absolutely fine. Telling me about making herself something for tea, and how she was looking forward to going to Wilmslow with me for some shopping and beauty therapy.'

'Is Abigail able to express herself verbally to that extent, Mrs Buller? Or do you use Makaton when you speak to her?'

'We don't use any of that hand signal stuff with our daughter,' Buller said dismissively. 'Her mother understands her perfectly well without, don't you, dear? Mothers do.'

'Mrs Buller, I don't want to upset you, but the information we have to date suggests that if you spoke to your daughter just a couple of days ago, then the body was already in her kitchen. It could have been there for up to a week. Are you sure there wasn't anything Abigail might have said, or tried to say, which could have indicated she needed help with a problem?'

'I don't like your tone, inspector. You should think about who you're dealing with here. One phone call from me to a person in high authority and you could find yourself off this case faster than you might imagine.'

'Are you threatening me, sir?' Ted asked him, his tone polite. 'If so, please don't. I don't like being threatened when I'm doing my job.'

He turned calmly back to the wife and continued, 'Anything at all, Mrs Buller? Was there anything Abigail said or gestured which was out of the ordinary in any way?'

She looked confused now, looking rapidly from Ted to her

husband and back again.

'Well, no, not that I recall. But I was in a hurry. Frank, my husband, and I, were going out and he was getting impatient. He'd got the car out and I could hear he was revving the engine. I promised Abigail I'd see her as soon as I could, but I haven't had the time to arrange anything since then.'

'That's right, woman, blame it on me. It's always my fault,' Buller retorted.

'I really don't think this is helping. My main priorities at the moment are identifying the deceased and ensuring Abigail's welfare at all times. With that in mind, I think I should now go and see what progress, if any, has been made in finding her an interpreter, and if the doctor is here yet.

'I would ask you both to please stay in this room for the moment. I'll try to arrange some tea or coffee for you, but you must understand we have an ongoing serious incident in the town centre. Councillor Buller, please feel free to call a solicitor for Abi, although of course they cannot be present while she is examined by a doctor. But above all, please stay here. It won't be helpful to anyone if you start wandering around the station. I promise to keep you informed at all times.'

Ted went first to the Control room. Irene was still there but the Ice Queen wasn't. Things seemed to be calming down somewhat, by what he could see on the monitors.

'Where's the Super?'

'Back in her office updating the top brass on the situations we have going on here. Your sign language lady has arrived, and the doc. They're both with Abigail now, with Jezza sitting in. How's it going with Buller? Is he as bad as his reputation suggests?'

'I seriously think he should ask for a refund on his Charm School course,' Ted said with a grin. 'How's the injured officer?'

'Discharged and gone home. He should be fine. It might even have knocked some sense into him finally, and there was certainly a need for that.'

'I'd better go and update the Super. Irene, I know you're still flat out, but if you could please find someone to take a cup of tea to the Bullers in Interview Room 1, I'd be really grateful. Especially if someone could keep half an eye out to make sure he doesn't start wandering round opening doors. The last thing we need is for him to blunder in on his daughter being intimately examined by the doctor, and perhaps breaking all the trust she's built up in us so far.'

Irene gave an exaggerated sigh as she said, 'Because of course my officers have nothing better to do than be fetchers of tea. But since you are one of the few CID officers I've worked with who always remembers to say please and thank you to us humble minions, I'll see what I can do.'

Ted went and tapped on the Super's office door, before putting his head round to see if she was free. She was on her mobile phone but waved him in and indicated a chair.

'As soon as I get any update, I'll let you know. She's with the doctor now.'

When she ended the call, she told Ted, 'The ACC. I thought I'd better take it to a higher level straight away, in view of the involvement of Councillor Buller. I suspect he will lose no opportunity to make political capital out of this, however it turns out. We shall all have to tread very carefully.'

She stood up and went to refill their coffee mugs in a reflex gesture.

'He's already threatened to have me thrown off the case. He reckons he could do it with one phone call.'

She gave a snort of contempt. 'Perhaps he could, with some officers. Unfortunately for him, you are the Force's secret weapon, Ted. A squeaky clean and excellent record. Everything always by the book. And astute enough never to beat the Chief at squash.'

Ted had to laugh at that. 'I couldn't, even if I wanted to, although I always try my best to.'

'Precisely, which is why you have his respect.'

Ted's blushes were spared by a knock on the door. Jezza came in, in response to the Ice Queen's summons.

'Ma'am, boss, I thought I'd update you with what we know so far. The doctor's still examining Abi. There are no signs of violence to date. But the doctor did find something which might complicate things a bit. She's pregnant. She clearly had no idea. We're not even sure she understands what it means but she's quite calm about the whole thing. She's very docile. It's easy to see how she could be manipulated by someone, in so many ways.'

'Thanks, Jezza. How's it going with her? How's the Makaton interpreter doing?'

'She's very nice and very helpful, boss, but she says herself her vocabulary isn't going to be anything like enough to cope with questioning Abi about possible sexual assault. Or even about her relationships in general on that kind of level. She works in an elderly care home so what she knows is geared at that level of client, where pregnancy doesn't often come up in discussion. We're going to need someone with much more specific training and I doubt we're going to find anyone at short notice, certainly not at this time on a Friday evening.'

'This potentially complicates things even further,' the Super said. 'Sit down, DC Vine. Would you like coffee?'

'Thank you, ma'am, but I think I'd better get back. I seem to be building something of a rapport with Abi which might be useful to us, perhaps.'

'Your thoughts, Ted?' the Ice Queen asked him as soon as Jezza had left them.

'Until I hear more from either Professor Nelson or Ms Chowdhury at the scene, we've no way of knowing if Abigail is a murderer or a victim of something, who was acting in self-defence. We've certainly nothing at all to charge her with at this stage. Equally, we clearly can't let her go back to her flat.'

His mobile phone interrupted him. He glanced at the screen.

'It's the CSM. I'd better take it. It might hopefully give us something more to go on.'

'You asked me to call you if anything else came up as we worked the scene,' Priya Chowdhury began, by way of greeting. 'The body's been recovered now so we've been able to get at some of the cupboards which it was blocking us from opening.

'So does your "anything at all which might be helpful to us" include what to my inexperienced eyes looks like a very valuable stash of Class A drugs?'

'Drugs?' Ted echoed, looking towards the Super as he spoke. 'Right, thank you for that. If you can let me know when you've finished on site I'll need to arrange for specialist officers to come and recover them to get them analysed.'

'Well, at least it gives us our reason to hold her for questioning,' the Ice Queen said dryly as Ted rang off. 'Do I understand drugs have been found on the premises? In which case you will need to proceed to a caution before you can question her further.'

'I don't see how we can, without a specially trained Makaton interpreter. If Buller calls up his solicitor, they're not going to allow Abigail to say anything at all. Could we look at releasing her on pre-charge bail, conditional on her living at her parents' address?'

'We could. I'd be happy to sign off on that. I think I should be present when you tell them, and we should perhaps wait for the solicitor to be there as well. That way, as far as I can see, we've covered all bases.'

'I agree. I don't see that there's anything else we can usefully do for now. I'll come in tomorrow and we'll make a start on identifying who our victim is. We'll begin with door-to-door of the neighbouring flats. With any luck, a building like that has plenty of security cameras in place which might help us. And I might as well let Jezza go home. She's looking a bit tired.'

'I noticed that. Is she all right?'

'It can't be easy, living with her brother Tommy. He doesn't seem to need sleep like most people do and I think it takes its toll sometimes.

'Debs, it's early days, but it seems to me possible that we're looking at a case of cuckooing here. An unidentified young male in the flat, perhaps crashing there, with a stash of drugs. Abigail is the perfect target. Living alone, vulnerable, perhaps eager for friendship. She might have let him in easily enough without understanding she was being used.'

'It certainly has all the hallmarks,' she replied, then rose majestically to her feet, towering over Ted.

'Right, let's deal with this and then we can all go home to our nearest and dearest. And at least we know Abigail should be relatively easy to find and in a place of safety if she's at her parents.'

'Hello, Mr Policeman. Are you in bed yet?'

Trev's voice in Ted's ear via the mobile, sounding as if he was having a good time.

'I'm still at work, as it goes, but getting close to calling it a day. Did you want picking up?'

'Well, I couldn't possibly ride the bike now after the odd wine or three. I left it at home, in case that happened, so I was hoping for a lift. I was going to walk back but the place is full of some nasty thugs throwing things at one another, so I had to take refuge in the nearest pub in the hopes that a kind policeman might come to my rescue.'

'Give me ten minutes to finish up here then I'll come and get you.'

'I can walk up to the station in that time. I'll meet you in the car park.'

'Just be careful. There are some nutters around tonight.'

To Ted's relief, Trev was waiting for him, perched against the bonnet of the little Renault, when he left the station. Trev was smiling the inane smile of the slightly happy-drunk. It had clearly been a good evening.

'Hey, you,' he greeted him, wrapping his arms around Ted, then recoiling in horror. 'Oh, my god, you smell revolting. What have you been up to?'

'Sorry. A particularly nasty suspicious death. I didn't realise it had got into my clothes that much. I'll chuck my jacket in the boot, then it should be a bit better.'

'Put your trousers there as well. You smell disgusting.'

'Trev, I am not taking my trousers off on the car park outside the nick and driving home in my kecks.

'I'm not.

'Trev ...'

Chapter Five

'Boss, I'm so sorry to be late,' Jezza panted, as she burst through the doors of the main office.

Ted was just about to start briefing the team members who were there, DS Mike Hallam and DC Virgil Tibbs. He hadn't yet called everyone in. They normally worked half on, half off for weekend days. He was waiting until he knew for sure that the case fitted their Serious Crime remit, rather than being another sort of unfortunate incident. Although it was looking more likely, with the Professor's initial comments, that it would be one for them.

'I know it's no excuse, but I've had the night from hell with Tommy. The quiz judge said he'd got a question wrong. Nat had to drag him out because he went ballistic. He then wouldn't go to bed until he'd used up all the computer paper and ink printing out internet searches to prove that he was right. Lough Neagh is the biggest lake in the British Isles, not Great Britain. So I'm sorry. But at least you all now know the correct answer if you ever get asked that in a quiz.'

Jezza went to her desk and sat down. She looked much worse than the evening before, when she'd already appeared to be in need of a good night's sleep.

'Right, we'll crack on, now you're here, Jezza. If anyone's not yet met the term cuckooing, I'll give you a brief outline,' Ted began.

'It's getting increasingly widespread, but I think this is the first case to date on our patch. Certainly the first that's come to light, if that's what it turns out to be.

'It's usually groups of young people, who go out of their way to befriend someone lonely and vulnerable. Often someone isolated and with learning difficulties. Like Abigail Buller.

'They gain their confidence. Sometimes even move in with them, if they've nowhere else to live. They might use their home to stash things, such as drugs or stolen goods. And drugs seem to be the factor in our case, although I'll need to get detailed analysis of what was found there to know what we're dealing with.

'They'll also often be taking money from their victim. They might even take over full control of any benefits they receive, as well as their bank accounts, credit cards, that sort of thing. We know that Abigail comes from a wealthy family. Her flat is an expensive one. Depending what arrangements her parents have made for her, she might have a fair bit of money, which would put her at increased risk.

'In at least one recorded case to date, it's ended up with the targeted person being killed by the people who befriended them. Even at its mildest, it's a nasty and cynical crime. One that preys on the most vulnerable victims.'

'So what's the priority for today, boss?' Mike Hallam asked him. 'Identify the victim if we can?'

'As good a starting point as any. All we know so far is that he goes by the name of Latte, which seems to be a reference to him being tall and skinny. And he appears to be young. Perhaps late teens, but that can't be confirmed until the post-mortem. All of which probably isn't going to get us very far without something else to go on.'

'D'you want me to run it through the system, boss? The description and the nickname?' Jezza suggested. 'In case it shows up anywhere. Mispers, perhaps, or even on his record, if he has one.'

Looking at her, Ted suspected Jezza would welcome the

chance to spend at least the start of the day at her desk. She looked about out on her feet, so he nodded his agreement.

'Mike, if you and Virgil can make a start with neighbouring flats to Abigail's, see if any of the occupants have seen or heard anything suspicious there at any time. Particularly anyone coming and going to Abigail's flat. Find out if that was a common occurrence. Start with the person next door who reported the smell in the first place. See what they know.

'I imagine Uniform will be busy dealing with the aftermath of last night, but if I can get you any help, I will do. I'm going to concentrate on finding out who owns or maintains the building and getting the security camera footage out of them. Plus I'll call up any CCTV from round about. I'm curious about who tipped off Councillor Buller. He turned up here last night, not long after we brought Abigail in. Does he have some connection to the building? Or has he arranged for someone to keep an eye on his daughter? I'll look into that, first off.

'It seems as if the parents don't go there very often. Their contact with Abigail appears to be largely from the mother through FaceTime. She told me she spoke to Abigail a couple of days before we were called to the scene. She said Abigail was telling her about making herself some tea and was looking forward to going shopping with her.'

Jezza gave a snort of scorn. 'Well, I know she's her mother so she knows her better than I do, but from my experience with Abi – and don't forget that within a very short time she was declaring undying love for me – I can't see how she could convey all of that in a phone call, even on visual. Unless the mother is proficient in Makaton.'

'The husband says not, but claims Abigail and her mother understand one another without.'

'She might nod and sign yes to everything her mother says, but that could be the sum total of it.'

'We'll keep an open mind on that for now. First let's see

what you can find out about this Latte, and if there are any more young people who might be hanging round. Whoever dumped a stash of drugs there, if that's what they are, they're not going to walk away and leave them. They've got too much money invested. The cuckoos might also have some dangerous types chasing them if they can't deliver or sell whatever they've got stashed.

'I'd quite like to have another look at the inside of the flat myself later today, now the body has been removed and there should be more room to look around. We'll regroup later in the day and see what we've come up with between us.'

Ted worked from his desk to start with. He could get a lot of the information he needed from phone calls. He was making some progress when his door opened. He looked up in surprise to see Jim Baker, the Big Boss, looming into his small office.

'Hello, Jim, I wasn't expecting to see you here this morning.'

'Yes, you were,' Jim told him with an exaggerated wink. 'That's why you phoned me at home this morning and asked me to come in to discuss the case. At least, that's what I've told Bella. So I need you to alibi me, if she ever asks.'

He lowered his frame warily onto the spare chair, ignoring its creak of protest.

'She wanted to take me shopping all day. A posh place in Cheshire, where everything costs twice as much as it needs to, even though Bella says it's cheaper there than in most shops.

'Shopping, lunch, more shopping. She's buying outfits for our honeymoon. Honestly, Ted, we'd need to go for a couple of months for her to wear everything she's bought so far, never mind more shopping today. So I said you needed me in this morning but I promised to meet her there in time to eat, and shop this afternoon.'

Ted stood up and put his kettle on.

'Coffee?'

'Not the piss-water you make. Make it a tea, and none of

that green stuff. Stick two bags in and leave it to brew. And while it's doing that, tell me everything you have to date.'

'How do you want to do this, sarge?' Virgil asked Mike as they left their parked car and walked towards the converted mill where Abigail's flat was situated. 'Shall I start on the ground floor and you take the first floor?'

'Your legs are younger than mine, Virgil, and you're a lot fitter. You take the first floor, in case the lift's broken.'

Virgil grinned at him as he trotted out his catchphrase. 'Is it because I is black?' Then, looking appreciatively at the imposing building, he added, 'I'm betting everything works in this place and there's a hefty service element in what the residents pay to make sure it stays that way.'

'We'll meet up when we've done those two floors to compare notes.'

Virgil went first to the flat next door to Abigail's. There was no sign of police activity there for now and no 'crime scene' tape on the front door, although it was securely locked up. Ted and Debra Caldwell had decided between them that it would be a good move politically not to make any such public declaration, which might give Councillor Buller an excuse for complaint. He'd apparently made several attempts to contact Ted's Chief Constable, Jon Woodrow, who was so far refusing to take his calls.

It took several rings on the doorbell and some discreet knocking before the neighbour's door was opened and Virgil found himself facing a walking definition of 'bed hair.' A wild shock of bright red, framing a pale freckled face, with piercing green eyes.

'Ms Aherne?' Virgil asked her, having read the name under the doorbell, holding up his photo ID. 'DC Tibbs, Stockport Police. Sorry if I woke you. I understand it was you who phoned to complain about the smell coming from your neighbour's apartment. Would it be all right if I came in to ask you some questions about it, please?'

'Oh god, what time is it? Is it even daylight yet? Yes, I did report it. I have to pass her door every day and if she had the door open, even a crack, the stench was making me gip.'

She stood back and held the front door open enough to allow Virgil to enter. 'You'd better come in. Give me time to make coffee before you expect any sense out of me. D'you want some?'

She turned away and padded barefoot down a tiled hallway. She was wearing what looked like an oversized man's nightshirt, which hung off one shoulder and came down to mid-calf. Virgil wondered fleetingly if he was putting himself at risk of allegations of impropriety, being alone with her in the flat, dressed as she was. But she was potentially their most important witness so far and he'd ask permission to record their conversation to cover himself.

She prepared an Italian Moka pot and started it going on the gas range, opened a window a fraction then sat down at the kitchen table, taking a cigarette out of a packet there and lighting up.

'Strictly prohibited by the terms of my lease, officer,' she told Virgil, blowing smoke towards the open window. 'Are you going to arrest me for it?'

'Cigarette? What cigarette?' Virgil turned on the charm as he grinned at her. 'I would like to video our conversation though, if you have no objection, Ms Aherne. It's just a formality.'

'Oh, bugger,' she said, stubbing out her cigarette and moving the ashtray out of the way. 'Go ahead then. And please call me Roisin.'

'Do you know your next door neighbour at all?'

She'd got up to close the window now she wasn't smoking, and to get mugs ready for the coffee.

'How do you take yours?'

'As it comes, please, nothing added.'

'I make it strong,' she warned him. 'I need something for a kick-start in the mornings.'

'Strong is fine. Tell me about your neighbour.'

'I don't know her in any sense of the word. I don't even know what her name is, to be honest. The first time we passed on the stairs, I said hello and introduced myself, because I knew she was my neighbour. Then I realised she's very deaf and has difficulty speaking. She gave me like a sideways wave and pointed to herself but all I got was a short A sound, so I avoided trying to address her by name, but I always said hello and did the same sort of a wave back. I tried to tell her my name but even English people with good hearing sometimes get it wrong. She always used to say just "Seen" when she said hello. I still don't know what her name is.'

'Abigail,' Virgil told her, then took a sip of the coffee she'd put in front of him. She wasn't exaggerating when she said it would be strong.

'Did Abigail have many visitors, do you know? Were you aware of people coming and going from her flat.'

'Oh, god yes. All the time, and at some very anti-social hours. It got noisy in there often, too. Lots of shouting and banging. Loud music thumping. I would normally have banged on the wall to get them to shut up a bit, but then I figured she probably couldn't hear how loud things were and I didn't want to upset her. She didn't seem to go out much, so I suppose it was nice for her to have friends coming round.'

She took a swallow of her own coffee then asked, 'So what was the smell in there? Rats or something like that? I could have told the concierge but he's not exactly dynamic. I really wasn't trying to stir the shit, certainly not by calling the police. But I thought I'd better, just in case there was a dead body, other than a rat's, in there.'

She laughed at the idea, then saw Virgil's face.

'Oh my god! Is that what it was? I honestly had no idea. Was it on the news? I phoned up during the day, then I got home very late last night so I never saw any TV or listened to the radio. There was a body? Gross! Was it Abigail?'

'Not Abigail,' he assured her. 'All we know at the moment is that it was a young male. What about her visitors? Male or female?'

'Lads, mostly. Late teens. Stereotypical moody youths with hoodies and bum cracks on view. I assume most of them could speak but all of them chose not to if I passed them on the stairs, or shared the lift with them. There were some teenage girls, too, but not as many. Real hard-faced bitches. I found them far more intimidating than the lads, to be honest.'

'Did you ever go into Abigail's flat? Or invite her in here?'

'Oh, heck no. I mean, I'm trying not to sound discriminatory here, but it was such hard going even trying to say hello and introduce myself to her that I decided it was about as much as I could manage. It probably sounds really selfish but I didn't want to get sucked into maybe having to babysit her or something. She seemed lonely and vulnerable, apart from the teenagers who came round. And I got the impression they weren't real friends. More like they were using her, if you know what I mean.'

'And did ...' Virgil didn't get any further. He was interrupted by hammering on a door, loud shouting, and what sounded like someone kicking something.

'Right on cue,' Roisin told him, 'that sounds like one of the delightful characters in action. Presumably because Abigail is deaf, I've been treated to that racket a lot more than usual this week. As if she wasn't opening the door to anyone, for some reason. But then if you say there was a body in there ...'

'I'd better go and see what's happening. Thank you for all your help so far. I might need to come back at some time and ask you some more questions, if that would be all right?'

She gave him a smile and said, 'That would be absolutely fine.'

There was no sign of the noise from next door dying down

so Virgil paused inside the flat to make a quick call to Mike Hallam.

'Sarge, there's someone banging on Abigail's door. I'm just going to investigate, but perhaps you can watch the bottom of the stairs for me.'

Roisin opened the door for him and he stepped out. There was a young woman – late teens, early twenties, maybe – still kicking seven bells out of the door of Abigail's flat. She too was a hoody wearer, but the hood of hers was down, showing the worst epic fake tan fail Virgil could ever remember seeing.

She did little more than glance at Virgil in a dismissive way, despite the size and bulk of him. She kept her finger pressed to the bell push, one booted foot kicking away at the bottom of the door, occasionally shouting, 'Abi, open up, ya fat slag.'

'Are you looking for someone?' Virgil asked, his voice deep and smooth.

'What's it to you?'

He reached for his ID card.

'Police ...' was all he managed to say before she whirled and ran, faster than his grasping hand, which closed on thin air. She bolted down the stairs, leaping them two at a time. Virgil bellowed, 'Coming your way, sarge!' as he raced after her.

Mike Hallam appeared at the foot of the stairs, arms outstretched to stop the runaway. But Mike, on his own admission, was not sporty in any way. Not into rugby or anything useful in such situations.

With her running straight towards him, propelled by her own velocity, he couldn't miss.

But he did. With his arms wide and out of play, the rest of him was entirely unprotected. So her knee coming up caught him right between the legs, knocking the wind out of his sails as he doubled over, the breath gushing out of him in a loud 'Ooph'.

Even on the ground and in evident pain, he instinctively

lashed out with his feet, making her stumble. Virgil was onto her in an instant, grabbing her by the back of the hoody, shoving her, face forwards, none too gently up against the wall as he reached for his handcuffs.

'I'm arresting you for assaulting a police officer,' he told her, as she screamed back at him, 'Take your hands off me, you fucking black pig!'

Virgil ignored her until he had her safely immobilised. Then he asked, 'Are you all right, sarge?'

'Bloody marvellous, Virgil. Never better. Let's get her to the nick so we can charge her.'

He was just on the right side of rough as he took her by an arm, bundled her out of the building and into the back seat of their car.

Chapter Six

Mike and Virgil's passenger refused to give her identity. She refused to say much at all on the short drive back to the station. Most of the words she uttered were of the four-letter, Anglo-Saxon variety.

She was slightly more talkative when they got to the nick, demanding a solicitor persistently, in a loud voice. They booked her in, asked for one to be called, then left her to stew while they went upstairs, Mike wincing visibly as he did so.

Ted heard them come in and went out of his office for a catch-up. Jezza was just finishing up a phone call.

'We brought a suspect in, boss,' Virgil told him. 'She kneed the sarge in the nuts so we've got her on an assault charge, whatever happens. She was knocking and kicking at Abigail's door, and shouting her name, so she clearly knows her, but she's not talking now.'

Ted made a sympathetic face. 'You all right, Mike? You'll need to get yourself checked out anyway for the charges against her.'

It was Mike's turn to make a face. 'That should be fun – not.'

'We might as well pool our findings to date while we're all in. Jezza, any luck with finding out who this Latte might be?'

'A couple of possibles, boss, but one very strong contender. A lad called Giorgio Mantone. Tall and thin. So, with an Italian name to boot, my money's on him being our tall skinny Latte.

'Originally from the Druid's Heath area of Birmingham.

Seventeen and with a string of juvenile offences to his credit. Nicking cars, often torching them after a joy ride. Lots of theft of all sorts. Some burglary, some drug offences. He was put in care at the age of thirteen and has been a frequent absconder from homes since then.

'Here's where we get to the part where some bureaucrat somewhere had what they thought was a brilliant idea. Only it wasn't. Giorgio Mantone was known to be involved with various gangs around Birmingham, mostly on the drugs scene. He was thought to be selling for at least one of the top people. The bright idea consisted of taking youths like Mantone and removing them to children's homes in remote parts of the country, away from the gang contacts.

'Mantone was never going to be adopted or even fostered. Too difficult, too much baggage, so it was a children's home for him. And they decided to send him to North Wales to get him away from his contacts. Some remote place in the hills with lots of L's and W's in the name.

'Long story short, he legged it from there within a week and the trail went cold. There was a brief trace of him on Merseyside not long after. His fingerprints are on record, of course, and they were found on a burned-out car. But since then, nothing.'

'Good work, Jezza. I don't know from the state of the body whether his prints will be retrievable. But if he's got a record, his DNA should be on file too so that might get us confirmation of his ID. That's a good start.

'And now we have your assailant, Mike. It at least seems she knew Abigail, which is another hopeful lead. Once we charge her, we'll have her prints, so they can be compared to any found in the flat. She might even be able to tell us something.'

'Doubt it, boss. I'd say she definitely has a record. She seems to know all the ropes. But I'd be surprised if she was the talkative type. We'll have to make all the running, I'm pretty sure,' Mike told him.

'With a bit of luck, if she's local and she is on our books, someone from Uniform will recognise her. Especially if we've had her in before.'

'Boss, I spoke to the neighbour. The one who reported the smell. She said there were teenagers coming and going all the time there. Noisy. Playing loud music. Knocking and kicking the door to be let in.'

Ted frowned. 'Did she say if that's been happening all week? I'm wondering if they were still going round since the death. If not, that rather suggests some of them, at least, may have known what happened. They may even have been there at the time of the killing.'

'The immediate neighbour works long hours, she told me, so she's not at home much and when she's there, she certainly sleeps through noise. I had to ring and knock quite a bit to get her to open up. But she did mention hearing the same racket this past week.'

'Or they were going round and Abi wasn't opening up to them,' Jezza suggested. 'Although as she doesn't seem to have registered that Latte was dead, why wouldn't she let them in? She let Sergeant Morgan and Stuart in with no problem, remember.'

'When I was in the kitchen of her flat I saw that she had one of those video links to the front door. There was a red light, which presumably lets her know when the doorbell rings, then she can look on the screen and see who's there. Plus there's the spyhole in the door. She would have seen they were both in uniform.'

'Yet she wasn't keen to talk to Susan, who was in uniform,' Jezza pointed out. 'Although she may simply not have understood her sign language as well as my very basic efforts.'

'So she's not afraid to let the police in, but she doesn't want to let any of the teenagers back in,' Virgil concluded.

'And that might perhaps indicate that it was one of them who killed Latte, not Abigail herself,' Mike suggested. 'They'd want to get back in to recover the drugs and remove all traces of their presence. But Abigail might be afraid that she would form part of the clean-up operation. That she might be the next body in the kitchen. Can she reason at that level, Jezza? You seem to know her better than anyone so far.'

'Hard one to call, sarge. She corrected me when I made the sign for man instead of boy. But as for the rest of it? I honestly don't know how much she understands, but my overall impression is not much at all. Possibly enough to feel afraid in some circumstances, although she was very passive and trusting being examined by the doctor. And that was a very intimate examination, of course, in the circumstances.'

'I think, before we get ahead of ourselves, we need to wait to see what the PM tells us on Monday. And Jezza, since you've been in on this one since the start, I think you should come with me for that. I know you say you're not interested in promotion but a case like this can only look good on your portfolio.'

Jezza made a face. 'Boss, I know I shouldn't let my personal life get in the way of work, but if it's one of the Prof's dawn starts and I've had another night from hell with Tommy…'

'You're in luck. She's got something on first thing so it's late morning. Are you off tomorrow? Can you catch up on some sleep?'

'I am and I hope so. Nat, bless him, has offered to take Tommy out for the day while I sleep. So I will try to be back to my usual bright and breezy self by then. Or at least to something resembling a functioning human being.'

'Virgil, you're going to be tied up for a bit now with your assault case, because clearly, Mike, you can't be involved in that interview. Not as the victim. We can ask for someone from Uniform to interview her for now and Virgil, you keep an eye on it and make sure they cover all bases.

'Mike, you'll need to get your statement sorted as well as getting yourself examined, of course. I want to go back to the flat later on for a proper look round now CSI have finished. If you're up to it, perhaps you could come with me. When we've done that, we could knock on a few more doors, to see what else we can find out.

'I've managed to get a fair bit of information about the building. It's owned by a property development company of which, no surprise there, Councillor Buller is a major shareholder. Some of the flats have been bought outright, but at least some of them are rentals, and the rent is a bit eye-watering. Plus there is a full service contract, with a caretaker living on site.'

'Concierge, boss,' both Mike and Virgil corrected him at the same time, then Mike went on, 'Nowt so common as a caretaker there. I saw the sign on one of the ground floor flats but no one was in when I knocked. I was planning to go back later.'

'Right, let's you and I do that. So that's most of us with plenty to be getting on with for now.'

'Boss, if it's all right with you, I'd like to dig a bit more into this Giorgio Mantone. I know it could be a false trail, but it's surely worth me pulling up his file. I thought I'd also ring the home in Wales and see if they can tell me anything, or if they have details of his previous social worker or probation officer or anything. Maybe see if I can turn up any known associates in and around here. It might just lead us to some of the other little charmers who've been pitching up at Abi's place.'

Ted nodded his agreement. 'Well worth a shot, I would say. Right, in the meantime, I'll go and see who's in downstairs who might know your assailant, Mike.'

Long-serving local officers like PS Bill Baxter, now retired and in charge of the reception desk for a living, or PS Eric

Morgan would no doubt have known the identity of Mike's attacker. Neither was in on a Saturday. Ted went downstairs to see who else might know.

He found PC Dick Higgins having a cup of tea while he was busily transcribing notes from his pocket book. Dick had been at the station for as long as anyone could remember. Long enough to have vivid memories of Ted's arrival as a Detective Sergeant in his first ever post out of uniform. Unsure of himself, covering it by bravado, which had made more than one person mark him down as a 'cocky little sod'.

'Dick, do you know who the young lass is who assaulted Mike Hallam? He and Virgil brought her in earlier. She won't give a name but I thought you'd know, if anyone did.'

'Ronnie? Of course I know Ronnie. She's a regular here. I heard about what happened to Mike, poor bugger. Not sure which he'll find harder to live down. Getting kicked in the bollocks by a young lass like her, or having to get his tackle photographed for the file.'

'Ronnie? Is that short for Veronica?'

Dick laughed. 'No, it's what everyone calls her. Ronnie, short for Ronseal. She must go to the worst tanning place on the planet. She's always the colour of something you might put on your decking to keep the rain out. She's got some sort of a Pola ...'

He pulled himself up short, remembering what Ted could be like with anything disrespectful, changed the word he was about to say quickly to 'Polish' and went on, 'Polish name, but she never uses it. Zofia, or summat. With a Z. Surname has a Z or two in it somewhere as well, but don't ask me to spell it from memory. Family's from up Reddish. Decent enough folks. Dad has a decorating business, I think. Ronnie went right off the rails. No idea where she lives now. A squat somewhere, probably.

'So what's this suspicious death case you've got on, Ted? Cuckooing, did I hear on the grapevine? Maybe that's where

Ronnie's been living. In the flat where the body was found. I hear she was trying to get in there when Mike and Virgil found her.'

'Could Ronnie be a killer, do you think?'

Higgins took a thoughtful swallow of his tea, then said, 'Would I turn my back on her if there was a weapon to hand? No bloody fear! Does she have a record of violence? Well, Mike's not her first assault, for sure. But I don't remember her using a knife before and I hear your body is a likely stab victim.'

Ted had long since ceased to be surprised at how fast word got around within the station. It's why he often tried to chat to the Uniform officers to bring himself up to speed.

'Thanks, Dick. The surname. Is the Z at the beginning?'

'Starts with a W, I'm pretty sure. The Z's in the middle somewhere, and it ends in an -eck or something like that.'

Ted went back upstairs to give Jezza the information he had so far. It would be helpful to have as much background as they could before the solicitor arrived and Virgil briefed a Uniform officer for the initial interview. His mobile phone rang as he headed for his office.

'Hey, you. Did you get arrested for indecent exposure in a police station car park?'

Ted laughed. 'If anyone saw anything on the cameras, they've not said anything to me yet. And I've not had any knowing looks, so I think I got away with it.'

'Good. I was just looking up recipes for suitable cakes in which to conceal a file. But actually, I've just dropped your stinking suit off at the cleaners and I'm on my way into town. I fancy having lunch with my husband, if you can make time for me?'

Ted hesitated. 'It's a bit full on. I was going to grab a sandwich to eat at my desk.'

'Take half an hour off and meet me in The Grapes for a sandwich instead. Please, Ted. I've not seen much of you all week and I'm practically walking past there on my way to town.'

'You're walking?'

'I've decided to be more virtuously green. And also to spend less money. I've still not recovered from having to show you my credit card statements. Nor the knowledge that your ACC has seen them, too. So have we got a date? I promise not to disrobe you in public again.'

'Shame. That was going to be the clincher. All right, give me a bell when you're nearly there and I'll come round and join you.'

'We'll try this caretaker – sorry, the concierge – person first, then go back up to the flat,' Ted told Mike as he parked his car later and the two of them walked into the building. 'Given Buller's connection to the development and what seems to have been happening to his daughter, I wouldn't be surprised if he's lying low a bit for the time being.'

It took a couple of rings and a bit of patient but persistent knocking on the door of the concierge's flat before it opened and a man looked out, his expression wary.

'Mr Boyle?' Ted asked, photo ID in his hand, held up so the man could see it clearly. 'DCI Darling, DS Hallam, Stockport Police. Could we come in and ask you a few questions, please?'

'What's it about? Only I have to do my rounds of the building. There are a few things I need to attend to ...'

'What's it about?' Ted echoed, wondering if the man really was trying to claim he knew nothing of the recent goings-on in the building he was paid to maintain. 'Perhaps we could come inside to talk about that. We shouldn't keep you long.'

His reluctance evident, the man stepped back and let them in.

'Go through to the kitchen at the back. We won't be disturbed in there.'

The kitchen was empty but there was music coming from behind a closed door nearby. Boyle nodded towards it and made a face.

'Teenage son. My turn to have him at the weekend. The ex always forgets to send him with a functioning volume control. I can't complain too much because his waking hours are limited. But it's generally noisy when he is awake. Unless he's eating.'

He didn't invite them to sit down. He simply stood facing them, arms folded across his chest.

'Mr Boyle, as concierge, you surely must know that the police were called here yesterday and recovered a body from a first floor flat?' Ted began.

'Well, yes. But people do die. Anywhere. Even in a block like this.' His tone was defensive.

'But this was a suspicious death, Mr Boyle. And if you make regular patrols of the building, you must surely have been aware of a noxious smell coming from the apartment where Abigail Buller lives. I take it you know her; you know who she is.'

'Yes, of course. But that's part of the problem. Abi's … well, I don't know how to put it politically correctly, but she's not the full shilling. I don't think she copes on her own, to be honest. The flat's not always very clean, I don't think. But she's an owner-occupier. At least, her father owns it, so it's very tricky.'

'Was it you who called her father last night, Mr Boyle? To say she was being taken away in a police car?'

He didn't reply. His shifty look meant he didn't need to.

'Were you aware of a lot of young people frequently visiting Abigail's flat, Mr Boyle? Perhaps staying there? Lots of loud noise and banging? Music being played very loud?'

Ted had looked round the room as soon as he'd entered it. He'd seen the monitors, covering the main and rear entrances.

'Your flat is right by the stairs and the lift, plus you can see on the screens anyone who comes and goes. We've already recovered security footage which is being examined. You must know that. And you must have been aware of the comings and goings too, surely?'

'Like I said, it's difficult. Abi's technically an adult, but you wouldn't want her to babysit your kids, if you know what I mean. She's entitled to her friends and her private life. Just as long as the other residents weren't complaining.'

'But you were aware of young people coming and going?' Ted pressed him.

A shrug. A non-committal, 'Like I said, owner-occupancy. Nothing to stop her having people to visit or to stay over. I'm the concierge for the block, not her babysitter.'

Ted was looking out of the kitchen now, towards the source of the noise.

'How old is your son, Mr Boyle? And how often does he stay with you?'

'He's seventeen. Weekends, and any time the ex fancies taking off somewhere exotic with her new bloke. Then our Ricky gets sent round here.'

'I wonder if you'd mind calling him in so I could ask him just a couple of questions please, Mr Boyle.'

Chapter Seven

'Right, Ronnie, you know me well enough already, but for the recording, I'm PC Higgins and this is ...' he turned to the young probationer sitting next to him, trying not to dwell on the fact that she looked younger than his own daughter. 'Can you give your name?'

'PC Papadopoulos.'

Higgins was glad he was able to leave it to her to pronounce. He was never sure how many syllables there were. He'd been heartily relieved when she'd invited him to shorten her first name, Eulalia, to just Lia. He could cope with that.

'Okay, then, Ronnie ...'

The solicitor she'd asked for had arrived. A duty solicitor, and a new one. Keen. Eager to make his mark. Definitely trying to establish his Alpha male status from the start.

'Officer, as a courtesy, please address my client by her correct name. She's already given it for the tape.'

'All right, Zofia, let me ask you ...'

The scowling young woman interrupted him this time. 'Not my first name. We're not mates or nothing. You wouldn't like me calling you Dick, would you? Dick.' She put heavy emphasis on it.

'Let's get on, shall we? What were you doing at the building where you were arrested?'

She leaned back in her chair and folded her arms. 'No comment.'

'Who do you know who lives in that building?'

'No comment.'

It was exactly what Dick Higgins and Virgil had been expecting when they'd discussed how the interview should go. Virgil was in another room, watching over the monitors. He could talk to Higgins through his earpiece.

'Tell her we have all the camera footage for the building, so we're going through it to see how many times she's visited, especially in the last week,' he told him.

'You clearly do know someone who lives there. An officer witnessed you knocking at the door of a flat on the first floor and calling out a name. Why did you run off when the officer tried to speak to you?'

'Are you fucking kidding me? Some big black bloke built like a brick shithouse tries to grab hold of me and you wonder why I legged it? I didn't know he were a pig.'

Her solicitor leaned closer to her and spoke quietly, cautioning her to stick to 'no comment' answers for now.

'The thing is, Zofia, we have camera footage not just from the building but the surrounding area as well. You're clearly in the habit of visiting the occupant of one of the flats. We just need to know about your connection to that person. You might be able to clear yourself of a potentially much more serious crime than assaulting a police officer. Although that charge will stand.'

'Exactly what are you accusing my client of, officer?'

'As you've been told, Zofia has been arrested for assault on a police officer. I'm trying to establish, Zofia, what you were doing in that building.'

'No comment.'

'We could be in for a long session, Dick,' Virgil said dryly through the earpiece.

'Have you seen the news today, Zofia?' Higgins asked her.

The suspicious death had made all the local press and media and had even had a brief mention on the national news.

She scowled at him. 'I don't watch that shit. Too depressing.'

'So you're not aware that a body was found in the flat where you were knocking at the door?'

She couldn't disguise her reaction to the news. Unless she was an outstanding actor, she clearly wasn't aware. In an involuntary movement, her body straightened up slightly. Her eyes widened. Subtle indicators not lost on someone of PC Higgins' experience.

'What does that have to do with my client? I've only been told about the police assault,' the solicitor cut in. 'If you have something else, I need to be informed so I can properly advise her.'

'Mr Denby,' Higgins explained patiently, 'Zofia was seen knocking on the door of a flat in which there had been a suspicious death, and calling the occupant by name. You can see why we would want to speak to her in that connection, surely?'

'I need time to take further instruction from my client. This interview was supposed to be about the alleged assault on a police officer.'

'It still is, Mr Denby. The purpose of my questioning is to establish why your client was at the flat in the first place, and why she was apparently so keen to avoid the police.'

Denby opened his mouth to speak again but Higgins went on, 'But I'm quite happy for you to take a break for more instruction now. You can use this room. I'll make sure the recording equipment is turned off to give you some privacy, and I'll see if I can arrange a cuppa for you both.

'Interview suspended. PC Higgins and ...' the probationer again obligingly supplied her name for him, 'leaving the room.'

He left them to it and went to find Virgil.

'She didn't know about the body, did she?' Virgil asked him by way of greeting. 'The neighbour who reported it said she could smell something when the door was ajar. Perhaps it wasn't that strong if it was shut.'

'I'd bet my miserly pension on her not knowing. Like I said, I've known Ronnie a while. Arrested her a couple of times. Interviewed her a few times. That was news to her, I'd swear to it. But now I'm going to have to leave you to it, Virgil. Contrary to rumour, us Woodentops do have our own crimes to tackle and there aren't enough of us to do that properly.'

'Yes, thanks, Dick, I appreciate your help. I need to start going over all the camera footage to see exactly when we can place Ronnie in the building. I'm hoping to get Jezza to talk to her next, if she's finished phoning round to find out more about the victim.'

Dick Higgins laughed at that. 'Ronnie versus young Jezza? Now that I would pay money to watch, and I've no idea which way I'd place my bet.'

'Ricky, is it? I'm Detective Chief Inspector Darling, from Stockport police. This is DS Hallam. Is it all right if we ask you some questions, please?'

The teenage boy, who was still half-dressed despite the time, corrected him swiftly.

'Rick. No one calls me Ricky, not since junior school. Except him.' He lifted a scornful chin in his father's direction as he spoke.

'Sorry. Rick. Do you visit your father here often?'

He shrugged and headed for the kettle. 'Most weekends. A lot of the school holidays. And whenever my darling mother feels like dumping me while she goes off somewhere.'

'And where's home when you're not here?'

'Cheadle Hulme. But her bloke doesn't trust me enough to let me stay in his house when they go away. I'm a teenager, so clearly I must be dangerous and certainly not to be trusted in his posh property.'

'Do you have friends here? People you see when you're staying with your father? Maybe someone who lives in the building, or friends who visit them here?'

Rick finished making his drink, threw the spoon towards the sink, which it missed, and turned to face Ted. 'No, no and no. It was three questions, wasn't it? I lost track.'

'You don't have any contact with any other young people who live in the block or any who visit here?' Ted pressed him.

Rick Boyle leaned against the nearest worktop and eyed Ted appraisingly. He didn't seem in the least intimidated by being questioned by a senior police officer.

'Do all adults make assumptions? I'm a teenager so by definition I must know every other teen who comes into the building?'

'I apologise if that's how it came across,' Ted told him, to his apparent surprise. 'It wasn't my intention. It's just that, with the cameras here, you must at least occasionally see people coming into the building. I wonder, in that case, if you'd ever seen anyone you know.'

'Still no. Despite what the Aged Parent might tell you, I'm the studious type. He just hears the noise in my room. He doesn't understand that my generation can multi-task. I'm studying while I listen to music, even if it is a bit loud. I'm trying to get my grades up to study Law at Uni.'

'I know you work hard,' his father told him. 'He's a bright lad, inspector, does very well at school.'

'You made a judgement,' Rick told Ted dismissively. 'So did I. I saw a procession of knuckle-draggers coming and going, making a lot of noise, and decided we might not have a lot in common. So I avoid them like the plague. And I haven't seen anyone I recognise, looking at the monitors. I try not to go out when I hear them around. I'm not the bravest of souls.'

'A bit different on the inside, eh, boss?' Mike Hallam remarked when he and Ted had taken a first detailed look round the interior of Abigail's flat after talking to Boyle and his son. It was easier to get a good look at the place, now the body had been recovered and CSI had packed up for the weekend. They clearly had a lot of work still to do but it was the usual problem of resources and available time. The smell was strong but windows must have been opened at some point as it was marginally better than it had been.

'I've seen squats in better condition,' Ted agreed. 'And it looks as if quite a few people have been crashing here, at least from time to time. It will be interesting to see what shows up from the security cameras. I think we're going to have a lot of people to trace and interview, once CSI has finished with all the fingerprinting.'

Ted and Mike had shoe covers and gloves on while they picked carefully over anything they could see. The drugs which had been found had gone off for testing for identification and valuation purposes. A sniffer dog had been used to make sure any and all stashes were found.

The flat had two bedrooms. One was clearly Abigail's own room, although from the bedclothes and a couple of sleeping bags scattered about, it looked as if she didn't always have it to herself. What was evidently a guest room also showed signs of multiple occupancy. Both rooms were in a state of squalid disorder.

'No computer anywhere. Is Abigail computer literate?' Mike asked.

'I honestly don't know. She clearly has an iPhone to FaceTime her mother. There's a lot about Abigail we don't yet know and we need to find out, before we go much further. We don't know her literacy abilities, for one thing. It would be helpful, from a communication point of view, if we knew if she can read and write, and to what degree. We might not always have the right level of Makaton interpreter available.'

'I'll get on to that once we're back in the office, boss.'

Ted was looking thoughtfully at one of the few areas of the

room which was not covered in sleeping equipment or detritus. He moved carefully towards it, studying the floor intently, then looked across at the bed, with its rumpled and stained sheets. He moved all round the clear space, looking from the floor towards the bed. Then he spoke to Mike.

'What do you make of this, Mike? These marks on the carpet.'

Mike went to stand next to the boss; to look at what he had spotted. Three distinct indentations on a carpet which, although stained and filthy, was clearly good quality and not all that old.

'A piece of furniture that's been moved?' he suggested. 'Although it's a funny place to put something like a side table. A bit in the way there.'

Then he looked again, as Ted had done, from the marks to the bed.

'Shit,' he said half under his breath. 'A camera tripod. You're thinking some kind of porn filming or something, then?'

'It must be my suspicious policeman's brain but that's the first thing which came to my mind. I'm open to other suggestions, though. More innocent ones, if you can think of any.'

'I must be the same because at the moment, I can't think of an explanation I like any better. Could that explain Abigail's pregnancy, and the fact that she didn't seem to know about it?'

'Let's not get ahead of ourselves. She may not have been involved. It could be others who've been using her flat for some kind of filming, perhaps when she's been out.'

'I hope so,' Mike said with feeling. 'She's such an easy target. So vulnerable. I hope Virgil can get something out of that girl we arrested. If we at least knew who and what we were dealing with, we could make a start at rounding up some likely names.

'With an indication of possible filming, and a dead body in the kitchen, you don't think we're talking about those snuff films, do you? Or is that too wild a leap?'

'I'm not dismissing anything until we get further evidence. The post-mortem is likely to be the most important step next, I think. Then we should at least know if the death was murder or some sort of an accident. Or even self-defence.

'We're going to need access to Abigail's financial stuff at some point, I suspect,' Ted went on, opening drawers of a dressing table, leafing carefully through the contents. 'There's a strong possibility, if this is cuckooing, that they've been fleecing her for all she's worth. Which would seem to be quite a lot.'

'How can the parents leave her on her own like this, boss? They must know she's not coping. When did they last come here, for god's sake? Look at the state of it. It's not got like this in just a week or two. That poor young woman. What must she have been going through?'

Ted was only half listening to his rhetorical questions. He'd pulled out a sheaf of papers from a drawer and was carefully looking through them. Words, often misspelt, in a large and childish hand. Brightly coloured hearts, crudely scribbled, and large X's, probably intended to show kisses.

'Well, this would appear to show us two things. Firstly it would seem that Abigail can write, although her spelling isn't good. And secondly, she seems to be in love with someone called Data. Whoever he, or she, might be.'

Four months earlier

'We need some quality, Igor. The pond life we have now are all right for street corner selling. But they're never going to be able to get into the places we need for them to shift the good stuff. That's why we're out here talent-spotting. Again.

'The new supply line's all set up and it's watertight. Squeaky clean. We're good to go. We just need the right front man. Or woman, of course. I'm not sexist.

'But where do they hang out? Some days, I despair of

finding exactly what I'm looking for.'

The man in the back seat of the parked black vehicle was scanning the road intently. Occasionally he ordered the man in the driver's seat to start shooting with the expensive camera in his hands.

'Now that, Igor,' he said reflectively, after a long period of sitting in silence, 'that is what I'm talking about.'

His eyes were locked onto a young man walking down the road towards them, seemingly unaware of their presence. He walked with his head high, a spring in his stride. Light brown skin, jet black hair. A certain arrogance in the way he carried himself.

The driver panned the camera to follow him. The man in the back seat swivelled round to keep him in sight.

'Oh my god, look at that arse. He's perfection, Igor. The camera will love him. Find him for me. Get one of the pond life to reel him in. I don't care how you do it, but he's the one I want.'

'Yes, Mister Big.'

'What's happenin', man? Did you get inside?'

The new arrival stopped next to the park bench. The speaker was sitting on the back of it, feet on the seat, thumbs working the keypad of his mobile.

'No way. The feds were there. Well, one of them was a short bloke, didn't look much like one. But the bloke he was with was one, for sure. He had one of them badge things round his neck. Anyway, I could smell pig, even from where I was.'

'So where the fuck is Latte? And where's the fat slag? Why's she not letting anyone in? The Big Man is having a fucking meltdown. If we don't get the stuff out of there and soon, we're going to have to get out of here, bro. Before they come looking for us.'

The second youth was looking round him. 'Where's the others?'

'They'll be here.'

'Has Data still got that trace on the fat slag's phone? At least if we knew where she was we could try to find her.'

The first boy was looking along the path now. 'Here they come. We might get some answers.'

Four figures were striding towards them. They looked to be all around late teens. Two girls, two boys. They came to a halt next to the bench. No greetings were exchanged.

'Have you heard?' one of the boys began, before anyone had chance to speak. 'I saw it on the news. There's been a body found. In the flats. Where the fat slag lives.'

'Was it her?' the first youth asked.

'Dunno, they've not said. But where the fuck is she, and where's Latte? And Ronnie?'

'You still got that trace on the slag, Data?'

One of the two male youths who'd just arrived had his mobile phone in his hand, his eyes glued to the screen.

'Yeah, it shows her being some place called Over Pee-over, wherever the fuck that is. I'm just looking.' He consulted the screen again, then looked back up. 'Some posh place out in Cheshire. What the fuck's she doing there? She's been inside the flat all week, even if she wouldn't open the door, the stupid bitch.'

'Maybe it's not her?' one of the girls suggested. 'Maybe someone nicked her phone. Maybe Latte did and he's done a runner. He was always flaky. Ready to leg it.'

'Maybe the two of them have gone together, and taken all the gear with them,' the other female said.

'So who's the body?' the second youth asked. 'I couldn't get near. The feds are there.'

'And Ronnie's not turned up to say how she got on. Maybe the feds got her. So how the fuck are we going to get inside the place to get the stuff back, before the Big Man comes looking for us?'

Chapter Eight

'Right, for the recording, I'm DC Vine. How would you like me to address you? As Zofia or Miss Wieczorek?'

The name tripped effortlessly off Jezza's tongue. As soon as she knew she was going to be taking over the interview, she'd done her homework online. She had a good ear for words, accents and pronunciation from her drama training. It came in useful.

Ronnie tried to look scornful but clearly there was going to be no fun in asking to be addressed by her surname by someone who could master it perfectly. Instead she shrugged and said, 'Whatever.'

'So, Zofia, you've now had time for further consultation with your solicitor and we've had time to look through some of the security camera footage from the building where you were arrested. We're interested in your reasons for being in the building. We've seen that you've so far visited it four times this week.'

As she spoke, Jezza was placing printed-out stills, date-stamped and showing the young woman in the entrance to the building where Abigail Buller's flat was. Ronnie merely shrugged.

'For the recording, Ms Wieczorek has not made any answer other than a shrug. Zofia, it would be helpful if you said something.'

'No comment, then.'

'Where do you live, Zofia? Because we have you down as

of no fixed address and that's going to present us with a problem. You're facing a charge of assaulting a police officer, for which you could receive a prison sentence. Especially with your record. Which raises the question of whether to release you on bail pending further enquiries, or to apply to have you remanded in custody. And as your solicitor,' she made an elaborate show of looking at her notes for his name, 'Mr Denby, has no doubt already told you, we would seldom willingly bail anyone without a fixed address.'

She looked from Ronnie to her solicitor and back again, then went on, 'So do you have an address to go to, Zofia, and if so, may I have it, please?'

Denby leaned closer to her again, reminding her once more that she didn't need to say anything.

'But if I've got an address to go to, I'm more likely to get bail, yeah?'

'I'm not saying that, Zofia. That's not for me to decide. I'm just saying, in general terms, that it could go in your favour if you have an address. And also if you're seen to be cooperating with the police.'

Ronnie hesitated, weighing up her options. Then she said, 'I got a mate there. In them flats. I stay with her sometimes. I've not seen her for about a week now. So is it her that's snuffed it, then?'

'You say you haven't seen her for a week, yet the security camera footage shows you've visited the flat several times in the past week.'

'Yeah, well, she's a mate, innit. I ain't seen her for a bit so I was checking up on her. Only I never got no reply. Is she all right? Where is she?'

'Can you tell me the name of this mate, please?'

'Abi, she's called. She lives on the first floor. Where that black bloke tried to grab me. I legged it 'cos I didn't know he were a fed.'

'We'll come back to that point, Zofia. But for now, could

you please tell me how you came to meet Abi.'

'At the shops. I'd got to the till wi'me stuff but I couldn't find me purse. She were next to me in the queue so I asked her to lend us some money. And she did. So I helped her carry her stuff back to her flat and she asked me in. We got talking.'

'I see,' Jezza replied, keeping her tone neutral. 'How, exactly, did you communicate?'

She saw the questioning look the solicitor gave her and went on, 'Zofia, how exactly did you "get talking" to someone who is profoundly deaf and has limited speech?'

'We got on dead well. I talked, she nodded. We understood each other. She said I could stay there if I wanted. I had nowhere to crash.'

'Do you know any sign language, Zofia?'

Her expression a sneer, she raised a middle finger and made a gesture with it towards Jezza.

'I know some,' she said.

'So despite almost certainly limited understanding between you, you say that Abi allowed you to move in and stay there. Is that right?'

'Yeah. Well, not all the time. Sometimes I went to see other mates. But she let me move my stuff in there and I stay there sometimes. She likes the company.'

'Does anyone else stay there?'

Her expression turned wary in an instant.

'She's got loads of friends. Always people coming and going.'

'Can you give me any names of anyone?'

'No comment.'

'But you say Abi let you move your stuff in there. So there's a chance that anything we find in the flat which isn't Abi's might belong to you, is that what you're saying?'

'Where is this going, detective? This seems to be well outside the circumstances surrounding the assault for which my client has been arrested. And that was a very leading question.'

Jezza turned to face the solicitor and spoke in the firm but patient tone she often had to use with her brother Tommy.

'Mr Denby, you've been watching too many American cop shows. The correct way to address me is DC Vine, please. Or Detective Constable.

'Zofia, I need to tell you now that inside the flat, where you say Abi was allowing you to stay and to store your stuff, we found a large quantity of drugs. An amount far bigger than could possibly be deemed as being for purely personal use. I can't emphasise enough that it will only work in your favour if you tell me now anything you know about those drugs, or about anyone else who might use that flat.'

Ronnie wrapped her arms protectively around herself and seemed to shrink down into her chair in a defensive gesture.

'I ain't saying nothing more. If I tell you owt now, I'm dead.'

'I'm happy to sign off on a twenty-four hour remand in police custody for her for now,' Ted said when they met up to discuss progress. 'Denby will complain but we clearly can't let her go, with no known address. We can charge her with the assault on you, Mike. That's enough to hold her on for now. But we need to know more about her involvement with the drugs. You did a good job, Jezza, but she's clearly scared to say anything more.

'With what we have so far, we can't yet make any direct link between her and what happened in the flat. And until the PM on Monday, we don't know if that's a murder or not.

'As far as the drugs go, if we're looking at a drugs gang connection, which her fear would seem to indicate is distinctly possible, this might be one for Drugs rather than us. It's possible there's an ongoing operation we don't know about and we don't want to go blundering in treading on any toes. I'll see what I can find out about that.

'What I suggest we all do now is write up everything we have so far then get off home to our families while we can. I'll come in again tomorrow to brief Jo and the others and we can take it from there. See what else turns up.'

'Boss, if it does turn out to be Abi who killed Latte, is this even going to get to trial?' Jezza asked. 'I mean, if we don't find any witnesses or evidence to what exactly happened. And there's only Abi to try to tell us what really went on there. Is it actually a goer?'

'I don't know, Jezza, is the short and honest answer to that. That would be up to CPS. It's our job to build a file to go to them and for them to decide on what course of action, if any, to take, in the public interest.'

The desk phone next to Mike Hallam rang. He answered, said, 'Yes, he's here. Put him through,' then put his hand over the mouthpiece. 'Rick Boyle, boss, asking for you in person.'

'Interesting,' Ted said as he reached for the phone, then, 'DCI Darling.'

'Hello, again. This is Rick Boyle.'

There was a slight hesitation, so Ted prompted, 'Yes, Rick, what can I do for you?'

'I didn't lie to you when I said I didn't see anyone I knew. I didn't want to get involved in anything. But if I'm going to go into law, I need to consider that not disclosing everything, even something perhaps insignificant, isn't very honest, either.'

'Go on.'

'Well, I did see a girl on the security cameras here in the kitchen once, and I thought I recognised her. I went to the chippy, a few weekends ago now, and she was hanging about outside, trying to get people to give her money. She said she was hungry and hadn't got any cash. It sounded like a scam to my suspicious mind, so I wasn't falling for it. She was trying to chat me up. Hinting that it could be my lucky night if I bought her chips. She was very persistent, but in the end I decided to give up on the chips and go somewhere else instead.'

'Thank you, Rick. Is there anything else at all you can tell me about her? I don't suppose she gave you a name or anything?'

'She did. She said it was Beth, but she pronounced it like Beff. Y'know, more like a southern accent than from round here. Unless it was put on.'

'That's excellent, Rick, thank you. Can you give me a description of any sort, for us to be going on with, please?'

'White, late teens, about your height, maybe an inch or so shorter. Long straight hair, light brownish. Average build but, erm, this sounds bad, I know, but well-endowed. Y'know. Big boobs. Hard not to notice.'

'Good, thanks, Rick. By any chance would you be free at any time tomorrow to come into the station and have a look at some of the security tapes? To see if you can point her out to us? The person you think you recognised? I'll give you my direct number, then you can call me in the morning to arrange a time. Will you be at your father's tomorrow? You're not going out, or going back to where your mother lives?'

'Not until late. They tend to forget about me until the last minute. So I can come in. I'll be studying most of the day, despite what my father believes. I'm sorry I didn't mention this earlier. I needed time to mull it over.'

'That's fine. It sounds as if you have the right credentials for studying law. Thank you for this, and I'll see you tomorrow.'

He ended the call and told the others, 'Rick Boyle. The lad Mike and I spoke to earlier, who said he'd never seen anyone he knew at the flats. He was phoning to correct himself. No one he knew going in and out, but there was one girl he thought he'd seen before. He's given me a description and will come in tomorrow to pinpoint her on the tapes. Says she gave her name as Beth but pronounces it Beff. I'll ask Uniform. If anyone knows her, someone there will.'

'Hey, you, two meals in one day with my husband? I am honoured,' Trev greeted him as Ted strode into the kitchen, moving carefully to avoid the cats who came swarming round, scooping up Adam who writhed in delight at the shameless favouritism.

'Make the most of it,' Ted told him, planting a kiss on the cheek Trev turned towards him, deftly avoiding the knife in his hand from preparing a meal. 'I'm going to have to go in again tomorrow, I'm afraid. We still don't know if this case is a murder or not, but it's going off in several directions at once, so I need to pull the threads together to present to Jim, probably on Monday after the PM. Then he can decide who gets what bit of it to work on.'

'Well, I can't complain. I'll be getting my revenge when I'll probably have to work all next weekend. It's this week Geoff goes off for his operation. I still haven't plucked up the courage to ask him what it involves. I'll have to cover his usual Saturday shift, and because he does all the grown-up admin stuff and leaves me to do the charm offensive, I thought I'd go in on Sunday, too. That way, if I try to set a day aside to keep on top of the paperwork, I shouldn't either bankrupt the business or leave the books in too much of a sorry state before he gets back.'

Ted had carefully put Adam down, stroked each of the others in turn for balance, hung his jacket on the back of his chair – his tie had already been relegated to his pocket – and started to lay the table.

'Have you got some wine on the go or do you want me to open a bottle?'

'I haven't yet. It's part of my new resolution. One glass with the meal and that's it.'

'Times aren't that hard, you know. If you want to cut down, that's great. But the household budget can run to a few glasses of wine for you, if that's what you want. You enjoy it, and I don't mind.'

Trev stopped his food preparations to wrap Ted in a hug.

'I know you don't mind. I just think I sponge off you too

much. Time for me to start adulting a bit more. Beginning by living within my means. Especially now I actually have to play at being a business partner, instead of just swanning about and playing with big bikes, like I usually do.'

Ted was in early on Sunday morning. He wanted to catch the Uniform briefing at the start of the new shift. That way he could ask as many officers as possible at the same time. One of them would certainly know who Beth, or Beff, was. Once retired Sergeant Bill Baxter was in on Monday morning, Ted planned to get him to view security camera footage from the flats to see what familiar faces he could pick out. Bill was the station's fount of all knowledge.

When the duty inspector had finished briefing, Ted stood up and went to stand next to him at the front of the room.

'I need your help again, please, to identify a potential suspect.'

He gave them Rick Boyle's description of the young woman and finished up, 'She gave her name as Beth but pronounced it with two F's at the end, rather than a th, if that helps.'

An officer in the front row, with a good few years' service under her belt and her pension firmly in her sights, said, 'Busty Beff? I think a good many of us have felt her collar a time or two, guv. What's she done this time?'

'She's a person of interest in this suspicious death we have in the old mill flats. What can you tell me about her, Julie, please?'

'She must be eighteen or nineteen now, I think,' she said, looking round at her colleagues for confirmation. A few heads nodded in agreement. 'We've known her since juvenile days. She comes from up Portwood way, originally from outside the area. But the family kicked her out long ago. Religious lot, didn't approve of her having two kiddies before she was sixteen, to different lads who were never seen again. Kids were taken into care. Probably just as well.'

'What's her form for?'

'Public order offences. She's inclined to drink too much then lamp anyone who looks at her the wrong way. Petty theft and shoplifting. Some drugs stuff, but she's lucky enough to have been treated lightly as it's mostly been small enough amounts to pass as personal use rather than supplying.'

'Any connection to Ronnie?'

'Not that I know of from the top of my head, guv, but you'd find more on her file. Bethany Hayes.'

'Thank you. I'm going to need some help identifying visitors to the building from the security cameras. I'll start by asking Sergeant Baxter tomorrow.'

Everyone in the station, from the top down, still called Bill Baxter by his rank, although he was retired. He was an institution there and had earned the respect of all.

'If he doesn't know any of them, I'll need to ask you all again.'

There were chuckles in the room and the duty inspector said, 'Guv, there isn't anyone on our patch that Sergeant Baxter doesn't know. Not unless they've literally just landed here from somewhere right outside the area.'

Chapter Nine

'I'll get a twelve-hour extension to continue questioning Zofia, also known as Ronnie, but we need something of a miracle to get her to say any more for now. She's clearly scared and that fear seems to be linked to the drugs find. Much more so than the suspicious death,' Ted finished off his summing up to the team members present.

Jo Rodriguez, Rob O'Connell, Maurice Brown and Steve Ellis were in for the day. Ted still hadn't called everyone in at once, always conscious of his budget. Time for that if and when they got the green light that it was a murder case. Or at least a serious crime of some sort.

'She's many things, but not stupid. She's going to know that the only safe way for her to tell us anything which might help save her own skin is to agree to tell us everything, and then to testify in court. She's smart, street-wise, so she'll know the risks she's taking. The only way she'll consent to those terms, no doubt, is if we can offer her a witness protection programme.

'But to get anywhere near that stage, she's going to have to find someone she might be willing to trust to start the dialogue. Which is where you come in, Maurice. Have a catch-up from the notes on where Jezza was up to with her and see if you can take it any further. Just don't make her any promises, and check with me before you start discussing what, if anything, we can do to help her.

'If she's likely to talk to any of us, it will be to you in

Daddy Hen mode. Give it your best shot, please.'

'Boss, from what you've told us, there's a pattern emerging. Both Ronnie and Beth seem to use the old "oh, whoops, I forgot my purse, lend us a few quid" ploy to get near to potential targets. It's not exactly original but if we can find out which shop Ronnie was talking about where she claims to have met Abigail, and which chippy for Rick Boyle, I could perhaps start doing some digging. Maybe ask around some other shops, if anyone's noticed that sort of thing going on.'

'Mind-reader, Jo. I was about to come to that,' Ted told him. 'Yes, well worth a look, I would say. It might lead to some others, as it's clear from the flat that there's been more than a couple of them staying there with Abigail.

'Steve, can you run face recognition on all the footage we have so far, please? We're trying to ID people the old-fashioned way but it's just possible you can pick up something much faster with the help of technology. The person I'm particularly interested in at the moment is this Data. Abigail's notes declare undying love for them, and Abigail is pregnant. So without jumping to conclusions, there's at least a strong possibility that Data is male and might possibly be the father of the baby.

'I'm interested in that nickname, too. Unless it happens to be a real name. Perhaps in a foreign language. It makes me wonder if it might be someone with the techie brains to be manipulating Abigail's finances, perhaps. To find out about that in detail, we're going to need access to her bank accounts and so on, if she has her own and they're not solely controlled by her parents. And until we know more from the post-mortem tomorrow about what we're dealing with, I'd rather not rattle Councillor Buller's cage.'

'On it, sir.'

'Rob, Jezza couldn't get very far yesterday in finding out anything more about our victim, who we believe to be Latte – Giorgio Mantone. People she needed to speak to weren't available and so on. I doubt you'll do much better on a Sunday but give it a go, please. Can you also collate for us. Go through everything we have to date and flag up any links we've missed. See if you can build a logical structure to follow, based on priority of what we need to track down first.

'Right, Maurice, you and I should talk in detail about your interview with Ronnie. Or Zofia, we should call her for the interview. I'll be watching while you speak to her, then I can guide you on the direction it needs to take. No pressure, but if you could get her to tell us about the drugs, that would be a big leap forward.'

'Right, Zofia, I'm DC Maurice Brown. You won't believe me, I know, but I really am here to try to help you.'

Ronnie made a scoffing noise. She was slouching with arms folded, not showing much sign of being ready to talk. Denby was with her once more. Maurice wondered whether he was on the duty rota for the day or if he'd simply decided to stick with the case, sensing it might be something big.

'You don't believe me, clearly. I didn't expect you to. You don't know me. I'm a copper, so I must be the enemy, right? But I'm not. I really do want to get you out of the mess you're in, if I can. And right now I think you need all the help you can get.'

Denby was quiet for the moment, weighing Maurice up and wondering what, if anything, he was going to offer his client.

'I told your mates already. If I talk, I'm dead.'

'You still won't believe me, but I don't want that to happen, Zofia. I want to try to help you here. Now, you'll have been told you risk a prison sentence for assaulting a police officer. But I expect Mr Denby is going to tell you to claim self-defence. You didn't realise the two men were police officers. You panicked. You were protecting yourself. You might very well get away with that. Possibly even be found not guilty. Or be convicted and get a lesser sentence.

'My bosses want you banged up. As soon as. A nice tick on the statistics. But I'm a big softy. I wouldn't like to think of you in prison if you don't need to be. Not a young lass like you. I know how dangerous it can be on the inside. So I'm going to press to have you released on bail.'

She opened her mouth to speak but he cut across her. 'Yes, I know you've been told you won't get bail, with no fixed address. But I'm going to try to get you conditional bail. Let you out, as long as you come and sign in at the station at least twice a day. And of course, if you don't turn up, I'll have to send Uniform out looking for you in an area car.'

'Are you trying to intimidate my client?' Denby asked him.

Maurice was the picture of wide-eyed innocence. He spread his hands as he said, 'Me? Intimidate a lass? Never. I'm just trying to help her out here.'

'If I talk to you, I'm not safe anywhere. Inside. Out. Wherever. They'll find me.'

'Who's they, Zofia?'

She snorted. 'I just said, I ain't talking to you.'

'That's a shame, Zofia. Because when you go up before the magistrates for a remand hearing, if I go to court to testify about how much you've been helping us ...'

Both Zofia and her solicitor interrupted him at the same time.

Zofia: 'Fuck sake don't do that, it's a death sentence.'

Denby: 'Stop threatening my client! This is entrapment and you know it.'

Maurice leaned back in his seat, doing his best to look offended that his offer of help was being refused.

'I'm just trying to help you, Zofia, like I said. Because at the moment, things aren't looking good for you. Assault on a police officer could turn out to be the least of your worries. We've got you present at the scene of a violent sudden death. A place where a substantial quantity of Class A drugs were being stored.'

'Outside the premises, constable,' Denby put in. 'Ringing the doorbell, so clearly with no means of access to the place without the consent of the occupant. So that's not going to get you anywhere.'

'We're working on fingerprints from inside the flat now. We've got yours on record, so it's only a matter of time before we find a match.'

'Change tack, Maurice. Ask her about Latte now,' Ted told him through the earpiece.

Maurice paused for a moment, looking at Zofia. Trying hard to look non-threatening.

'All right, let's leave the drugs aside for now. Zofia, do you know anything about someone called Latte?'

'It's coffee, innit. With milk.' She said it with a smirk of self-satisfaction.

'Do you know a person called Latte? Either as a name, or as a nickname?'

She was frowning now, ignoring her solicitor reminding her she didn't need to say anything.

'Is that who's dead? Someone called Latte? Did someone kill him?'

'So you know that Latte is male?'

'You said he was,' she said defensively.

'I didn't, pet,' he told her, his tone gentle. 'I said person. Mr Denby can confirm that for you. And we're being recorded. You know that. You said "him". So you do know the person, don't you? It might be time to think about talking to me, Zofia. Let me see what I can do to help you. Particularly to find a way to keep you safe.'

Zofia was sitting stiff with suspicion. Looking from Maurice to her solicitor and back. She was backed into a corner and she knew it. Looking desperately for a way out. Her eyes drifted back to Maurice, weighing him up.

'I want proper protection if I start talking to you. A safe place. A new identity. The works. I'm not kidding when I say I could end up dead for telling you anything.'

'You'll need to talk to my boss about that. He's the only one who can agree to it. But you can trust him, Zofia. He's all right. You help us and he'll do everything he can to protect you.'

Monday morning and the full team was back in. Ted was bringing them all up to speed on the progress so far.

'Maurice finally got Zofia to start talking. Not much yet, and it's still unclear how much she might know. But she is cooperating, so she's now in a safe house, under twenty-four hour protection.

'We're particularly interested in what she can tell us about the drugs. All she's said so far is that a lad called Kane, who seems to be the boss of the group she hangs round with, sets up deals to store drugs and sell them on. All she's been able to tell us about the contact Kane uses is that they all refer to him as the Big Man, but no one, except Kane who refuses to talk about him, has ever met him or knows his real identity. Which is clearly what we need.

'Kane is on record. Kane Lomax. I'll circulate all the details we have. Ronnie doesn't always know the second names, but Kane was easy enough to track down. It's not that common a name and he has a record. His name came up on face recognition so when she mentioned a Kane, it wasn't too big a leap from there.

'The big mystery so far is this character Data. There are a couple of faces which the recognition software couldn't identify. So he could well be one of those. Zofia only knows him as Data, although she's at least confirmed now that he's male. And she says he's fit-looking and can talk posh, as she put it.

'The fact that she's starting to cooperate means that there is a possibility, Mike, that we don't proceed with the assault charge involving you, I'm afraid.'

'Boss, I can't tell you how happy that would make me. She'd be bound to plead not guilty if it went to trial, and having to stand up in public court to discuss my battered bits is not exactly top of my bucket list.'

It raised a ripple of amusement and some heads nodding in sympathy.

'Right, Jo, priority for today, please, is tracing all the names we have so far and hauling them in for questioning. Whatever happens with the PM this morning, we have the drugs issue to deal with, so we might as well do the legwork on that for now.

'The plan is, depending on what the Professor can tell us today, to bring Abigail back in for questioning tomorrow. We're got an experienced Makaton interpreter lined up, and Jezza, I think you should be in on that, since Abigail clearly already relates well to you and trusts you. I'd like to take the lead on it for now, though.

'And don't forget you're with me for the PM later this morning, Jezza. Or that we need to be on time for the Professor, of course.'

'Not forgotten, boss. Looking forward to it. You certainly know all the best places to take a girl.'

Ted smiled indulgently. It was good to see her looking less tired than she had on Saturday. When it was time to set off for the post-mortem, he let her drive his service vehicle, as usual.

'Ah, here you are,' Professor Bizzie Nelson greeted them. There was an implied 'at last' in her tone, although they were, as usual, ahead of the appointed hour.

This time there were no eagerly-watching students lined up in the viewing gallery, hanging on to the Professor's every word as she spoke. Just Bizzie and her assistant, who was working away discreetly in the background.

'We've just done the preliminaries so far, whilst we were waiting for you to join us. I can get started properly now you're here. I hope you have your sweeties with you, or whatever you plan to use. He's not exactly our most fragrant guest, it has to be said.'

As soon as she made the first incision, Jezza clamped a hand to her mouth, blurted an apologetic sound and bolted out of the door.

Bizzie watched her go with a sympathetic expression.

'Poor lamb. Not the nicest one for her to have to attend. How far gone is she?'

She saw the surprised look Ted gave her and hurried on, 'Oh dear, whoops. Situation normal. Open big gob and insert brogue-clad foot right in it, Elizabeth. As per usual. I take it she's not made the news public yet?'

'First I've heard of it. Are you sure?'

'Edwin,' she told him patiently, using his full name, which she only ever used in private, now Jezza had left the room, 'I do know quite a bit about the human anatomy and how it works. More importantly, I have seen so many people get pukey in my autopsy suite. Believe it or not, not all of them behave in the same way. I may very well be wrong. It has been known. But that,' she nodded to the door which was still swinging slightly with the speed of Jezza's exit, 'was not your average post-mortem puke.

'So, do we bash on regardless, or wait for the unfortunate young lady to come back and join us. If indeed she feels able to do so.'

'We don't want to delay you, and I do need to know your findings as soon as possible. Carry on, please. We'd better not say anything for now. But I'll try to find time to have a long chat with Jezza at some point. See if there's anything she wants to confide in me. We get along quite well. She might well open up.

'I usually stop for a cup of tea and a bacon barm on the way back to the station after a PM. For some reason, they always give me an appetite, especially for meat.'

Bizzie's tone was dry as she told him, 'You might want to consider that that might not be the most tactful course of action in the young lady's presence, if I'm right.'

Chapter Ten

'Right, so, on with the business in hand. The body is that of a young white male. Estimated age is eighteen to nineteen, subject to confirmation. Below average weight for his size but we don't yet know if there is a pathological reason for that.

'I've sent off samples to confirm the identity, and I have asked for everything involving this case to be fast-tracked as much as possible. But I understand you believe this to be the body of Giorgio Mantone, known as Latte.

'As you can see, we have already removed the knife which appears to have delivered a single fatal blow to the thorax. It's been sent for fingerprinting and DNA testing, also marked for fast-tracking, which might help you to determine who was wielding it at the time the wound was inflicted.

'As usual, I've been playing around with the weapon and some cadavers – the fun part of my work – to try to reproduce as accurately as possible the wound and its direction of entry. All of which indicates that this was a single blow delivered by a right-handed person standing immediately in front of the deceased, although the blade has gone in at a slight angle. No great force would have been required as the knife was extremely sharp and very well made. I've made a note to get some of the same make. It's much better than anything I currently have in my kitchen.

'There's a total absence of any sort of defensive wound on the deceased's hands or arms, so it would appear that the unfortunate victim was not expecting any such attack and had no time to put up any sort of defence. The indications are that he clasped his hands to the wound after it was inflicted, rather than before, in any sort of preventive measure.'

The door opened quietly at that moment and Jezza crept back in, muttering an apology. Neither Bizzie nor Ted commented. Whether or not the Professor was right, Ted decided it was neither the time nor the place to take it any further.

Bizzie had cracked open the chest by this point and was peering inside with something of an air of triumph.

'I try not to go in with any preconceptions, but it's always pleasing when my initial ideas – I prefer to call them that as I don't do guesswork – prove to be correct. I'm seeing largely what I expected to see. The knife has gone in through this intercostal space, here,' she was poking a gloved finger into the entry wound as she spoke. 'It's passed cleanly between these two ribs without touching either of them. Luck? Or carefully judged precision? That's for your department to determine, Chief Inspector.' She was being formal now that Jezza had rejoined them.

'The blade has nicked a lung here – do you see? – then gone on to sever arteries and the aorta, as it penetrated the heart.

'Now, because I saw the body in situ, I know that this unfortunate young man, once stabbed, slumped first to his knees then pitched face-forward onto the floor. The pressure of his own weight would have been expected to cause the blade to pass right through and exit at the back. It's long and sharp enough. But there is no rear exit wound so I'm expecting to find, as I delve deeper, that the point lodged itself either against a rib or against the spine. If the latter, then depending on the damage it inflicted there, it could have considerably accelerated death.'

'Would death have been an inevitable outcome of a wound like that? Could he have been saved if medical assistance had been called at once?' Ted asked her.

'Unlikely in the extreme, I would say. We all know the waiting times for ambulances these days. Paramedics do an amazing job, but something like this would have required the immediate attention of a highly skilled cardio-thoracic surgeon. Not someone who would be routinely despatched to an incident like this. Not unless the person calling for emergency aid knew enough to indicate the nature of the wound and the likely ensuing problem. Even then a positive outcome was highly unlikely, given the amount of damage.

'A penetrating wound to the heart, such as this, causes a condition called cardiac tamponade. If you watch any of the dreadful hospital series on television, you might already know that that is
a clinical syndrome caused by the accumulation of fluid in the pericardial space. It results in reduced ventricular filling and subsequent haemodynamic compromise. It's an extreme medical emergency which can easily lead to death, if not given immediate emergency intervention.'

'Would it have been obvious to the person who stabbed him that he was dying, Professor?' Jezza asked. She still looked pale, but at least she was now watching and listening attentively.

'The most obvious immediate sign of cardiac tamponade would probably have been distended neck veins and some difficulty in breathing. Then a clinical examination would reveal low arterial pressure and distant, muffled heart sounds. Both of which would require specialised knowledge and equipment to detect.

'And we are still talking about Councillor Buller's daughter being the principal suspect here, I take it? Pending the findings from the knife, of course. If that were to be the case, then I would find it unlikely in the extreme, based on what I have heard about her, which is admittedly not a lot. It really is very specialised knowledge. Unless she is an avid watcher of said medi-soaps, then I'm not sure where such knowledge would come from. Even if she had it, she could have done nothing, single-handedly, to prevent this person's death. Whether or not she caused it, either deliberately or accidentally.

'In conclusion, this young man has been killed by other than his own hand. But whether in an act of murder, or of self-defence, is beyond my realms of science to answer. Your best hope now rests on what the knife itself can tell you. Although I'd venture to suggest that, unless you have some witnesses, it would be difficult, perhaps impossible, to rule out self-defence.'

'Can you pull over here for a moment, Jezza, please. You're about to witness my guilty secret. I usually stop here for a cuppa and a bacon barm on the way back from a PM which, for some reason, always gives me a ravenous appetite.'

'It's a survival reflex, boss. Some people, confronted by death, become rampantly randy. I should be grateful your instinct is nothing worse than to eat dead pigs.'

Ted laughed then asked, 'Can I get you anything?'

'Just a tea, please. No milk or sugar.'

She was quiet and thoughtful when Ted got back to the car and handed her the drink.

'Will it bother you, me sitting here eating my greasy dead pig? I can open the window ...'

'It's fine. Don't worry.'

Ted took a first eager bite of his barm, trying to work out in his head how he was going to broach the subject. He was worried about saying the wrong thing. Blundering in and spoiling the good relationship he had with Jezza.

He swallowed his bite of sandwich; washed it down with a mouthful of tea, then began, treading carefully, 'Are you all right, Jezza? Because I hope you know you can always talk to me. About anything. Not just work stuff. If it would help you at all.'

Of all the reactions he was expecting, it wasn't her turning to him, eyes flashing in evident anger, and spitting, 'Oh, for god's sake! Yes, I am pregnant. No, it wasn't planned. And no, I don't have a bloody clue yet what I'm going to do about it, except I know I don't want to have a baby. So the last thing I need right now is you wading in like a bloody great hoofwanking spangletwat making me feel ten times worse.'

Then she burst into noisy, anguished sobs which shook her whole body, making her black tea slosh alarmingly close to the top of the paper cup.

Wordlessly, Ted put down his roll and his own drink and took Jezza's tea from her, carefully storing it in the car's cup holder. Then, still saying nothing, he reached for the clean, perfectly-ironed handkerchief which Trev always put in his pocket, and handed it to her.

She took it. Wiped her eyes. Blew her nose. Then she reached out her left hand, not looking at Ted, took hold of his right one and gave it a squeeze.

'Sorry,' she said quietly. 'Can we put it down to hormones?'

'Jezza, I want to help but I'm useless at this. I've no idea what to say or do. Is there anyone you can talk to who would know the right things to say to be supportive? Certainly not to make you feel worse, for which I can only apologise.

'Have you told Nat, and what does he say about it?'

'Oh, he's over the moon. He'd love to have a child. But, bless him, I know he'll accept whatever decision I make. It would be so much easier if he was the dominant type who would tell me what to do then put his foot down to make me do it. Only of course, I don't really mean that. Hormones, again, I suppose.'

'Close female friends you can talk to?'

'I'm not really the girlfriend type. Yes, there are girls I go kick-boxing with. Ones I go out and get pissed with, on occasion. But no one I could talk to about something this big.

In fact, you're the first person I ever told about what my father did to me.

'This was a monumental mistake. One which should never have happened. Certainly not planned. And now I have to think about all of the consequences of this mess.

'I just don't think I can do this. Even with Nat's help, and he's wonderful. Autism runs in families. What if the baby is like Tommy? Worse, perhaps. I can barely cope with Tom a lot of the time. I certainly couldn't do it without the help I get from Nat. Not forgetting what Maurice and Steve have done to help. Steve still rallies round when he can but Maurice has enough on his plate now with the new twins.

'Maurice is my best friend. But can you imagine me talking to Daddy Hen about killing an unborn child?'

'And is that what you want to do?'

'Yes! No. I don't know. I don't know who I can talk to. A grown-up. But not someone who's going to judge me.'

While she was calming down and the violent shakes of her body the sobs had produced were diminishing, Ted risked another bite of his barm, washed down with more tea, both already starting to go cold.

'What about the Professor?' he suggested.

Jezza's look towards him suggested she thought he'd lost the plot.

'No, I'm serious, Jezza. She helped me through a dark and difficult time. She's become a great friend to me and Trev. She calls a spade a bloody shovel but she really does have a heart of gold.'

'But that really is weird, boss. I'm thinking about killing my unborn child and you want me to talk to a pathologist about it. Talk about cutting out the middle man!'

'I'm sorry. Everything I say sounds more and more tactless. But you honestly can talk to her. She knew, straight away. She mentioned it to me because clearly she thought I'd know already. Hence me blundering in like a … what was it, hoof-spanking something or another?'

Jezza's laugh was spontaneous and genuine. Much more like her old self. She grinned at him as she said, 'Best not dwell on that, boss. Sorry.'

'Right, if you want me to, I'll phone the Professor and ask if she would speak to you. Whatever you decide to do, Jezza, you know, I hope, that you will have my support. But for now, I need you to be on top form tomorrow for the interview with Abigail. So I want you to get your notes together and take them home to read through them. Then take some time to do whatever will help you. A nice long soak in the bath ...'

'The hot baths and gin remedy is a bit old hat these days, boss.' There was another spark of the old Jezza in the way she said it, smiling at him as she did so. 'But I don't need to go home ...'

'You will do as your senior officer instructs you, DC Vine,' he told her, trying to sound stern, despite the fond smile towards her. 'Tomorrow is going to be a challenging day for all of us. Councillor Buller will no doubt engage the best solicitor money can buy and we'll be facing challenges to the interview every step of the way. We need to have our game plan sorted, and you and I will need to get our heads together first thing tomorrow, before we do anything else.

'So go home, read up, get some rest. And I'll ask Professor Nelson to give you a call.'

Jezza drained her tea and reached up to put her seatbelt back on. Then she leaned across and planted a kiss on Ted's cheek.

'You really are the best boss. D'you know that?'

Ted had caught up with the progress of the team from Jo Rodriguez, once he got back to the station. Or rather, the frustrating lack of it.

'It seems like all the cuckoos have flown back to their own nests, wherever they are, for now, boss,' Jo told him. 'Still no clue at all as to who Data might be, or even whether it's a name or a nickname. It may possibly be something you can find out from Abigail tomorrow.'

'I don't think we should get our hopes up too high for results tomorrow, Jo. I think it's going to be something of an initial fishing trip for both sides. Whatever solicitor Buller brings in will be top rate, you can be certain of that. The Professor has pushed for early results for any prints or traces on the knife, but unless we get those in time, we have very little.

'We also don't know, until we sit down and make a start, how much, if anything, Abigail is going to be able to tell us. Never mind knowing whether she's willing to tell us anything at all. I'm talking to Her Majesty and Big Jim last thing today to see where we're going. We'll also conference call with CPS. I'd say there's a strong possibility, short of a frank and detailed admission from Abigail, that they may decide this one is not in the public interest to proceed with. Her legal team would be bound to go for diminished responsibility, anyway.

'So, give me some good news to throw their way. What's been achieved today?'

'We've got a bit more of a picture of Giorgio Mantone, if that is who our victim is. Sad and depressing. Not a good start in life. Easily led into trouble, which seemed to follow him everywhere.

'Busty Beff seems to have gone to ground. No further sightings of her so far. But I did find out from various shops that she's well known for her trick of sponging off anyone kind and gullible enough to believe her story of having lost her purse.

'No sign either of Kane Lomax, Sarwar Dabiri or Reece Williams, the other names we've found so far. They've all got records so we got an ID on them from face recognition, confirmed by Uniform. So far there's one girl no one knows, not even Bill Baxter, believe it or not. Plus the mysterious Data. Bill doesn't know of him either, not from the name or from the still from the security camera. It looks like he might also be new to the patch.

'As far as the drugs connection goes, not much to go on there so far, but we are still digging. Virgil's gone out round his contacts to see what he can find out. We don't think Stockport has any more or less of a drugs problem than anywhere else. But the way Ronnie is freaking out, we're concerned that something's moving up a gear somewhere.

'The Big Man isn't helping us much so far. It's a pretty common expression for anyone in charge of anything. Certainly no one, not even Bill, knows who it might refer to in a drugs context. And speaking of the drugs connection, Drugs have been on, returning your call, while you were out. They don't have any ongoing ops on our patch, covert or otherwise. They're not aware of any escalation in drugs supply here and they don't know who the Big Man might be in our context. But they have got an op on in Manchester, so I suppose it's just possible that that's where the cuckoos were selling stuff, if that's what they've been doing.

'They did get a rush-through analysis on at least some of the stuff found in Abigail's flat. Enough to tell me it's very good stuff. Some of the best quality they've seen recently. So now their interest has gone up several notches, in tandem with their anxiety to get that supply route closed down as soon as possible.

'They're anxious to be kept informed. So with that end in mind, they'll be talking to Big Jim and the Super about a possibility of some of them working with us on this.

'Wherever this case is going, Ted, it looks like it's going to be a biggy.'

Chapter Eleven

Ted tapped briefly on the Ice Queen's door and hurried in apologetically. She and Jim Baker were sitting waiting and had already established the conference call with one of the senior Crown Prosecutors from the CPS.

'Sorry to be on the last minute. Afternoon, Tony,' he said towards the screen. 'I've literally just got the results on the fingerprints from the knife handle. Abigail's are the only ones on it. We took hers, of course, for elimination purposes, while CSI were working in the flat.'

'I can see us hitting a problem right there,' Tony Alleyne, the prosecutor, said gloomily. 'Did she understand what she was consenting to when she was asked to provide her prints?'

He saw Ted open his mouth and went on, 'Yes, I know you'll say you took every reasonable care and you had an interpreter and everything. But if this even gets as far as a preliminary hearing, the defence are going to jump all over this part right from the start.'

'So can we ask her again, tomorrow, when her solicitor's present?' Ted asked him.

'Let's cross that bridge when we come to it. Mention tomorrow that we have her fingerprints on the knife and see what her solicitor says to that. What else?'

'The elephant in the room,' Ted told him. 'Abigail's pregnancy. We're not sure if she knows herself that she's pregnant. Let alone if her parents know. It's not the easiest thing to raise with someone even when there are no communication issues.'

He was thinking of his own recent efforts.

'We can't tell the parents. It would be a breach of all sorts of Abigail's rights. But at some point, it's going to have to come out. I'd quite like to raise it with her tomorrow because I suspect there's a strong possibility that the father might well be this lad Data, one of the ones we can't trace.

'Having said that, I also think there's a possibility of some sort of porn film-making having gone on in the flat, but that's just speculation at the moment. If that was happening, then there's a chance that even Abigail doesn't know who the father is. Always assuming she knows the basics of how these things come about.'

Tony Alleyne turned his gaze up towards the ceiling and groaned.

'Dear god in heaven, this case just gets better and better. We now have a learning-disabled, abuse-victim mother-to-be, protecting her unborn child against all comers like a she-wolf. We may as well throw the towel in now. Certainly as far as a murder charge goes.'

'We need some expert evaluation of her ability to make deductions and judgements,' the Ice Queen put in, her voice measured. 'The fact that the parents seem happy for her to live independently, rather than in some sort of supported living scheme, is surely rather telling?'

'Plus she pulled up DC Vine for saying man rather than boy, didn't she?' Jim Baker put in. 'That must indicate some degree of basic understanding and judgement.'

'I wouldn't want to see that point argued in court, Jim. It's too subjective. I suspect even the four of us might have a different opinion about when a boy becomes a man, so we might all use a different term. It's too flaky to amount to much.

'What about her educational levels? What do her school records show?' Alleyne went on.

'We're working on getting those. She was educated at a

residential special school. Exclusive and expensive. They're proving a bit reluctant to hand over any records without the permission of the parents. Jo's dealing with that. He's reminding them that Abigail is of age so there would be confidentiality issues if they discuss anything with her parents. But I suspect it will take a warrant to get all the records.'

'Either Debs or I can sort that, Ted. Leave it with us,' Jim told him.

'Do it as a matter of urgency. It's going to be pivotal to how we proceed,' the prosecutor urged them. 'How were you able to find out where she went to school? Was she able to give you such details?'

'There's been quite a bit about her in the papers over the years,' Ted told him. 'A lot of controversy about her not being vaccinated and her disabilities having been caused by a preventable childhood illness. Councillor Buller has, of course, spent a lot of time taking action against various press and media and there have been some apologies and retractions. But there's still enough out there on the internet to find out a good deal about her. We are, of course, checking thoroughly that anything we find is accurate. I've got Steve Ellis on that. He's a demon for detail, especially when it comes to the internet.'

'I thought it couldn't be any worse. Now it seems that it could, with all that to contend with. Who's doing the interview tomorrow?' Alleyne asked.

'I will be,' Ted told him. 'Together with DC Vine. She's already built something of a rapport with Abigail so that should make it easier. And we've got a Makaton interpreter booked.'

'No doubt Abigail's team will insist on bringing their own.'

'I hadn't thought of that,' Ted admitted. 'What's the procedure? Would they be entitled to?'

'They will claim that anyone brought in by us can't be considered to be impartial. It's a moot point,' Alleyne told him. 'But they must presumably have their own, for when their solicitor talks to Abigail, so they might well insist. I'd be inclined to agree, if they do. Let's be seen to be doing everything in our power to be impartial and without pre-judgement. And especially to be doing whatever we can to ensure Abigail has the same level of protection as any other witness or suspect from inadvertently incriminating themselves through lack of proper understanding.

'It might, of course, turn into duelling hand signals between the two Makaton experts if they disagree over the interpretation of anything she says. But that's a risk we'll have to take.'

'That would mean too many people to squash into a normal interview room,' Debs Calder pointed out. 'I would suggest, therefore, that you use the vulnerable witness room, Ted. Then we really are seen to be doing all we can to enable Abigail.'

'Nice PR touch, Debs. I would agree with that,' the prosecutor told her.

'I'll be watching over the monitor, too, Tony. We need to be right across this from the start,' Jim Baker told him.

'No pressure, then?' Ted asked with a touch of irony.

'Hey, you. Supper can be ready any time you want it. You could have it now, or chill a bit first,' Trev told him when Ted walked into the kitchen. He turned to give him a brief hug and a kiss on the cheek, then put a lid on the simmering pan and turned the heat down underneath it. Adam was already halfway up Ted's leg, needle claws clinging to his trousers.

'I'd really like a shower first. It was the PM this morning on the body from Friday. It didn't smell quite as bad but I'd still like to freshen up and get changed before we eat, if that's ok?'

'As I said, it's ready now but it can simmer for a while yet before it starts to spoil. Do you want company in the shower?'

'It sounds tempting, but I feel like I still smell bad, so perhaps later on, when I feel more fragrant. Anyway, I'll be quicker on my own and I'm quite hungry now. I only remember having a bacon barm early on and that went cold before I got chance to eat it all.'

'Make the most of the home cooking,' Trev warned him when he came back downstairs. 'We may be living off takeaways for a bit. Geoff's had his operation confirmed. He goes in tomorrow so I'm likely to be getting home later than usual.'

'Do you know yet what he's going in for?'

'Oh, heavens, no, I still daren't ask. I mean, Geoff and I get on really well but I don't need to know about his plumbing or anything else intimate.'

'It could be ingrown toenails,' Ted suggested, smiling.

Trev gave a theatrical shudder as he dished up their meal.

'Don't! You know I hate anything like that. But I'm just a bit worried about Wednesday and the self-defence class. I'll do my best to be there on time, but it depends how things are going at work. I can usually leave Geoff to close up while I swan off. In fact, I think I'm about to find out exactly why he is the senior partner and how little work I really put into the business in comparison.'

'This is good,' Ted indicated his plate. 'Just what I needed.'

'Does it need more pepper? I couldn't decide.'

'It's fine. Delicious, in fact. And you do a lot for the business. You've brought in some good service contracts. You could sell coals to Newcastle. Even the Ice Queen admitted she was nearly tempted to buy from you. Except she had her heart set on a Ducati.'

'Is there any chance at all you can get to the dojo on Wednesday? Just in case I'm held up for any reason? I'd hate to disappoint them all. All those eager young faces, waiting for one of us to turn up and teach them.'

'All I can promise is that I'll try my very best and if for any reason I can't get there, I'll try to phone you early on to let you know. But you know what it's like, with work. I can't guarantee anything.'

'If I don't know that by now, after living with you for years, there's absolutely no hope for us.'

Ted was expecting Abigail's legal representative to be high calibre. When he saw her and her parents entering the station preceded by the imposing pin-striped figure of Rafe Stewart-Smith, he almost groaned aloud. He had a fearsome reputation and a price tag which made Ted's eyes water just thinking about it.

He'd not been available at short notice when Abigail had first been brought in. It had been a minion from the same firm who had come in on that occasion.

There was another man with the family. Not as tall as the solicitor but big and solid, with shoulder-length hair and a bushy full-face beard. As soon as Ted saw him, he was reminded of a TV series he'd watched as a boy. A fugitive from justice, living in the American backwoods, with a bear as his sole companion.

Ted was about to go across to greet them when Councillor Buller strode over to him, his face furious.

'Right, we're here. Now can we get this farce over and done with?'

Ted nodded to them in greeting. He was about to speak when Abigail rushed forward towards him and Jezza, beaming, signing and trying to articulate.

She looked totally different to when they'd seen her on Friday. Her hair had been recently cut and styled. Her face had a discreet touch of make-up. Her clothes looked new and she smelled of a light citrus fragrance.

Ted and Jezza had agreed between them not to attempt any sign language in case they made mistakes. They would simply speak and leave their expert to interpret.

The bearded man stepped forward and said, 'She said Hello, darling, and hello, then what sounded like Jess. I'm

Christy Madden. I'm here to help Abi with communication.'

'Thank you, Mr Madden. We do, of course, have our own Makaton expert, but we have no objection at all to you being present for the interview.

'Councillor Buller, Mrs Buller, if you'd like to take a seat over there, please, I'll make sure that someone brings you a drink at some point. Abigail, if you would like to come with us, with your solicitor. Mr Madden, could you explain what's happening, please.'

'We're sitting nowhere,' Buller said angrily. 'We're coming to make sure our daughter is being properly treated.'

Ted had started to move away but turned back to him and explained patiently, 'Councillor Buller, as I've said to you previously, and as no doubt Mr Stewart-Smith has explained to you, Abigail is an adult in the eyes of the law. Therefore you don't have the right to be present. Her solicitor is there to protect her interests and we are doing everything we can to allow for her special needs.'

'And I've told you before, I don't like your attitude. I've a good mind to make an official complaint about you.'

'Please feel free to do so, sir,' Ted told him calmly. It was water off a duck's back to him. Such things went with his role. 'Some of my senior officers are currently in the station. If you ask at the front desk, I'm sure arrangements can be made for you to speak to the Assistant Divisional Commander, Superintendent Caldwell. But for now, unless I receive orders to the contrary, I'm not prepared to allow you to be present when we interview Abigail.'

The hint of a smile passed over Stewart-Smith's lips. He and Ted had met, and clashed, before. It had ended in a bloodless draw and they now had a grudging mutual respect.

'He's absolutely right, Frank, I have to say. At present, you don't have the right to be in there with Abi. I did warn you of that. That's what you're paying me for. And you can trust me, I promise. I will look after Abi's interests.'

Ted led the way to the vulnerable witness room, then stood aside to let the others go in. A woman waiting there stood up as they entered. She looked surprised to see the bearded man and addressed him first.

'Hello, Christy, I didn't know you were on this one, too.' Then she turned her full attention to Abigail, smiling at her, speaking clearly and signing as she spoke, 'Hello, Abigail. I'm Emma. I'm here to help you.'

Abigail smiled at her and at the bearded man. She seemed perfectly relaxed.

'Can we just have a few ground rules first?' Christy Madden asked. 'I can understand you wanting two interpreters to avoid any conflict of interest,' he looked at Stewart-Smith as he spoke. 'But Emma and I have worked together before, and I'm quite happy that she will interpret accurately and without bias. So, much as it would be nice to take your client's money, do you really still need me here as well? Might it be a bit overwhelming for Abigail, for one thing?'

'Those are my instructions, Mr Madden,' Stewart-Smith told him. 'In the circumstances, I would propose a compromise. I would suggest that Emma here does the interpreting and you follow closely. But please let me know immediately if you feel anything at all requires further clarification or is open to differing interpretations.

'Shall we all sit down and get started now?' Ted asked. 'We can move the chairs round if we need to, so Abigail can see to lip read.' Then he looked directly at Abigail and began speaking slowly and clearly. 'Abigail, I'm Detective Chief Inspector Darling, this is Detective Constable Vine. You met us both before, on Friday. We're going to be recording this interview. Is that all right with you?'

While Ted spoke, Emma's hands moved in rapid explanation and she mouthed his words clearly for Abigail to follow. Abigail nodded happily and beamed at them both, as if at old friends she was pleased to see again.

'I need to ask you about the man – the boy – who was found in your kitchen. Do you know what happened to him?'

Emma listened then spoke for her, faithfully interpreting exactly what she said and signed.

'Bad boy. He hurted me. Shouted in my ears. I was frightened. He said bad things. I thought he would hit me. I hit him. He falled down.'

'Abigail, do you know what happened to the boy when he fell down?'

'He bleeded. Then he went to sleep. Not woken up.'

Jezza and Ted exchanged a look which spoke volumes. Could Abigail really not know that the boy she called Latte was dead?

Ted was more than a little surprised that so far Stewart-Smith hadn't challenged anything his client had been asked nor advised her to say nothing. It seemed clear that he would be relying on claiming that his client had been acting purely in self-defence. Without any witnesses, it was going to be extremely difficult to prove otherwise.

'What did you hit the boy with, Abigail?'

This time she didn't speak, simply mimed something which was easy to understand. The movement of a corkscrew being turned.

'Could you please clarify what exactly she means, Emma?' Ted asked her. He was starting to get a glimmer of why the solicitor was sitting so passively.

'A thing for bottles, she says. He wanted beer so I took bottle thing to take top off bottle.'

'And who was this boy?'

Emma frowned. 'She's signing coffee but saying what seems to be Latte.'

Ted nodded. 'Thank you.' Then he went on, 'Abigail, can you please tell me again why you hit Latte.'

'She said he frightened her. He was a bad boy. Then she said her daddy told her that if a bad boy tried to hurt her she must pick up a thing near to her and hit him with it.'

'Abigail, do you know that Latte is dead?'

She smiled at him, shaking her head as if she'd just heard something silly.

'She says not dead. Latte sleeping. Latte falled down and now he sleeping.'

Chapter Twelve

'What d'you think, boss?'

Ted had called for a short break to go and consult with Jim Baker. It was a tricky case and he wanted to make sure his Big Boss was thinking along the same lines as he was at every stage.

'What do I think?' he rumbled. 'I think that bastard father has spent the entire weekend schooling her in what to say. Except he clearly forgot to tell her not to mention his bloody great idea of virtually telling her it was fine to stab any bugger who bothered her.'

He looked across at Jezza with his most stern expression and said, 'And you didn't hear me swearing then, did you DC Vine?'

'Not at all, sir. Perish the thought.'

'I would love to get him on an inciting charge, but I know that's just a pipe dream. The question is, where do you plan to go from here, Ted?'

'We need to explore Abigail's pregnancy, which will certainly be opening up a can of worms. If the parents don't know about it, it will put Stewart-Smith into an ethical dilemma over whether or not he should say something to them. But we are going to have to broach that subject with her because so far it's our only route to identifying this character Data, as far as I can see.

'It's going to be difficult to handle, especially as we're not sure if Abigail knows herself yet. Or rather if she understands

107

what it's all about. Jezza and I have discussed at length how that part of the interview will go. She already has Abigail's trust so she's going to do the bulk of the questioning next. It's one of the reasons we need those school records, so we have a better idea of Abigail's level of understanding.'

Jezza and Ted had had a long discussion earlier on the way they planned the interview to proceed. Jezza had seemed in better spirits. Ted wasn't going to pry but she appeared to be quite happy to talk about her situation to him, in the privacy of his office.

'The Professor was bloody marvellous, boss. Thanks so much for that. She made time for me last night. She even invited me round to her place so we could talk in private. I felt I could say absolutely anything to her. In fact I pretty much did. She told me all the current statistics for the possibility of me having a child with autism. They were a bit more worrying than I'd thought from my own research.

'So after talking about all the options with her, I've decided to have a termination. Next week.'

She was looking anxiously at Ted. Scanning his face for judgement. Not finding any.

'The timing's just not right for me. One day, maybe, I will have a child. But for the moment, I can't do it. There's my career, for one thing. You know I'm not looking for promotion now. Maybe the dizzy heights of DS sometime in the future, but I'm honestly not that bothered.

'I love my job. I love all of the team and being part of it. Maybe that makes me a selfish bitch, but I don't want to take a break from it just yet.

'And then there's Tommy. Not just the risk that any baby I have might well be the same as him, if not more challenging. I've no idea how he would react to sharing living space and attention. Perhaps if Tom goes to boarding school in the future or something. I don't know. All I do know is that the timing isn't right for me now. Not at all.'

'Jezza,' Ted told her gently, 'It's entirely your decision. I told you. I'll support whatever you decide. Just let me know when you need time off. And I'm glad you talked to the Professor. She's very easy to talk to. Even I've managed to tell her things, and that's something I'm not good at.'

'We seemed to get on like a house on fire. She's amazing. Not at all how I expected her to be. Different altogether, away from work.'

'Are you going to be all right talking to Abigail today about her pregnancy? If you'd rather not ...'

'Boss, it's fine. Really. I feel relieved, more than anything, now I've made the decision and booked the appointment. Nat and I had another long talk last night and he was as supportive as ever. I honestly don't deserve him. So I'm quite happy to talk to Abi. And as she says she loves me, I might be the best person to do it.'

'Sorry for the short delay. I hope you've all had something to drink while you were waiting?'

Ted and Jezza retook their seats, rewarded once again by beaming smiles from Abigail. Ted turned his attention to her and said, 'Abigail, Jezza would like to ask you some questions now, if that's all right with you? If you're happy to talk to her?'

Abigail nodded enthusiastically and signed something which Jezza and Ted both now recognised without needing the translation of Emma. Two hands over her heart, then pointing to Jezza.

'She said I love you.'

Stewart-Smith frowned at that then addressed Ted as if neither Jezza nor his client were present in the room.

'Can I just clarify, is there some sort of special relationship between this officer and my client? If so I may need to request that she is questioned by someone else.'

'Don't we need to consider Abi in this, and what she wants?' Madden put in.

Emma nodded agreement, and added, 'You certainly need to make sure Abi can lip read what you're saying and give me time to interpret for her, rather than speak about her in her presence.'

He inclined his head in her direction but made no comment. He did, however, turn to Abigail and say, slowly and distinctly, 'Are you happy for this officer to ask you questions, Abi?'

There was no mistaking the enthusiastic expression on Abigail's face as she nodded her head vigorously.

'Thank you, Abigail,' Jezza began. 'Can I ask you, please, do you have a boyfriend?'

A blush and a child-like giggle. Then a nod of the head.

'Do I need to interpret that for you?' Emma asked. 'Abi is saying yes, if so.'

'And what's his name?'

She signed and spoke, though not clearly. 'Data.'

'And are you sleeping with Data?'

Abigail's face took on a puzzled frown. Emma and Madden both started to speak at the same time. Emma indicated that she was happy to let him go first.

'I'm sure Emma and I were both about to say the same thing, officer. Makaton isn't like British Sign Language. It's rather more limited as it's designed partly with people with learning disabilities in mind. To that extent, it's not quite as nuanced. A question like that is open to misinterpretation.

'Emma and I will be able to interpret in some detail any specific questions to do with sexual activity, but they will need to be quite direct. No euphemisms.'

'I agree,' Emma confirmed. 'We might have to make it much more basic than that. It is possible to be quite explicit. But euphemisms do indeed present a problem so they're probably best avoided.'

'We're happy to be guided by both of you,' Ted confirmed.

'Abi, do you have sex with Data?'

Emma repeated the question, her hand movements explicit. More giggling from Abigail, her eyes downcast, her head nodding.

Jezza looked to Emma rather than at Abigail as she said, 'I need to deal with the subject of consent. If Mr Stewart-Smith and Mr Madden have no objection, I'm happy to be guided by you as to how to convey that meaning, and whatever answer Abi gives.'

Jezza sat back and watched the exchange between the two of them. Abigail seemed quite animated. Jezza recognised the now familiar gesture for 'love' as Abigail signed and said, 'I love Data and Data loves me.'

'Right, at this point, I'm going to have to raise an objection about the line of questioning. With the greatest respect to this officer,' Stewart-Smith made no pretence of remembering Jezza's name, 'my client uses the same word and phrase about loving her and loving this person Data, whoever that might be. It's not clear to me at this stage, therefore, what her level of comprehension is.'

'I'd be happy to leave this particular topic for now and come back to it in a second or subsequent interview,' Ted told him. 'I think it might be better to carry out the interviews for shorter times than we would normally use. Please carry on, DC Vine.'

'Do you have any photos of Data, Abi? On your phone, perhaps?'

She shook her head then signed. Emma interpreted.

'No photo on my phone. Data shy. Not like photo.'

'Can you tell us the names of any of your other friends, Abi? Would it help you to write them down for us, or is it easier for you to tell Emma?'

Emma only got a single-handed gesture to the heart, Jezza noticed, as Abigail signalled her willingness to speak through her. Jezza pressed on. It was going to be slow work, with Abigail's poor speech and not knowing how well she could spell each name.

When she'd finished reeling off a list, with a lot of stammering which clearly made it harder to interpret, Emma repeated: 'Data, Latte, Kane, which she signs with a C rather than the more usual K so I don't know which is correct. Then Onnie, and she's not clear on the first letter; Beff, Arwar, Oren and Rhys, I think, although that's unclear. Are you happy with those interpretations, Christy?'

He nodded. 'That's pretty much what I made them too. We might need to confirm in writing at some point.'

'Would any of your friends have photos of Data, Abi? Perhaps a nice photo somewhere of the two of you together?'

Abi nodded enthusiastically and rattled away with attempts to speak, and accompanying hand gestures. Emma looked shocked for a moment, then the professional mask returned.

'She says Kane has pictures of them. Her and Data together. He takes pictures when they're in bed. When Data is loving her. And she says she doesn't love Kane.'

'I see. Thank you,' Jezza said, then turned her attention back to Abigail. 'Abi, do you know you're going to have a baby?'

Stewart-Smith looked surprised. He opened his mouth to speak but Abigail was already replying. Emma interpreted as Abigail made an unmistakeable rocking motion with her arms, whilst at the same time shaking her head vigorously.

'No baby. Jezza is silly.'

'Yes baby, Abigail. The doctor you saw here says very definitely yes baby.'

Eyes wide in wonder, Abigail looked directly at Jezza as she asked and signed, 'Baby? Here?' pointing to her own stomach.

Ted sensed rather than saw the sudden change in Jezza's behaviour. Heard her swallow hard before trying to speak. He immediately took over.

'I think, everyone, that might be enough for today. Abigail, you've had a surprise. Mr Stewart-Smith, you might perhaps like to go somewhere with your client to take further advice. I'm sure I don't need to remind you of the confidentiality question which arises, in view of her age.'

'I hope you're not lecturing me on points of law, Chief Inspector?' he asked, although his tone was ironic. 'But I do think it is in my client's best interests – indeed it is essential in view of where she is currently living – that her parents are informed as soon as possible. Christy, perhaps you and I can go and discuss further with Abi before talking to her parents.'

'You're very welcome to continue to use this room for the time being, if that would help you. Abigail, we will need to speak to you again tomorrow, please. At the same time.'

Ted sent Jezza up to the main office to start writing her own notes of the interview while he went to speak to Jim Baker once more.

'Bloody hell, Ted, what a nasty bunch of little shits this lot seems to be. Bullying the lass, sponging off her, living in her flat, stashing drugs there. And now this filthy business. Porno films of her, by the sounds of it. What in the name of god are we dealing with? And why weren't the parents keeping a better eye on her? How could they convince themselves she was coping on her own? I'll tell you what, it makes my blood boil.'

'Well, try to stay calm, Jim. We don't want you having another heart attack. Bella would never forgive me, for one thing. As your best man, it's my duty to take care of you, right up to the moment you put the ring on her finger.

'And now we have some names to be going on with, it's time for me to go back to the team and see how many of them we can round up. Plus find out what any of them who've already been found have had to say for themselves.'

'Wind this one up fast, Ted, for god's sake,' Jim told him. 'It's as nasty as it gets, and I don't want it on our patch.'

'Doing my best, Jim, as ever. I don't think it's helped that

Buller went storming off to find Debs to complain about me.'

'I'll give him bloody complaining! What in the name of god were the parents thinking about, giving that young lass chef's knives like those? I'm not judging her, but was she really some sort of *cordon bleu* cook? Even if she never took them out of the drawer, didn't it occur to her bone-headed father that he'd put a weapon there which anyone going into that flat could use against her?'

'The problem we've got is that she clearly did take it out of the drawer and quite possibly used it to defend herself, with the consequences we're dealing with.'

'And you've not yet put that to the defence? The fact that we have her fingerprints and only hers on the weapon used? What's your reasoning for that?'

'I made a judgement call. It may or may not be the right one. The news of the pregnancy was clearly a surprise to Abigail, so no doubt the parents are still in the dark. I thought it was probably enough of a bombshell for them to digest in one day.'

'When she says she hit the lad with the corkscrew, do you think she really believes that? Or is it something the father drummed into her? With hindsight, we probably shouldn't have let her go home with her parents.'

'We didn't have enough to hold her in police custody, never mind anything else at that stage, Jim. And can you imagine if we'd gone down that route and got it wrong? We'd have both been tethered to our desks for the rest of our service, coming up with neighbourhood community policing schemes or some such.'

'So how are you proposing going about establishing whether she really does have the intellectual capacity to know the difference between a corkscrew and a bloody big knife?'

'I need those school records. To give me a background on her abilities. I think the only way to check is to show her various kitchen utensils, or photos of them, and get her to identify things. But if, as you say, she's been coached by the father, it might not get us anywhere.

'For now, I'd better go and see if they've left the premises, and if Buller really has lodged a formal complaint against me. Or tried to.'

Jim fell into step next to him, telling him, 'He's not got a bloody snowball in hell's chance. We all know you can be an annoying little bugger, but you're about as by the book as it's possible to be when it comes to procedure.'

The vulnerable witness room was empty now, so the two of them headed towards the reception area. They caught up just as Abigail, her solicitor and her own interpreter were walking towards where her parents were sitting waiting, her father still looking disgruntled and impatient.

As soon as she saw her parents, Abigail broke into an ungainly trot and hurried over to them, smiling widely, looking pleased and proud.

'Baby, here,' she announced, making the same rocking movement and pointing to her stomach. 'Baby!' Then she tapped her own chest and said, 'Mummy. Me. Baby.'

Ted thought he'd seen Buller angry already. His earlier display was as nothing compared to the state of him now.

'What's this bloody nonsense? What have you put into her head? I've already made one complaint about you today, but this is just outrageous. Now I'll have you off this case faster than you can say ...'

'Councillor Buller?' Big Jim stepped forward and placed his considerable bulk directly in front of the ranting man. 'Detective Superintendent Baker. I'm in overall charge of this case, and if you think you're going to remove my best officer from running it, then you and I need to have a long talk.'

Chapter Thirteen

It was a working lunch over sandwiches for most of the team. A time for a catch-up on any progress made so far.

Virgil was still out working round his contacts to see what he could find out about the drugs and the likely supplier. Maurice was at the safe house, talking to Ronnie. He'd phoned in to report on what she'd said. She was slowly opening up to him, but it was clearly going to be a long process.

'So we have one previously unidentified female. Ronnie's told Maurice there's a Lauren, and Abi mentioned an Oren,' Jezza summed up. 'Is that too big a leap to assume it's the same person? I've searched online for anything like Oren as a girl's name. The name exists, but usually for boys. Although we all know the fashion for giving kids the most bizarre and trendy names.'

'We'll put it down as a distinct possible,' Ted agreed. 'Do we have any trace of her? A second name? Anything else to go on?'

A few heads shook.

'Ronnie either doesn't know her second name or isn't saying for the moment. Similarly Abi said Arwar and we know from face recognition that Sarwar Dabiri has been to the flat on several occasions. Abi often drops the first letter of a name so that's surely too big a coincidence for it not to be him. We've not found him yet, nor Kane Lomax, but we're still looking.'

'I've found Busty Beff, boss,' Jo told him. 'The lead on her hanging round shops trying to get people to buy her things was a good one. She actually tried the trick on me and got the shock of her life when I pulled out my ID. She's cooling her heels downstairs while we decide who's doing which interview.'

'And we've got Reece Williams too, I gather, Rob?'

'We have, boss, but bloody hell! That lad can sprint. I had to chase him halfway along Petersgate to get him. And I only succeeded because he ran into someone with a dog, tripped over the lead, then the dog bit his ankle and wouldn't let go.

'He's downstairs too. I'm getting him seen by a doctor, just to be sure. He's bleating about wanting a rabies jab, so I think he watches too much television.'

'Jo, I'll let you decide who interviews which one, but the priorities are to find as many of them as we can. In particular, we need to find Kane Lomax, if he really is the boss of them, as Zofia said. And if he's the one who has the drugs contacts, and who does the filming when Abigail is in bed with Data. It goes without saying that we need to find Data, too.

'Good work, everyone. We'll regroup at the end of the day to see what progress we've made.'

'I'm actually going to be late home for a change,' Trev told Ted when he phoned him, towards the end of the afternoon. 'This being a grown-up stuff is harder than it looks, isn't it? I've got a prospective client who wants to talk service contracts but isn't free until he's finished work for the day. So I'm going to grab a takeaway while I wait for him. If you get home before me, there's plenty in the fridge.'

'I'll probably do the same. I might as well stay on and sort out some paperwork.'

'What about the cats, if neither of us is home to feed them at their usual time?'

'If you fed them this morning, they'll be absolutely fine. They might pretend they won't, but they really will. You be careful what sort of a takeaway you get. You might put your client off if you knock them out with curry fumes.'

Trev laughed. 'I'd better avoid the *sag aloo*, too. Nothing worse than spinach in your teeth when you're trying to woo a new client.'

Ted was still chuckling to himself when there was a brief knock on his door and the Ice Queen strode in. He'd been trying to avoid her so far, not sure he really wanted to know if Buller had made a formal complaint about him or not. Although he was fairly sure he'd have heard about it earlier, had he done so.

She sat down in the spare chair and told him, 'I wouldn't say no to a green tea, if you have some on the go, Ted.'

Ted stood up and put the kettle on. She was being relaxed and informal, so he hoped the news was reasonable, at least.

As if reading his mind, she said, 'First the good news. I managed to persuade the delightful Councillor Buller that he really has no grounds to make a formal complaint against you. Everything you've done has been within the correct procedure, as I would have expected.'

Ted dropped teabags into two mugs and said, 'But I'm sensing there's less good news.'

'Politics, Ted. I know you know all about that. Politics and diplomacy. It would be a good move if you were, without in any way admitting your behaviour was at fault, to offer an apology for having been misinterpreted. Something along those lines.'

Ted could hardly kick another one of his waste-paper baskets to death in front of her, although he had an overwhelming desire to do so. He contented himself with throwing the used teabags into it with more force than was necessary.

'I know. It's a pain in the backside.' There was some sympathy in her tone as she saw his gesture. 'It's simply that, as you well know, it's sometimes better to make a small concession to reach an objective. It doesn't mean, in any sense, that I or anyone else thinks you've done anything wrong.

'Let me know when they're back in the building tomorrow and you and I should greet them together. Perhaps even with Jim there, too. A show of solidarity while you make your little speech. Then you can get on with doing your job.'

Despite the early hour, Ted was already up, dressed and having tea and toast in the kitchen the following morning when his phone rang.

Trev had been right about the cats. Despite having enough dry food in the bowls to see them through a day, at least, they'd been following the unwritten cat law: food at the bottom of the bowl is for dire emergencies only. All seven felines had been sulking, even young Adam, when Trev had got back, much later than usual, but with the new contract signed and sealed. They had at least thawed slightly by the time Ted returned home even later.

'Duty inspector, guv. I hope I didn't wake you. We have a body for you. And it's definitely one for you. The victim appears to have been tortured.'

Ted gulped tea to wash his toast down before replying. 'Where's the scene?'

'Heaton Mersey Park. Well, down in the Bowl there, to be precise. Found by an early morning jogger, as usual. One good reason never to go out jogging, eh? Uniform are in attendance, CSI are on their way. Do you want me to call anyone from your team or can I leave that to you?'

'It's fine, Roly, leave it with me. Thanks.'

A few more swallows of his tea was all he'd have time for now. He decided to call Rob O'Connell for this one. Time to stretch him a bit more, let him have a go at something challenging.

'Morning, Rob, sorry to wake you. How does a dead torture victim appeal to you?'

Rob's voice initially sounded sleepy when he answered.

The details Ted relayed to him appeared to snap him fully awake.

'I've had more appealing invitations, boss, it has to be said. D'you want me to pick you up?'

'It's fine, I'll meet you there. That way I can go back to the nick independently. I need to stick with the Abigail interview for now. So I'll have to leave you to run the scene.'

There was a slight hesitation at the other end, so Ted added, 'If you're up for that?'

'Well, yes, boss, if you think I can handle it.'

'I wouldn't suggest it if I didn't, Rob. I'll see you there shortly.'

He and Rob arrived at the scene within minutes of one another. Crime scene tape was already in place. At least at such an early hour there were no curious members of the public around, trying to find out what was going on.

Ted signed them both in and they walked down the slope, following the direction indicated by the uniformed constable with the clipboard. Ted instinctively reached for his menthol lozenges, knowing there was a torture element involved. He offered one to Rob who accepted, seemingly grateful. They weren't sure what sight might be waiting for them.

Once more, the Crime Scene Manager, who looked up at their approach, was Priya Chowdhury. Ted made a point of waiting this time to catch her attention before entering what she would no doubt remind him was her crime scene until she handed it over. Doug was still off work with his back injury and likely to be so for some time yet, so Ted would have to learn to get along with his stand-in.

One of her team interrupted her concentration. She looked up, then came across to Ted. All he could see, beyond where she'd been working, was a body hanging from a tree, upside down.

'Thank you for waiting this time, Chief Inspector,' she told him. Ted wasn't sure whether there was a note of irony in her tone. He introduced her to Rob then asked, 'Can you tell me what we have, and can we enter the scene, please?'

'The body's your concern, rather than mine. It's a male, I can tell you. And even without the signs of several people having been here, I'd say it would certainly have taken more than one person to string him up like that.'

'Killed on site?'

'Unlikely, I'd say. But go and have a look. Just use the stepping plates. And don't touch anything.'

'I wish I had Doug to work with for my first solo run,' Rob told Ted as they made their way carefully over to the tree where the body was hanging. 'I'll be scared to ask her anything, or even to move, for fear of getting it wrong.'

They'd reached the tree and stood for a moment, looking up at the body. A young man, at first glance. Strung up by the ankles, so the face and hands were low enough down for Ted and Rob to get a good look.

'Tell me what you see, Rob. Your first thoughts.'

'His face has taken quite a beating, for sure. I doubt his own mother would recognise him like that. IC1 male, possibly, but it's hard to be sure. There's a lot of blood around the mouth, too. And look at his hands, boss. The ends of his fingers have been burned away by something. A blowlamp, perhaps? Why would they do that? They must surely realise we can identify a body without prints these days, from the DNA. As long as it's on record somewhere.'

'Purely for the torture element? Or as a warning?' Ted suggested. 'The good news for you is that a case like this, definitely a suspected murder, means it will be Professor Nelson doing the PM. She'll almost certainly want to view the body where it is, I imagine, before it's recovered to her domain. And she's very easy to work with. Approachable, knowledgable. She'll be a big help to you, so don't be afraid to ask for her advice.

'Anything else jump out at you about the body?'

'The head's a bit over to one side at a funny angle. Broken neck? Hung the right way up first, then repositioned?'

'Possibly. But I agree, I'd suspect a broken neck as the likely cause of death.'

'So who shall I call to work with me on this one, boss?'

'The short answer, Rob, is that you're on your own. Sorry about that, but you know as well as I do what staffing levels are like. And we really need to wrap up the Abigail Buller case, one way or another, as soon as we can.

'We'll get Uniform to help with a detailed site search, but there's no sign of any eye witnesses, other than the jogger who phoned it in. Get a detailed statement from them, to start with. I'm going to be tied up and not able to take calls, but liaise with Jo if you need guidance.

'Like I said, the Professor will almost certainly come out to this one herself and she knows as much about working a scene as any of us. You'll be fine, Rob. You've got this.'

The main office was still empty and in the dark when Ted walked through to his own small working space. He went straight for the kettle. He fancied a builder's tea, for once, to wash down the sticky bun he'd picked up quickly on his way in. He'd decided a sugar rush might be a good way to start what was probably going to be another demanding day.

The kettle had only just boiled when there was a quiet, hesitant tap on his door. It could only be Steve. When he called out a, 'Come in', it was the young DC who appeared, looking as uncomfortable as he always did.

'Morning, Steve, you're in early. What can I do for you?'

'Sir, I decided to do a bit of research when I was at Océane's place last night. I know I should have done it on my work computer, but I only had the idea on the way there so I didn't want to come back in. And I didn't want to bother you with it in case it came to nothing ...'

'It's fine, Steve. I trust your judgement. Just be careful if you have anything contentious on your personal computer, but I know how careful you are. Especially working with Océane. Do you want a brew? And boss is fine. You really don't have to call me "sir" all the time.'

Try as he might, he'd never yet found the key to getting Steve to fully relax in his presence.

'Nothing to drink, sir, thank you.'

Steve sat down on the edge of the spare chair, still looking nervous. Ted invited him to carry on.

'Well, sir, in theory it's possible to find anything – anything at all – on the internet if you know where to look and what search terms to use. When I went round to see Océane after work, I asked her for some ideas. I hope that was all right? I mean, I know she has full clearance ...'

'It's fine, Steve,' Ted repeated. 'Good initiative. Well done.'

'Only, you saying that about signs of a tripod being used and mention of some sort of porn filming. It made me think. But this is why I wanted to try the theory out on my own computer first. Some of the search terms are ... well, not anything I would ever use and not something I'd want anyone else to see on my computer, unless it was an official part of the enquiry.'

Ted was starting to wonder if he'd ever come to the point. It was always tricky, where Steve was concerned. He was an excellent officer, but his obsession with always doing the right thing had often led to long dialogues like this one. All round the houses and back, before he made his point. It was always worth waiting for. Especially when he'd been working in tandem with his girlfriend, Océane.

'I understand that. Please go on.'

'I don't know if you know ... well, I don't see why you would ...' then he rushed on, his words blurting out, falling over one another in his discomfort to say them. 'Disabled porn is a thing. There's lots of it out there. There are even some sites exclusively for that. Although it's called something much worse than that.

'And I found her, sir. I found Abi on there. It's not nice, and it doesn't look remotely consensual to me. She looks drunk, or perhaps drugged, for one thing. It's, er, it's like an orgy, too. Group sex. Several of them at the same time. Including some girls.

'The faces are pixelated out, all except for Abi's. I recognised her straight away from the security camera footage at the flats. There's quite a lot of separate videos, clearly not all taken at the same time. More than one of the lads has sex with her, but the main one – so possibly this Data – appears in all of the clips and always gets first go with her. There's no way to make out his face but it's possible to see he's, erm, brown-skinned. So possibly Asian or mixed race or something like that.

'The free access videos are only short. Teasers, really. There are others, behind a paywall, with hints that they're much more hard-core. I wasn't going to get into that on my own computer.

'I've got the links to the trailers on my personal phone, sir. I can send them to you from that, but again, I was worried about putting things like that on my work phone without getting authorisation first. It was just that the idea suddenly came to me ...'

'Steve, it's all right. You've done very good work here. This could be a huge breakthrough. Please send me the links now and I'll have a look before my next interview with Abigail later this morning.'

Ted's phone pinged almost immediately as Steve shot the links across. He'd clearly prepared the email in advance. As Ted looked at his phone, Steve stood up to go.

'They really aren't nice, sir. And these are just the teasers. No wonder she turned on one of them with a knife.'

Chapter Fourteen

'Is there a chance this latest body is connected to our case?' Virgil asked. 'We're still missing three lads – Data, Kane Lomax and Sarwar Dabiri – and suddenly we get a young male body on our patch. Only, all I'm getting from my contacts is that whoever the Big Man on the scene pushing drugs turns out to be, he's new to the area and people are already afraid of him.'

Ted was updating the team on their latest body before he went downstairs for his next interview with Abigail. He would need to talk to Jim Baker, to bring him up to speed, and to have the usual discussion over additional officers, on his way.

'We can't get even a partial ID yet,' Ted told him. 'The body is male and probably IC1 but it's hard to tell.

'Maurice, I know you'll be careful, but when you go and talk to Ronnie today, make sure she doesn't hear about this latest body by some means. Even if it turns out to be unconnected, she might be worried enough to stop saying what little she is doing. Hopefully whoever's looking after her is sensible enough not to let her have access to watching the news or phoning her mates.'

'I'm not sure our Ronnie is the news channel watching sort, boss,' Maurice replied. 'According to the lass babysitting her yesterday, she spends her time watching daytime soaps and shopping channels. We've got her phone, though. I told her it was for her own safety, so no one could trace her through it, which is true enough, even if she wasn't too happy.'

He pulled an evidence bag out of his pocket, containing a phone in a pink, sparkly cover.

'I got her to sign a receipt for it, and to agree we could look through it to find out if there is a tracker on it.'

'Good. Steve, this one is for you, please. Can you give it priority attention and tell us anything we need to know. Will you be able to tell if there's a tracker on it?'

'I can do that easily enough.' The only time Steve sounded confident and even forgot the 'sir' was when he got onto one of his specialist subjects. 'Depending on how skilled the person who's planted any tracker is, it may not be easily possible for me to trace who they are, though.'

'Could Océane do it?'

The fondness and pride in Steve's voice wasn't lost on any of them. 'Oh yes. If she can't, it's not likely anyone could.'

'Right, thank you. And speaking of Steve and Océane, they've got us quite a breakthrough between them. A new twist on this case, and not a very nice one.'

Ted briefly highlighted what Steve had told him earlier and added, 'I've looked at some of it. It's not good, to say the least. Clearly someone is going to have to go through all of it, to see if it gives us any more clues as to the identity of the people in the films, apart from Abigail. For example, we now have an ethnicity indicator on the person we think might be Data. But we need more. And that will mean going in behind the paywall to something much worse than we've already looked at. Any volunteers?'

'Boss, if Mike takes over with Beff, as she calls herself, I'll do it. I can at least shut myself away in my office so no one else has to see it.'

'Thanks, Jo, I'm happy with that,' Mike told him. 'I don't envy you, by the sound of it.'

'Mike, we need names from Bethany, if you can persuade her. Virgil, Rob's going to be tied up at the new crime scene for most of the morning, I imagine, so can you please take over the questioning of Reece Williams? And the same goes for him. We need names. If they've been our guests for the night, at least they won't have heard about the body, in case it is one of their own. We need to keep a tight lid on that info for as long as possible.

'If anyone has a few spare minutes, please check out Mispers for any missing males. Probably late teens, but the body wasn't in much of a state for us to see any details to speak of.

'Jezza, I need to talk to the Big Boss first but I'll see you later, when Abigail arrives. Today we need to drill down a bit more about the weapon. And I need to tell Mr Stewart-Smith we have his client's prints on the knife which inflicted the fatal wound. Which he isn't going to like.'

'Are we remotely likely to get anywhere with this, boss?' Jo asked him. 'Surely we'll never get as far as getting Abi considered fit to plead.'

'We have to continue on the basis that we might. And with that in mind, Jezza, can you please chase up her school records, as a matter of urgency. We should have had those by now. Inform the school, in your most tactful manner, that we can always send over uniformed officers in a police car, armed with a warrant, if they really want to go down that route. Hopefully they're just too busy and short of resources to sort it all, rather than being deliberately obstructive.'

'Will do, boss. I've also come armed with some props for the interview.' She opened a folder and pulled out laminated pictures of various kitchen items – knives, corkscrew, egg beater, spatula. 'I got Tommy to help me. At least it kept him quiet for half an hour.'

'Excellent. But I expect we're going to have to fight Stewart-Smith every step of the way on this. At some point he's going to want her cautioned, but how we go about that in a way she can understand is currently a mystery to me.'

'Bloody hell, Ted, what are we dealing with here?' Jim asked him, after Ted had finished outlining Steve's discovery. 'Apart from anything else, this is handing Stewart-Smith the perfect defence on a plate. Diminished responsibility, protecting herself against abusers. We don't stand a cat in hell's chance of any kind of a case against her. But we need to carry on with it for now, at least. Take it as far as you can today, then we need to talk to CPS again for further guidance.

'Steve's a bloody good lad, though. If only he'd learn to trust himself a bit and speak up more. He's still with that Ocean lass then, is he?' Jim had never got the hang of her name. 'That's a couple of times the two of them have made some progress in a case for you, working off their own initiative. The Dynamic Duo, eh? And before you ask, no, you can't have her back on the team. You're lucky to keep the officers you've got already, the way things are going.'

'We might need to bring some specialists in on this one, though, Jim. Drugs, for a start. This looks like being some serious stuff on our patch and none of us has the necessary experience. Virgil's done a bit in the past but if it's a big new operation, he can't run it on his own.

'I've been reading up a lot about cuckooing. Given that Abigail is a wealthy soft target, I'm expecting to find they've been at her finances, too. I'm going to ask if we can take a look at her phone, to see what that can tell us. Or rather what it will tell an expert in such things. I think it's likely we'll also need someone more experienced with financial crimes than any of us.'

'DC Ahmed, you mean?' Jim asked him, referring to one of Ted's former team members, Sal Ahmed, who had left them to go back to Fraud.

'DS now, I hear. What are our chances of borrowing him back for a bit?'

'Bugger all springs to mind. But I'll at least consider it and make some enquiries. You clearly are going to need extra officers, whatever the powers that be might say.

'So, are we going to make a start? They should be here by now. I gather Debs and I have to accompany you while you do your smoothing ruffled feathers bit. It's a load of old bollocks, Ted. You know it and we know it. Just say your piece and let's crack on with the real work.'

The Bullers were waiting in reception with Abigail, her solicitor and Christy Madden. Councillor Buller had a face like thunder once more. Ted was starting to think anger was his default setting.

Ted stood there, flanked by both his senior officers looming over him, and began speaking. Abigail, as usual, beamed at the sight of him. Her trusting nature was clearly her greatest vulnerability, which had been exploited to the full by the cuckooing gang.

'Councillor Buller, allow me to apologise if I've allowed my words or actions to be misinterpreted. I can only assure you once more than I am trying to consider Abigail's rights and welfare at all times whilst interviewing her.

'Mr Stewart-Smith, if possible, could I have a quick word with you, before we start? Abigail, perhaps you and Mr Madden could go to the same room as yesterday. You'll find Jezza there, waiting for you.'

'This is all a bit cloak and dagger, Ted,' the solicitor said, lapsing into informality as the two of them went to find an available empty room.

'I thought I should update you on what we have so far. I know you're probably going to advise your client to say nothing at all. The weapon which inflicted the fatal wound was a kitchen knife, not a corkscrew. And the only prints on it are Abigail's.'

'Are you proposing to charge my client with murder? If you are, it's probably time to piss or get off the pot, Ted. If she's now being treated as a suspect rather than a witness, you should proceed to a caution before any further questioning.

You know PACE as well as anyone.

'And you're right. Even without all the inherent difficulties Abigail presents us both with, I would most definitely tell any client to say nothing at this stage. Without trying to teach you your job, I can think of a couple of plausible reasons to explain away the fingerprints, and that really is all you have, it would seem.'

His smile was almost friendly as he went on, 'This is a beggar of a case though, isn't it? Poor young lady is clearly very vulnerable. And I'll give you a little piece of advice, without charging you an exorbitant fee for it. Be careful with Councillor Buller. He hates the police at the best of times, and he clearly currently has his sights set on you in particular.'

'I noticed,' Ted told him dryly. 'What's his problem with the force?'

'Don't you know? He got pulled for drink-driving a few years ago. Didn't take kindly to the twelve-month ban and the hefty fine. He should have been grateful he didn't get a prison sentence. He seemed to think his position might give him some form of immunity. Clearly it didn't. But you didn't hear that from me, of course.'

Jezza produced her laminated pictures and spread them out on the low table. Emma, the second interpreter, was back, sitting close to Abigail, who was looking at what Jezza was doing with nothing more than mild curiosity.

'Abi, if it's all right with you, I'd like to ask you about some of the things you might have in your kitchen.'

Enthusiastic nods and smiles. She leaned forward, staring studiously at the pictures as Jezza pointed to different ones in turn. Abigail's speech was often indistinct, but there was no mistaking from her gestures that she could recognise many of the things Jezza pointed to.

'Knife.' She made a gesture of holding a knife and fork, cutting with the knife, lifting an invisible fork to her mouth.

'Thing for bottles.' She made a twisting gesture with her hand. The photo Jezza was showing her was of a corkscrew with a bottle opener at the top. The sort used to take the cap off beer bottles.

There were some she didn't know by their correct name, although she seemed to know, or to guess, their purpose. An egg whisk. A spatula. But when Jezza checked again, she still got 'knife' and 'bottle thing' the correct way round.

Jezza looked to Ted to continue. In discussing how they wanted the interview to proceed, they had agreed at what point he would take over. Stewart-Smith was being surprisingly quiet, not yet advising his client not to reply.

'Abigail, the boy in your kitchen. Latte. He wasn't asleep. He was dead.'

Her puzzled look appeared genuine enough. She looked from Ted to Emma and queried, 'Not sleep? Dead?'

'That's right. Do you know ...'

'And this is the precise point where I must stop you, Chief Inspector. Abigail, please do not say any more. Chief Inspector, you must caution my client before proceeding any further. I've been tolerant and accommodating thus far, but you are about to step too far over a line.'

Abigail was opening her mouth, trying to articulate words, but Ted spoke to her. 'Abigail, your solicitor is right. I now need to caution you.'

Then he looked from Emma to Christy and back as he asked, 'Is that even going to be possible?'

'It's theoretically possible,' Madden answered for both of them. 'It might just take a little longer than usual.'

'Would you just excuse me for a couple of minutes before we proceed, in that case?' Ted asked, standing up and leaving the room.

He went straight to find Jim Baker.

'Charge her, Ted,' the Big Boss said as soon as he went through the door. 'Charge her with murder. I just spoke to CPS.

I'll agree to bail, as long as she stays with the parents. She's not a flight risk. She's not likely to start interfering with witnesses. There don't seem to be any, for one thing. We're never going to get a conviction on this one, if it even gets to court. It's clear that the lass is the real victim here, in so many ways. But we have to be seen to try. In a sense, all the more so because of who her father is. Charge her.'

It was the most protracted caution Ted had ever sat through. It took all the skills and ingenuity of both interpreters to ensure that Abigail understood exactly what was going on. Even so, none of them could be one hundred per cent sure. She was still smiling and signing undying love for Jezza. But at least Stewart-Smith had accepted that the letter of the law had been followed within the limitations of the situation.

Only Steve was in the office when Ted and Jezza went back upstairs, working away on Ronnie's phone. Abigail had been more than happy to hand hers over and Stewart-Smith had raised no objection when Ted had explained about the possibility of it having a tracking device, which might be putting his client in danger. And that it might also help to lead them to other people who had been using the flat.

'How are you getting on, Steve?' Ted asked him as he put Abigail's phone down carefully on his desk. 'This one's Abigail's, and needs the same sort of attention, please.'

'There is a tracker on it, sir. I don't have the means to trace who's at the other end. That really does need to be Océane. Do you want me to take it up to Central Park straight away, or wait until after work?'

Jezza laughed. 'Nice try, Steve. A trip to see your girlfriend, in work time, on expenses.'

Steve immediately went red and opened his mouth to reply. Ted cut across.

'Wait until you've gone over Abigail's then you can take

both at the same time. I don't know if it's something you can unravel but I'm wondering if someone's been using Abigail's own phone to get at her finances, or something like that.'

'SIM-jacking, you mean, sir? That would definitely be one for Océane rather than me. She's much more up to date on it than I am. But I'll have a first look and then see if she's free to take over. It shouldn't take her long to do, once she has the phones.'

'I'm not sure I even know what SIM-jacking is, but it sounds like the sort of thing I was thinking of, without knowing the name. Thanks, Steve, keep me posted.'

He was about to head to his office when Steve added, 'There's a delivery for you, Jezza. I think it's the school records you were waiting for, about Abigail.'

'Let me know as soon as you find anything relevant, please, Jezza. I'll be in my office,' Ted told her. He was interrupted by his phone ringing. He recognised the number and picked up the call as he shut the door behind him.'

'Hello, Ted, it's Jono. How are things in your part of the world? Actually, I was hoping to find that out for myself. That's why I'm phoning. I was wondering if I could come up next Monday to talk to your partner. About the paedo ring and this bloke Harvey Warboys. If that's convenient to you both?'

Jono. Ted's contact in the Metropolitan Police. Needing to talk to Trevor about the incident in his youth which had caused him so much grief and left a rift between him and his parents which had never healed. Trev had only agreed to talk to the police after his father had turned up out of the blue to talk to Ted about it. It had caused problems when Trev saw it as a betrayal, that Ted had even spoken about him to Sir Gethin.

Probably the last thing either Trev or Ted needed right now, with both of them up to their eyes in work. But there was no point in putting it off. It was something which wasn't going to go away.

Chapter Fifteen

Ted was in his service vehicle, heading for Heaton Mersey Bowl and the latest crime scene. Rob O'Connell was perfectly capable of running things by himself, but Ted needed an excuse to get out of the office for a bit.

He stopped to grab a sandwich; chucked it onto the passenger seat in the vague hope that he'd find the time to eat it at some point.

There were more onlookers there now, being kept the right side of the outer tape by two officers from Uniform. It was a waste of valuable resources. One they could well do without.

Necks were craning, mobile phones being held aloft. The modern fascination with being the first person to post something grisly on social media.

As soon as Ted put one foot outside the car, Penny Hunter, the shy, mousey local newspaper reporter, appeared out of nowhere and began with her customary greeting.

'Erm, hello, Chief Inspector.'

'Hello, Penny, and to save you asking the question, it's the usual answer from me, I'm afraid. You'll have to wait for the statement from the Press Office.'

'But it is a body?' Politely tenacious, as ever.

'We're investigating a suspicious death, yes. That's all I can tell you for now. I imagine there'll be an official statement later today.'

He signed himself in, ducked under the tape, and set off down the slope. One of the reasons he wanted to be out of the office was that at some point someone would need to do a press statement, and a piece to camera, about Abigail's arrest and now this sudden death. Ted always tried to avoid such things if he could, hence blatantly nicking off when he really didn't need to be on site.

He found Rob deep in conversation with Priya Chowdhury. They seemed to be getting on well. The body had been removed and she and her team were carefully examining the ropes used to hoist it, as well as every inch of the ground beneath where it had been hanging.

'I'm not checking up on you, Rob,' Ted told him. 'We've charged Abigail, and it's been quite heavy going and I needed some fresh air. So tell me where you're up to.'

They moved aside, Rob speaking as they walked.

'You were right, boss. The Professor came and she was very helpful. Something very interesting from her initial examination, once the body was taken down. All the blood around the mouth, you remember? She had a look and showed me. The teeth had all been broken to buggery and the end of the tongue had been cut off. A warning to anyone who might be thinking of talking, perhaps? She said, from the amount of blood, it was likely to have been done while the poor sod was still alive.'

'The warning idea is a definite possible, but let's not jump to any conclusions too soon. But the Professor was able to open the mouth? So *rigor* hadn't fully set in, or had already passed, perhaps? Did she say which?'

'*Rigor* had begun, but the jaw had also been broken and dislocated, so she could see enough of the mouth to tell me that. Once he was taken down, it was easier to see in his mouth.'

'When can she do the PM?'

'Not before Friday at the earliest, she said. They're backed up. She's going to put DNA samples through on fast-track for us, though. No chance of face recognition or fingerprints, so unless there's anything else to help with ID, that's all we've got.'

'What does the scene tell us?'

'The Professor confirms that the body was brought here already dead and strung up. Killed elsewhere. Priya says there are three distinct sets of boot prints but they may well not help us much. They look like Army issue boots and the treads suggest they're probably quite new. Easy enough to get hold of anywhere, including online. If they're new, they won't have had time to acquire any individual characteristics to help much with identification, like if they were worn down more on one side than the other. Then if they disappear straight away, to a charity shop or into the recycling – maybe even to a homeless ex-serviceman – we might never link them to whoever was wearing them.'

Ted noticed Rob's use of the CSM's first name. He obviously needed to brush up on his own charm skills as she was still being frostily formal with him. He thought they'd parted on better terms than they started the last time they had met. Clearly he needed to begin again from zero.

'Professionals, then. Or at least they knew what they were doing with this one.' Ted was looking round him as he asked, 'I'm assuming no cameras anywhere near here? What about up near the parking areas?'

'Nothing, boss. I've walked all round everywhere. Whoever did this definitely knew what they were doing. The guy who found the body saw nothing of them either, although he can't have been far behind them, going on the timings the Professor indicated. Probably just as well for him he didn't run into them, looking at what they did to this poor sod.'

Ted frowned. 'Does he usually do early-morning runs round here? Only if they were professionals, I'd have expected them to have done a recce for things like that.'

'First time he's been down here. He's new to the area. Exploring his options for the best places to run. He'll probably give this one a swerve after today, I imagine. I've got his full statement and contact details so I let him go as he needed to get to work. Was that okay, boss?'

'Yes, fine, you did the right thing. What else have you discovered?'

'That it's not as easy as it looks on the telly. Certainly not for my first solo effort,' Rob told him. 'I've had Uniform going all over the site and like I said, I've gone round everywhere myself. But I can't see anything any of us could have overlooked. What have I missed, boss?'

'Probably nothing, from the sounds of it. Sometimes it's a slow start, until we get an ID. We've started trawling Mispers, pending the DNA results coming back ...'

Ted was interrupted before he finished his sentence by his phone ringing. The Ice Queen.

'Chief Inspector. You appear to be AWOL,' she greeted him.

'Not exactly,' he said, a touch on the defensive. If she was looking for him, it was almost certainly about the press conference which he had been deliberately trying to avoid. 'I just came out to the recent suspicious death site to see how Rob was getting on.'

'Perfectly well, I imagine. And I need you back here. You need to discuss with Jim and me what we're going to tell the press today about both cases. And who's going to do it. Soon as, please.'

As Ted made to leave, Priya Chowdhury called after him, 'How are the cats?'

Ted turned back, surprised. 'They're fine, thank you. And your carnivorous plants?'

'Equally fine. There really isn't a lot to go on here, but we will do our best to give you everything we can, and as soon as possible.'

It was late afternoon before Ted realised, with a guilty start, that he'd completely forgotten about junior self-defence club and his promise to be there in time to open up, if Trev was delayed.

As he'd suspected, the royal summons had been to inform him that he would be speaking at the press conference later that afternoon, although the Ice Queen was also going to be there. It would simply take the form of a brief statement which Ted would read from the station steps to any press or media who turned up. They wouldn't be answering any questions. The Ice Queen's role was to quell any attempt to solicit further details. One look from her could usually silence anyone, even a determined journalist.

'Sorry. I should have phoned you sooner. But I'm not ...'

'... going to get to the dojo at all tonight, let alone in time to open up,' Trev finished for him, then laughed. 'It's just as well I know you so well after all these years, Mr Policeman. And for some bizarre reason, I still love you. Neville will just have to lock up for me. He knows how to do it in theory, although it's usually Geoff or me who does it. And what is it this time? Another body?'

'It's the follow-up on the one from this morning. I drew the short straw. I have to stand in front of the baying press pack and try not to scowl too much at the cameras. I'll try to be home before you are, though, so do you want me to pick up a takeaway? If so, what do you fancy?

'I'm in the mood for spice,' Trev told him, the familiar provocative tone in his voice. 'And also for some spicy food. Just make sure you don't forget about it. I'll no doubt be ravenous by the time I get back and I don't want to have to eat cat food. Or start on you.'

Ted rang off quickly. He didn't need images like that in his mind just before he had to face the cameras.

Ted had called a team meeting at the end of the day for a progress report. With any luck, the phones might start ringing soon after his press announcement had gone out. They might even get lucky with some genuine leads, instead of the usual time-wasters wanting their five minutes of glory.

Before that, he went to find Jo to see how he'd been getting on with the videos. With his Spanish ancestry, Jo's usual complexion was more olive than classic IC1. He looked paler than Ted had ever seen him before. His jacket was slung on the back of his chair, his tie pulled halfway down and there was a distinct smell of cigars about him. He'd clearly needed to sneak out for a crafty smoke to get through the ordeal, despite his constant assurances to his wife that he'd given it up years ago.

'Bad?' Ted asked, as he took a seat on the opposite side of Jo's desk.

'Very bad, Ted,' Jo told him. 'I can't be the only bloke who's not a stranger to watching a bit of porn from time to time. But this is beyond anything I would normally watch. No wonder it's behind a paywall.

'The thing which is troubling me the most about it is how compliant Abi is through it all. Even the worst bits. I know you say she's generally passive and willing to please, but this goes beyond that. Like Steve said. But is it drink or drugs? Are the cuckoos feeding her some of the merchandise to exploit her for the films? Or is she someone with a low alcohol tolerance? She can't surely be complicit in what's happening. Can she?

'Would you take a look at a bit of it, at least, Ted, to see what you think?'

'The thing is, if they've got her hooked on drugs to make her easier to do whatever they want with her, wouldn't she be showing signs of withdrawal by now? And wouldn't we have seen them when she's come in for interview? But yes, of course, I'll look at some and see what I think.'

His hand went instinctively into his jacket pocket for one of his lozenges which he put in his mouth as Jo turned his computer screen so they could both see it at the same time.

Ted could only stomach five minutes before he signalled to Jo to switch it off.

'I'm no expert but I would say drunk, rather than drugged. And compliant by nature. From the less violent stuff Steve showed me, and from her own notes, it's clear that Abigail thinks that what happens between her and Data is a normal loving relationship. Rather than just the warm-up to stuff like this. At least they can't get at her for now.'

'What about when this is over? We're never going to get a case to stick against her. We'd have to disclose this to the defence. She's going to walk, whatever happens. Even if she's on probation. But she can't possibly go back to living on her own. I can't imagine what the parents were thinking of letting her even try. And then there's her baby to consider. Unless they decide to press her into getting rid of it.'

'Not our circus, Jo,' Ted told him. 'Not our monkeys. We just have to make the bullets. It's up to the CPS whether or not they get fired.'

Five youths were grouped around a bench in the park. Closer together than usual. Almost huddled. Seeking comfort in the presence of each other.

One boy sat on the back of the bench, mobile phone in hand, digits flying frenetically over it as he sought answers. He looked up at the others.

'Where the fuck is everyone?' he demanded. 'I've lost the trace on the slag now, too. After she left where she was and headed into town. And Ronnie's off the radar as well. Latte's phone's been off since this started and now Kane's has gone dead. Beth, Reece, did you do like I said?'

One of the boys nodded then flipped his fringe back out of his eyes.

'Course we did. We're not fucking stupid. Ditched the phones and showed the feds the dummies. They let us out on bail but we have to report in twice a day.'

'Sarwar and Lauren, you need to do the same. It's only a matter of time before they lift you. I've brought clean ones, set up like yours. Give me the others.'

Sarwar hesitated for a second. It brought the other boy springing to his feet, jumping down from the bench and going at him in open aggression.

'Give me the fucking phone. I'm trying to save all our arses here, you twat.'

In the tension of the moment, none of them noticed the small figure coming towards them. A man. Not much above four feet tall. Mirror shades hiding his eyes below a large forehead. A white stick out in front of him, swinging from side to side, checking for obstacles in his way.

The well-endowed girl known as Beff saw him first. She looked towards him, a feral smile crossing her face. She tugged the back of the jacket of one of the youths who was squaring up.

'Hey, look at the Oompa Loompa. He'd look good in a home movie, if he's got anything down his pants worth filming.'

'Stop pissing about. We have more important stuff to sort,' the boy with the mobiles spat at her.

She sashayed towards the short stranger, swinging her hips provocatively, not knowing if he could see her or not, but going for maximum effect in case he could.

'Hello, darlin', how would you like to star in a movie with me? Is everything about you small? Or have you got a whopper hidden down there?'

She reached out a groping hand towards his crotch. As soon as her fingers touched the fabric of his trousers, the hand not holding the stick chopped down swiftly, knocking her arm out of the way, sweeping it well out of play.

'Ow, you bastard, that hurt. Right, so now I really need to know what kind of a beast you're hiding down there. Come on, gizza hand.'

Mobile boy was still protesting, telling them they were wasting time. The other two boys and the second girl, distracted now and laughing, rushed forward towards the man. He calmly stood his ground and raised the white stick so it was pointing towards them.

There was an ominous click. They found themselves staring at a lethal long stiletto blade which had sprung from the end of the stick, like a flick-knife.

'Listen to what Data is telling you, children. If you know what's good for you.'

'How the fuck ...' the one with the phones started to say.

'I know everything about you,' the small man told them. He turned his head from one to another of them. It was impossible to read his expression behind the shades. But it was clear he knew exactly who each of them was.

'Kane told us everything about all of you. Before he died. Slowly.

'Data, you think you're so clever with your little trackers. But you're an amateur. A child. Even if you look good on film.

'Sarwar. I can smell the fear off you from here. Have you pissed yourself?'

His gaze seemed to land directly on each of them in turn. They had no way of knowing if he could see them. They felt as if he could see inside each of them.

'Beff. One day I'll happily show you what's down my pants. And I can promise you, you won't like it. Lauren, don't think having no record makes you safe. And Reece, you pathetic little shit. You couldn't even outrun a pig.

'Now listen very carefully, kiddies, before I really start to lose my patience. I have a message for you from the Big Man. He's pissed off. Really, seriously, pissed off with the lot of you. Your fucking incompetence has cost him a shitload of money. And he wants it back.

'It's not up to me to tell you how to put things right. I'm

just here to advise you that you need to find a way to do it. And just in case any of you is stupid enough to think that talking to the pigs is a good idea, here's a little souvenir for you. From your friend Kane.'

He tossed something small, wrapped in paper kitchen towels, at their feet. Then there was another metallic click, the blade disappeared back inside the stick, and the man walked away, completely unconcerned.

Reece was nearest to the object and bent to pick it up. When he peeled back the paper and found the end of a human tongue lying in the palm of his hand, he was the first to vomit.

But not the only one.

Chapter Sixteen

Another kitchen.

Another body.

Headless.

Blood on the tiled floor.

No chance of a Forensics team for this one.

Just Ted. On his own. Standing surveying the crime scene.

Seven potential suspects. Each as inscrutable as the next.

Holding Ted's gaze without wavering. With no flicker of guilt.

'We've talked about this before,' Ted told the cats sternly. 'I don't mind the odd mouse, if you must, but you're supposed to leave the birds alone. Certainly not drag them in through the cat flap looking like this. And it's not as if you don't have enough to eat.

'Now I'll have to clean this mess up to have the place looking nice by the time Trev gets home. And Roger. A little tip for you. If you're going to lie to a police officer, make sure you wash the feathers off your whiskers first.'

He took off his jacket and tie, rolled up his sleeves and made a start on the cleaning. By the time Trev got home from self-defence and his own judo session afterwards, the kitchen was spotless once more. Ted was showered and changed. A takeaway, being kept warm in the oven, was giving off welcoming and inviting smells.

'Mmmmm, that smells so good. And very spicy. You might just possibly be forgiven for standing me up yet again,' Trev told him as he enveloped him in a hug.

He'd clearly had a shower before leaving the gym. His body exuded a rich, exotic scent and his black curls were still damp.

'It's Chinese chicken. With extra ginger,' Ted told him. 'I hope that's all right? I didn't open any wine yet. I thought you might prefer a lager with it. There's some chilling in the fridge.'

'Fabulous! I'm starting to remember why I married you. How was work. Any more bodies?'

'I came home to one,' Ted told him, and recounted the tale.

It was a warm and relaxed moment between them. Exactly the sort of thing which got Ted through the most difficult days of his job. But at some point he was going to have to risk spoiling the ambiance. He needed to check with his partner if he was still happy to talk to Jono about his experiences with a predatory paedophile. Someone he'd believed himself to be in love with at the time. And to tell him that the interview was due to take place in a few days' time.

He decided to wait until after they'd finished eating. He'd taken the safe option for dessert, with a selection of sorbets.

Once they'd finished, Ted stood up to put the kettle on then said, 'Jono phoned me. About interviewing you. He'd like to come up next Monday, if that's all right with you? I know it's tricky, with you in charge at work.'

'There's no point in delaying it, really. I imagine they'll want to crack on with the case. I can leave Neville at the helm again for a couple of hours. It shouldn't take longer than that, should it?'

'I wouldn't have thought so. I was going to suggest using the vulnerable witness room at the station ...'

Trev made a face. 'Too many people know me at the nick. If they see me coming in to be interviewed, there are bound to be questions. I'd prefer it if not too many people knew about that particular phase of my life. Could we do it here?'

'Of course, if that's what you want.'

Ted put mugs of tea on the table for both of them and sat back down. Trev reached out and took hold of his hand.

'And you will be there with me? This won't be another time when you promise me something then let me down at the last minute, will it? Because I really do need you there, Ted. And if you do break your word on this, it's not going to be something you can fix with even another riding holiday. Even somewhere much more exotic than Corsica.'

It was late morning when Kevin Turner walked into Ted's office and looked pointedly towards the kettle.

'I definitely wouldn't say no to a brew, Ted, if there's one going,' he told him, sinking onto the spare chair. 'I have work stuff to discuss, but first I need some legal advice. Hypothetically speaking, if a man strangled his wife for banging on incessantly about going on a cruise, for weeks on end, there'd be a solid defence of provocation there, wouldn't there? Asking for a friend.'

Ted laughed. 'As bad as that?'

'Bloody worse. Anyway, the work stuff which brings me up here. Houston, we have a problem. Or rather you do. Possibly. Ta,' he added, as Ted put a mug in front of him. The kettle had still been hot from Ted's last brew.

'You know we let Busty Beff and Reece Williams go on police bail. Reece went back to his mam's and Beff found an auntie to put her up. They're on twice daily reporting and they both came in yesterday, meek as little lambs.

'Today, no sign of either of them. Nothing.'

'It's earlyish yet, though. Overslept, maybe? They're not exactly known for reliable punctuality, from what I've read of them.'

'Ah, but there's more.' He took a loud slurp at his tea, wincing at the heat of it. 'We had a young woman come in this morning. Very apologetic that she hadn't been able to get in yesterday, only work stuff, bla-bla-bla.

'Yesterday she was exercising her dog in a park. Throwing a ball for it. She noticed a bunch of what looked like teenagers hanging around a bench. Nothing unusual there. Then she saw a man walking towards them. A dwarf, she said. With dark glasses and a white stick. The teens started trying to shove him around a bit.

'The witness has some bottle, I'll say that for her. She was going to go over to stop them bullying him. She's got a big dog. But she said the man didn't seemed bothered. He pointed his stick at them, said something, then walked off. But first he dropped something on the floor. It looked like some folded up paper, she said, and it seemed to freak them out when one of them picked it up to take a look. A couple of them threw up, then they all legged it at high speed.'

'How's this related to our case?'

'Two things. Well, three, really, but two very big things.' He gestured with his hands as he went on. 'Our witness was observant. She couldn't describe all of the youths but she said one of the two girls in the group was very well endowed. So we're thinking Busty Beff, especially as we haven't seen her today.'

'Tenuous, but possible,' Ted conceded. 'And the third thing?'

'I like this lady. As well as being on the ball to bullying, she also doesn't appreciate people dropping litter in our parks. She makes a point of picking stuff up and putting it in bins. She went to pick up the paper. The dog got there first and was very interested. She called it off, as it seems to be obedient, and had a look.

'The end of a human tongue, which she kindly brought in for us, without handling it. And didn't your body up in the Bowl have part of the tongue cut off?'

'And this one is definitely human? Not some sadistic animal torture thing?'

'You know I said I like this lady? You'll love her as a witness. She's a dental nurse. She's seen more than her fair share of human tongues. Based on her telling us it's human, I've sent it off for testing and for reuniting with your Bowl body, to see if it's an exact fit.

'But I'm guessing this is all a bit worrying now, though? An indication of a connection between both your cases. And the strong possibility of a threat to a group of teenagers, which appears to include Busty Beff and possibly Reece Williams, who've now gone missing.'

'That's not the only worrying thing about it. Something like this reinforces our ideas of some sort of gangland, or organised crime, involvement.

'When your witness says a dwarf ...'

'She was being literal, rather than offensive. She said she'd have put him at not much over four foot one or two. A new one on me, for sure. I've not heard of any sinister blind dwarves operating on our patch before. Like you say, something to do with the new drugs presence? Time to get Drugs involved?'

'Quite possibly. I'll need to talk to Jim and Her Majesty. Thanks, Kev, I'll get someone to liaise and take all the details from you. In the meantime, I need to take some action pretty sharpish. I don't suppose, by any chance, you have a spare unit to look for Beth and Reece?'

He saw the look Kevin gave him and went on, 'I know, I know. But can you at least get everyone to keep an eye out for them, please. I'll get some of my team out there, too. We need to round up these teens. Their lives might be in danger.

'Oh, and tell your friend it's not worth it. There are easier ways to avoid a cruise than getting banged up for murder. And I don't want any more killings on our patch. We've got enough on our plate as it is.'

Ted picked up his mobile. Made a call. Then spoke.

'Maurice? I need to get you and Ronnie moved to a new safe house. Soon as. No cause for panic but there's been a development which means I want to err on the side of caution. Just please be extra vigilant until I can arrange it. There's no reason to suppose your location is compromised, but I don't want to take any chances. I'll keep you posted. If you have any concerns at all, call for armed back-up.'

Ted went out to the main office to see who was available. They needed to find Reece and Bethany, urgently, plus step up their efforts to find Sarwar Dabiri and the as yet unknown girl, Lauren. Most importantly, Ted wanted to get his hands on Data, whoever he was. He had a feeling he was going to be an important part in solving several aspects of the case.

He called everyone together and told them what Kevin had reported on.

'I'm going to ask the Big Boss if we can get someone in from Drugs as a matter of some urgency now. Threats like this implied one make me think more and more that drugs are behind what's going on here. And if anyone has heard of a blind person of short stature working for whoever this Big Man is, to pass on messages and threats from him, they should know.

'I may be over-reacting but I'm getting Ronnie moved to a new safe house, just in case. Jo, can you run things from here. The rest of us – all of us – need to get out there searching. And can you see where we're at with the DNA results from our body at the Bowl, please? If that really is one of the same cuckooing gang, then it could be either Sarwar or Kane Lomax. Or possibly Data.

'Jezza, you come with me. If you drive, I can talk to the Big Boss and also make sure Ronnie and Maurice are moved to a safe location.'

Ted glanced at Jezza as he got into the front passenger seat next to her.

'Are you all right, Jezza? Only you don't look on top form.'

'Thanks, boss,' she told him as she backed the car out of its parking space. 'You always know how to flatter a girl. But seriously, though, if this is what being pregnant always feels like, I'm bloody glad I've made the decision not to play any more. After next Monday, I might be back to something resembling normal.'

Ted wasn't convinced she was taking it all as lightly as she appeared to be. But for now, they both had work to do. He phoned Jim Baker, while Jezza drove. They were heading first to Beth Hayes' aunt's house, where she was supposed to be living whilst on bail.

'Can we bring in someone from Drugs, boss?' Ted was being formal, with Jezza in the car. 'This is much more their field than ours. Even if they only come over to hear what we have so far and to brief us on what they might know about it. Meanwhile we're all out and about trying to round everyone up before someone else finishes up strung up from a tree with a part of their anatomy missing.'

'Get me some bloody results on this one, then, Ted. I can stretch the budget if you get some solid arrests, and preferably convictions. Or if we can show that lives were saved. Otherwise ...'

Jezza parked the service vehicle in a street on the edge of Brinnington. Her slight wince as she got out of the car wasn't lost on Ted's sharp eyes.

'Are you sure you're all right, Jezza?' he asked her anxiously.

'What is it you're always saying, boss? I'm fine. Don't fuss. It's just a touch of cramp or something. All perfectly normal, I'm sure. So, shall we go and do this?'

They had to knock several times before the door opened to a short, overweight woman. Even before they lifted their ID to show her, she clearly knew who they were by the look of open hostility.

'She's not here. I said she could come and stay but I'm not

her keeper. She's out with her mates somewhere.'

She made to close the door but Ted stepped forward to block her.

'When did you last see her, Mrs Mason?' Ted asked. 'She was meant to report to the police station twice a day and she missed this morning.'

'Not since she said she were going there to sign in yesterday. She never come home after that. Like I told you, I said she could crash here but I ain't keeping her locked up.'

'Do you have any idea where she might be? Who she might be with? Do you know who her friends are?'

An indifferent shrug. 'I ain't seen much of her in a while. We're not what you'd call close. I just said she could stop here, so she could get out on bail. She'll turn up. So she was late for her slot this morning. Means nowt. She's not what you'd call reliable.'

She was still trying to shove the door closed. Ted's foot might not have been a large size but it was very determinedly parked to stop her from doing so.

'Mrs Mason, we need to find Beth because we have serious concerns for her safety. We think she may be mixed up with the wrong sort of people and we need to see she's protected. Please, here's my card. If you hear anything from her at all, can you urge her to get in touch? It's important.'

He knew she wouldn't. Suspected the card would be in the bin the minute she shut the door behind them. But at least he'd tried.

As they walked the short distance back to the car, Jezza suddenly clasped both hands to her abdomen, swearing loudly and doubling over in evident pain.

'Jezza, are you all right?'

'No, I'm not. Is it meant to hurt this much?' Then she put a hand down to the inside of her thigh, where a dark stain was starting to show through the grey fabric of her trousers. 'Jesus, boss, I'm bleeding.'

'Get in the car. Give me the keys. I'll drive. We'll go straight to A&E.'

'The seats, boss ...'

'Bugger the seats. Get in.'

Ted put the blues on. Drove as fast as he dared. Nudging up close behind anything in his way and giving a short burst of the siren to make them give ground. At the same time he put a call through to Jo, Jezza begging him not to tell anyone what was happening to her.

'Jo? Slight change of plan. No sign of Beth at her aunt's but I'm now en route for A&E with Jezza.' He looked at her, saw the plea on her face. 'Suspected acute appendicitis. I'll update you as soon as I know anything.'

Jezza was rushed through as a priority, even though the wait seemed interminable to Ted. He paced up and down in his anxiety, desperate for news.

A nurse finally came to find him. 'Jessica is asking for you, if you'd like to come this way.'

Ted had seen Jezza at one of the lowest points of her life. He didn't think she could look any worse than she had done on that dark and dismal winter's night. But she did. She was pale and crying. She looked like a vulnerable child.

Ted moved over to stand next to the bed. Put a gentle hand over one of hers.

'I lost it, boss. I never wanted this baby and I was going to kill it on Monday. And now I've lost it and I feel like I've murdered it.'

She lifted both arms towards him, a little girl desperately seeking the reassurance of a hug from an adult she trusted. It brought back vivid, painful memories of that night. When the only thing she'd wanted from him was a hug. Which he'd not been able to give her.

This time he wasn't going to let her down.

He perched lightly on the edge of the bed. Opened his arms to her. She fell against him, hot tears on his neck. He had absolutely no idea of what to say to her. So he just held her. Hands gently stroking the shoulders which shook with raw, tearing sobs.

Chapter Seventeen

While Ted was waiting for Jezza's boyfriend, Nathan, to arrive from work, he simply sat quietly next to her as she clung to him.

He'd never felt as inadequate as he did during what seemed like another eternity. Not even on the dreadful night when Jezza had been raped. At least then he was acting as a police officer. Dealing with a crime scene and a victim of a violent attack. Even if he hadn't found the right words of comfort, at least he'd known the correct procedure to follow.

This time, all he could do was sit there in silence, feeling useless, occasionally giving her hand a gentle squeeze when she finally stopped hugging him, in what he hoped was a gesture of support and comfort.

He'd turned his phone off for the moment. No doubt Jo would be trying to contact him for an update about Jezza. For now, he couldn't bring himself to talk to anyone about it. Not even to send a text.

As soon as Nathan came hurrying through the screens, ashen-faced, to rush to the bedside, Ted relinquished his place and stepped back to give him room. As Nat approached her, Jezza once again held up her arms to be hugged.

'I'll be off then, Jezza, now Nat's here. Look after yourself. Don't hurry back to work until you're fit. And Nat, you make sure you take very good care of her, please.'

Nathan remembered his manners, turning to Ted to shake his hand before he left.

'Thanks so much for looking after her. I feel like I should call you boss. You do know you're my serious rival, don't you? She thinks the world of you.'

Ted hurried away. It was all getting a bit intense. At least Jezza was now safe and in the best possible hands.

He went straight to the reception desk when he got back to the station, to sign his vehicle keys back in and have a quiet word with Bill Baxter as soon as there was no one around to hear them.

'Bill, a little problem with my car just now. I had to take Jezza to Casualty and the front passenger seat needs cleaning.'

'Was she injured …?' Bill started to ask then read Ted's expression. 'Ah, ok, understood. I'll get it sorted. Total discretion. Count on me.'

'I know I can. Can you just please make sure that whoever cleans it understands that too. This is not to be made public, and if I hear even a whisper about it, the person responsible will have me to deal with.'

'Poor lass, though, eh? Last thing she's going to need is people gossiping.'

'Exactly. Now, I don't suppose either Beth or Reece have shown up, have they?'

'No sign. I gather having half a human tongue thrown at them in a park has rather put the wind up them.'

Ted wasn't surprised Bill was already fully up to date. There was little that happened in the town, let alone inside the nick, that he didn't know about.

'And Abigail's coming in daily as per her bail conditions?'

'Good as gold. The mother brings her, which is nice for all concerned, without Buller here winding everyone up. He's an odious piece of shit.'

'You'll get no argument from me on that. Something else you might be able to help me with. I'm sure you've heard about our person of short stature? The bearer of the severed tongue.'

'Person of short stature? Are we not allowed to say dwarf any more? Is that not PC these days? Anyway "Bearer of the Severed Tongue" sounds like something from *Game of Thrones*.'

Ted looked at him in surprise. 'You watch that stuff? I didn't have you down as a fantasy fan, Bill.'

'A man's allowed a few guilty secrets in his private life. Especially by my age. Young Steve got me into it. That and *Star Wars*. Passes the evenings when there's nowt else on t'box.

'He's a good lad, Steve. He'll make a brilliant officer one day, if he ever learns to believe in himself. He wakes up screaming in the night sometimes. Did you know?'

'He got badly assaulted that time, remember? When his teeth got broken. That's enough to give anyone nightmares, I would think.'

'I think this goes back much further than that. He sounds like a little boy when he does it. A child. And he keeps his T-shirt on in the shower. I walked in on him one time when he hadn't locked the door. Maybe he wanted me to see. To ask him about it. And maybe one day I will. In the meantime, I sit and watch his programmes with him.

'And what was it you said just now? If even a whisper about my viewing habits gets out, you'll have me to deal with. So think on, Ted. I remember your first day here.'

Ted laughed. 'Fair point. Not my finest hour. But have you heard anything about this character?'

'When I heard mention that you were all out chasing your tails for a blind dwarf – sorry, person of short stature – I thought it was some sort of an in joke. Because it's absolutely a new one on me. No one from Uniform has heard of such a person either. And it's not exactly a sight you'd forget in a hurry. Must be new to the area, I think.'

As Ted headed for the stairs, Bill called after him, 'Winter is coming.'

Ted turned back, puzzled. 'We've not had summer yet.'

Bill laughed in turn. 'It's a Thrones thing, Ted. You need to watch an episode or two sometime.'

Ted had phoned Jim Baker on the drive back from the hospital after he'd found several missed calls from him.

'I called Jo when you didn't reply,' Jim told him. 'He said something about taking DC Vine to hospital with appendicitis. Is she all right, poor lass?'

'Not appendix after all. Women's stuff,' Ted told him, knowing that would be the most certain way to stop Jim's questioning in its tracks. He'd been with the Big Boss at some of the most gory crime scenes and revolting post-mortems he could remember, without seeing him turn a hair. Any mention of anything with a gynaecological connection would be certain to shut him up. 'She's going to be off a fair few days though, for sure, so can I have a replacement?'

Jim sighed heavily. 'You can borrow someone. For as long as she's off. If this latest death is linked to your cuckooing gang, then it's only one case to work on, after all, not two.

'And on that subject, I've got two officers from Drugs who'll come and talk to you tomorrow. Listen to what you have; see if it matches anything they know about. But you can't keep them. They're busy people, with cases of their own. I want to be in on the briefing with them, so when's a good time tomorrow?'

'I was planning to try to get everyone together early afternoon for a progress report. Bring the CSM in to see what forensic results we might have by then. And with a bit of luck, with the PM tomorrow morning on the Bowl body, Rob will be back with something useful for us. Including, hopefully, DNA results and an ID on the body.'

'Let's go for two o'clock, in that case. You round up yours, I'll sort out the others. Any news on the missing young-sters?'

'I'll find out from Jo when I get back in. I'm nearly there. If there is any news, I'll let you know.'

Jo Rodriguez was on the phone when Ted went into his office. He raised a hand to indicate that he wouldn't be long. Ted sat down while he finished his conversation.

'How's Jezza?' was his first question when he ended the call.

'Not appendix after all but she's going to be off work for a few days at least. Any update on our missing cuckoos?'

'Just this very minute. And for once the "insert supreme beings of choice",' he made quotation marks in the air as he said it, 'are smiling on us. Beth and Reece were picked up an hour ago by motorway police, thumbing on a slip road just north of Birmingham. They're being returned to us, with various forces helping out with the relay.

'I'd circulated the details far and wide, including ports and airports, just in case they had the means. But of course Beff was originally from down south so it seems likely she was trying to head back down there, with Reece in tow.

'Of course now they've skipped bail, we can get them remanded in custody, which means two less of them to worry about.'

'So that just leaves Data, Kane and Sarwar to round up. Or to account for, if one of them really is the Body in the Bowl. Plus whoever Lauren is. What news from Maurice and Zofia?'

'Ronnie is freaking out, according to Maurice. She's not stupid. She knows she won't have been moved to a new safe house without a valid reason. And the most likely valid reason is a real and present threat to her safety.

'She's clammed up and is refusing to say any more without all sorts of assurances about her safety going forward. Her demands are getting ever more exotic. She currently wants to be relocated to South America, although I'm not convinced she even knows where it is, or what part she wants to go to.

Maurice is doing his best but she's not budging. She really does watch too much daytime TV as she keeps going on about the Fifth Amendment.'

'I'll go round myself. Perhaps a bit of rank might persuade her to be more cooperative. I don't want to threaten her, but if I did suggest to her that there was no point in continuing to put her up and look after her if she has nothing to tell us, that might just do the trick.'

'Who's he?' Ronnie craned her neck from where she was lolling on the sofa, watching TV as usual, when Ted walked into the room at the new safe house, followed by Maurice Brown who'd opened the door to him.

'This is my boss, DCI Darling. He wants a few words with you.'

Ted picked up the remote control from the low table and switched off the television. That made her sit up and take notice.

'Oy, I was watching that.'

'And now you're not,' Ted told her, sitting down. 'You're going to talk to me instead.' He put his phone on the table where the remote was and told her he would be recording their conversation.

'Zofia, I'm the Senior Investigating Officer on this case. As such, I'm in charge of the budget. So I'm here to evaluate whether or not we're getting our money's worth out of you. It costs us money to keep you protected like this. And so far, the information you've given to Maurice isn't worth the expense. We need more.'

'I'm scared, innit,' she told him. 'I need protecting. This lot, behind the drugs an' stuff, are well dangerous. They'd kill me if they knew I were speaking to you. Why was I moved from the other place? Does that mean they know I'm talking to you?'

'But you're not, are you?' Ted said reasonably. 'You've

not told us anything at all of any use so far. And you were moved from the other house because this is smaller and we needed a bigger one for another protected witness.'

It was a good job Ronnie was looking at Ted and not at Maurice when he said that. Otherwise she would have noticed the surprised look on Maurice's face at the ease with which the boss trotted out a blatant lie.

'I need to know I'm going to be safe, if I talk to you. I want to choose where I get moved to ...'

'That's not how it works, I'm afraid. You need to tell us something solid. Something of use to us to move the case forward. Once you've convinced me that you can come up with the goods, then I can start looking into what we can do for you in exchange. But we've been waiting all week for you to say something useful. So far you haven't.'

'I told you about the Big Man,' she said defiantly.

Ted made a scornful noise. 'The Big Man? That's straight out of some TV programme. It tells us nothing. I need more than that. Have you ever met him, this Big Man? Can you tell me what he looks like?'

'Well, no ... It were always Kane who went to see him. No one else.'

'Where did he go to see him?'

'Dunno. Not far. He were never gone long. He always got a lift back, with the stuff, like. So he never had to carry it anywhere. In case he got caught.'

'Did Kane ever tell you about the Big Man? Did he say anything about him?'

'Just that he were a right bastard and he'd slit you like a kipper if you ever tried to do the dirty on him. And Kane always said it with like a sneer. "The Big Man". Like he were trying to show he weren't afraid of him.'

'Right, this is getting to be more like it. Maurice, can you put the kettle on, please? And send the other officer in.'

'Does that mean I'm going to be okay? I'm going to get

protection, and moved somewhere new?'

'We've not even got going yet, Zofia. That's why we need a brew.'

Maurice went out to the kitchen to put the kettle on. He passed the PC who was on duty and nodded to her to go in. Both of them knew Ted would not want to be alone with Zofia. Despite the recording, he wasn't going to run the risk of her claiming she'd been offered all sorts of inducements to part with any information she might finally decide to give up.

'So when Kane brought the stuff back, where did you put it?'

'Wherever we was crashing.'

'Recently. Say within the last couple of weeks.'

'The flat in that old mill place in town. Where them coppers grabbed me. We've got a mate there. She lets us stay.'

'Which mate is that?'

'Abi, she's called.'

'And she's quite happy for you to store drugs in her flat?'

Ronnie turned evasive again.

'She ain't all that bright. She just likes having mates round, so she don't ask too many questions.'

The grilling went on for nearly an hour more. Ted's questioning was relentless. He wanted answers and Ronnie quickly realised that her best ticket to safety was to give him something – anything – which she hadn't come up with before. Her big problem was that it was becoming all too clear that she didn't know enough to be of much use.

As she started to realise that, she was falling over herself trying to say something which was what Ted wanted to hear.

Eventually, he stood up, turned his phone off and pocketed it.

'Zofia, it's clear that you're finally making an effort to cooperate. But at the same time it's also obvious that you really don't have any of the kind of information we want. So I need you to have a long, hard think about what it is you do know and could tell us. And weigh that up against the risks you run if we don't, after all, agree to put you under witness protection. We'll talk again after you've thought through all your options.'

'Maurice, walk with me to the car, please.'

'Bloody hell, Ted,' Maurice told him as soon as they were outside the house. 'I've never seen you play bad cop before. That was pretty convincing. You certainly rattled Ronnie's cage.'

'Desperate times, desperate measures,' Ted told him. 'Let's hope it will achieve something. She really hasn't told us anything much of any use so far. And that's no reflection on you, Maurice. I know you will have been trying your best. I'm just not convinced she knows much of anything.

'Let her stew in her own juice for the day tomorrow. Maybe the weekend, too. Until she's really keen to talk. Don't come here in the morning. Come straight to the station. We've got briefings which need your input. Leave her to Uniform. If she thinks we're going cold on her, she might try a bit harder to give us something useful. Mind you, there was one interesting thing she said.'

'Kane Lomax was the only one of them to have seen the Big Man face to face, you mean?' Maurice queried. He was a plodder and a skiver but he didn't miss much.

'Exactly. So he's the only one of them who could identify the Big Man. And since we've not found Kane and we have a body with what looks like a very clear warning, since we started sniffing about ...'

'It's odds on that the Body in the Bowl is Kane.'

'Well, this is a nice surprise,' Trev said as Ted appeared at karate club. 'I didn't expect you to make it this evening, with all you have going on. Not that I'm complaining, of course.'

'It's been a tough day. I thought some time spent kicking people would make a welcome change. And I have a takeaway in the car for us afterwards, in case you hadn't had time to plan anything.'

'I was planning to go out for a curry with Mark and the others afterwards. I'd far rather go home with my husband like any boring old married couple.'

'It doesn't have to be boring,' Ted told him with a suggestive smile.

Chapter Eighteen

Ted was just about to tell the team about Jezza being off sick when the door opened and their former colleague Sal Ahmed walked in, grinning broadly. Rob was at the post-mortem but Maurice and Virgil, who'd known Sal well and were still friends with him outside work, stood up to greet him. A man-hug from Maurice, an affectionate thump on the back from Virgil.

'I'm seconded, boss, but not for long. Hopefully I can be of some use while I am here, though.'

'Good to have you back, Sal,' Ted told him, 'And I'm sure you will be. There's a financial angle to this which needs unpicking, so perhaps you can liaise with Steve to start with. He's been going through our suspect's phone.

'Before we get started, I wanted to let you all know that Jezza was taken ill yesterday and will be having some time off. Don't look so worried, Maurice, I'm sure she'll be fine. She just needs a bit of rest for now. So perhaps give her a quiet day or two before you rush round there with grapes and a bunch of flowers.

'We'll do a full briefing this afternoon at two when we might all have a bit more to report on. We've got two officers from Drugs coming to join us, and I've asked the Crime Scene Manager to come in for a round-up of her findings on both deaths.

'I'm hoping to get a word with Mrs Buller this morning when she brings Abigail in to report. We need to get access to any and all of Abigail's financial affairs and she may be more willing to talk to us without her delightful husband in tow.'

'Do you honestly think she'll dare say anything, without him there?' Jo asked. 'He would seem to have her well and truly under his thumb, from what we've been told.'

'I'll just have to try my very best charm offensive,' Ted replied.

'If that doesn't work, boss, try your bad cop act. First time I'd seen that, yesterday. I don't know what effect it will have on Ronnie but it certainly rattled me,' Maurice told him, raising a ripple of mirth from the team.

'Hello, Abigail, Mrs Buller.'

As usual, Abigail's face lit up as soon as she saw Ted. Her school reports, which they'd now received and were working through, had said she was of an overly trusting and affectionate nature, with a total lack of judgement on boundaries in social interaction. The perfect soft target for the cuckoos.

She was frowning now as she asked, 'Ezza?' She signed the J but didn't pronounce it.

'Not here today,' Ted told her, trying to speak clearly. 'Day off.'

'S'eeping?' Abigail asked him, gesturing with her hands together, leaning her head against them.

'Yes, sleeping.' Then he went on, 'Mrs Buller, I wonder if I could have a quick word with you, please, if that would be convenient?'

She immediately looked anxious. 'Should I call our solicitor? And Christy? Perhaps I'd better get my husband to come in ...'

'You can, of course, if you wish to. But it's really not necessary. It's you I wanted to talk to, not Abigail. Just a few quick questions. Nothing incriminating at all, I promise you. Shall we go and sit down?'

He held his arm out, indicating the way to the witness room

they knew well by now. Mrs Buller was scrutinising his face. She clearly found reassurance in his expression as she headed in the direction Ted was indicating, Abi following docilely in her wake.

As soon as they took their seats, Abi sat down, put her head back against the cushion and appeared to fall asleep. Her mother smiled fondly.

'She's permanently tired these days, bless her. I was much the same when I was carrying her. And I didn't have all this dreadful stress and anxiety to cope with. When will it all be over?'

'We really are doing all we possibly can to bring this case to a conclusion, Mrs Buller. It's not an easy one for any of us. Especially for you and Abigail.

'May I ask a personal question? Which of course you aren't obliged to answer.' When she nodded warily, he went on, 'Will Abigail keep the baby?'

'My husband says not. He wants to get rid of it.'

'But isn't that rather up to Abigail? After all, in law, she is an adult.'

'But she isn't an adult at all. Not really. Look at her, bless her. She doesn't function at the same level of a normal adult. Never has, never will do.'

Ted tried to make his tone as neutral as he could as he said, 'Yet she lives alone. Which is partly what I wanted to talk to you about. Are you familiar with the term cuckooing, Mrs Buller?'

She appeared to frown but her frozen face didn't show a lot of movement. 'I know about cuckoos. Everyone gets nostalgic about hearing the first one in spring. But they're horrible birds really, aren't they? They lay eggs in another bird's nest. Then when their chicks hatch, they throw the other eggs out of the nest so they get all the food. They kill unborn babies. Murder them.'

Her voice broke and she stopped for a moment.

Wordlessly, Ted got up to bring a cup of water from the dispenser, which he put in front of her. Then he spoke again.

'Mrs Buller, it's also a term which refers to a disturbing crime which is sadly on the increase. Groups, or gangs might be more appropriate, of people, often quite young, will target someone vulnerable. Pretend to befriend them. But then they take advantage of them in many different ways. They might move into their homes. Stash drugs and stolen goods there. They'll get the person to buy them things. Food, drink, clothing. Clearly the more money their victim has, the better it is for them.'

'Is that what's been happening to Abi?' Her expression was horrified. 'When she told me she'd met some new friends, I was actually happy for her. She's never found it easy to make friends.'

'Who's in charge of Abigail's finances? Presumably she's in receipt of various living allowances, but does she have any other source of income? I'm sorry about the personal questioning, but it really would help us to know all of this.'

She made a snorting sound. 'Oh, Abigail has plenty of money. A large portion of it comes from the Bank of Guilty Father. He's in charge of keeping an eye on her bank statements and her spending levels. Every month he moans and groans when he sees how much money she's gone through. All I have to do to get him to shut up is suggest that if Abi isn't managing on her own, she should come back and live with us. That does it every time. He just transfers some more money to put her account back in credit and says no more about it. Until he next checks up on her spending.'

Abigail shifted her position in her sleep, making a small murmuring sound as she did so. Her mother smiled again as she looked at her.

'So to access her financial records, it's your husband we would need to speak to?'

Her voice took on a much firmer tone. 'You leave Frank to

me. I'll see that you have everything you need. We've clearly let our daughter down so very badly. I just hope it's not too late to put things right.'

'May I ask another personal question? You don't have to answer ...'

She interrupted him. 'Why doesn't Abi live at home with us? That's what you want to know, isn't it? The simple answer is that Frank is ashamed of her. Of what she represents. As evidence that he got things totally wrong, due to his own ignorance. He's not man enough to own up to his mistakes. And she was one of them.

'Frank's always jumped on bandwagons. To advance himself, socially and politically. The vaccination denial was one of his hobby-horses. "No need to pump our children full of all these chemicals. It's just a scam by big pharma". That's what he kept saying. So he chose not to allow our precious only child to have the MMR vaccine. I wanted her to have it. It's a mother's role to protect her children.

'He's not an educated man. He started out as a jobbing builder. A very good, hard-working one, it has to be said. Then he made his money – a lot of money – in property development. But suddenly he knew more than doctors and scientists and everyone else.

'Probably inevitably, Abi fell ill with the measles almost as soon as she started school. When she was very young and up to that time, perfectly normal in all respects.

'She was so very ill. We thought she was going to die. The doctors said she very well might. But she survived, against all the odds. And here's the result. She'd lost her hearing, her ability to speak properly, her understanding, just about everything.

'So like I said, you just leave Frank to me. I'll see that you get every single scrap of paperwork you need, before the end of today. And whatever happens to Abi in all of this mess, rest assured that she will be coming to live with me. Where I can keep an eye on her. Her and her baby.'

They were using the downstairs briefing room for the afternoon session. With extra officers joining them, it would give them more space in which to work.

Rob had got back from the post-mortem late morning with the news that the DNA results on their body from Heaton Mersey Bowl were a match for those on record for Kane Lomax. The section of tongue recovered from the park had also been confirmed as having come from Lomax. No great surprise to anyone, as he'd been the one in direct contact with the drugs supplier, the mysterious Big Man.

Priya Chowdhury was there. Her first time attending a briefing with them. She looked slightly less hostile, now she wasn't on her own territory. She even gave Ted something of a smile.

Shortly before the briefing was due to start, the door opened and two strangers walked in. They could only have been the two officers from Drugs. Apart from the ID tags round their necks, they looked nothing like anyone's idea of police officers.

One was male, very tall, and thin to the point of looking emaciated. He was scruffily dressed, with rings in one ear. He had tattoos on the sides of his neck, and on both hands, disappearing up the frayed and dirty cuffs of a washed-out denim shirt. There was a smell hovering about him of cheap rolling tobacco and something else. Ted found it familiar but in a whole different league to what he was used to.

The man was with a younger woman. Much shorter, slim rather than thin. The complete antithesis of her colleague. Everything about her was classy. From the expensively cut and highlighted hair down to the high-heeled boots with the bling logo, by way of an exquisitely tailored trouser suit.

The man looked round the room, saw Jim Baker looming at the front of the room with Ted and headed over to him.

'Are you the gaffer? I'm Ian Bradley, from Drugs. This is Gina Shaw.'

'Superintendent Jim Baker. I'm in overall charge, but DCI Ted Darling here is SIO. Thanks for joining us.'

'We can't give you long. As you might have gathered, we've come in from something else. But if we can help, we will.'

'We'll kick off with your input, in that case,' Ted told the two of them. 'Then we don't need to keep you any longer than we have to.'

'Right, first off,' Bradley began, 'I've had all the various reports sent through to you. But to sum up. The gear that was found at your crime scene was basically for two completely different target buyer profiles. There was plenty of the average stuff you can buy on a street corner in more places than you'd imagine. Better quality than some, so not the cheap end, but not highest quality. That's the dealers' bread and butter.

'The other stuff, especially the coke, was very classy gear. High purity. Expensive to get hold of. Some of the best quality we've seen in a while, which is why we think this is someone new to the area, with a new supply chain. As such, it needs jumping on, fast, before it gets out of hand.

'That's where they make their serious money. And it's certainly not sold on street corners. Which is where Gina comes in.' He jerked a thumb towards his colleague.

'You'll find stuff of this price-tag in posh pubs and clubs, and at private parties. You're all detectives. I'll leave you to work out which of us two, me or Gina, focuses on which market.'

'It might be helpful, Ian, for those of us with not much Drugs experience, if you were to explain how the supply chain works. Do our young cuckoos have to buy the supply in from the dealer and then sell it on? Because that would presumably cost them a lot of money up front, so do we need to chase down where they'd be finding that sort of cash to lay out?' Ted asked him.

Bradley shook his head. 'They're just go-betweens. The big dealers have been turning to the cuckoos more and more. If the dealers stash their own gear, they know there's always a real risk of us finding it and it getting destroyed. They let the kids have supplies on trust and wait for the money to come back, of which the cuckoos take a very small cut. That way the gear gets stashed in places we wouldn't be as likely to raid.

'They'll be watched, of course. There'll be some heavies, in the background, keeping an eye on their investments. Ready to move in as and when necessary. The kids are kept in line with threats of violence. And by random displays of it, to prove it's not just an empty threat.'

He turned and looked at the board, where all the available information to date was displayed. Including the photos of the body, now identified as Kane Lomax, hanging upside down from the tree at Heaton Mersey Bowl. Bradley tapped it with a dirty, nicotine-stained finger.

'Like that. Showy. Unnecessarily so. A real "this is what happens to anyone who steps out of line" warning. How did he die?'

'Tortured first. Finger ends burned with a blowtorch. The end of his tongue cut off while he was still just about alive. Then his neck was broken cleanly, manually, by someone who knew exactly what they were doing,' Rob O'Connell gave him the broad outline of the morning's PM findings.

Bradley was looking at the board again. At the security camera stills of the various named and unnamed members of the cuckooing gang.

'They're the visitors to the building who we suspect are our cuckoos,' Ted told him. 'We've been working with the concierge to rule out residents and any of their known regular visitors. These are what we're left with so far.

Ted went to stand next to him to indicate photos as he spoke.

'Two are now dead. Kane Lomax, the Body in the Bowl, and this one, Giorgio Mantone, known as Latte, who was found dead inside the flat. Of the others, we have one in a safe house, talking to us, but not enough to be of much use yet. Two are in custody and two are still in the wind. We're concentrating on finding those two.'

'Most of these aren't going to be able to sell the high-end stuff. They'd stick out like a sore thumb in the right locations to sell it. It would be like me swapping places with Gina, without either of us changing our looks. This one, though,' Bradley tapped the photo of the person believed to be Data a few times, his expression thoughtful. 'He's different to the others. He might be more the sort to mingle in high places. Who is he? Gina, have you see this lad before?'

She stepped closer for a look, then shook her head. 'Impossible to tell from that. He wouldn't be dressed or looking like that in places where I might have seen him. Is there any better footage?'

'That's as good as it gets, I'm afraid. And we don't have an ID on him yet. All we know is that Abigail, the young lady whose flat they were using, calls him Data and thinks she's in love with him. Film footage that our DC Ellis found online tells a completely different story, though. It seems they've been using her for online porn films, probably with Data as the warm-up act, or whatever you'd call it, although the faces are usually pixelated out. Two-tier porn. Some of the softer stuff is readily available. But it links through to much harder core stuff behind a paywall. Abigail features heavily in it. I gather disabled porn is now a thing.'

'Certainly is,' Bradley agreed. 'Although it has much worse names on the street. But this is an interesting new angle. Gina, are you thinking what I'm thinking?'

'I am. You're right, it is getting to be a thing. You're probably all too aware that some people will pay a lot for, shall we call it, unconventional sex. The rougher the better, and this added aspect could well be an extra incentive for some. I can see some well coked-up flash gits jumping at something like that.'

'And that opens up other possibilities too. Extortion and blackmail, for one. They'll be promised anonymity, told their faces won't be shown. Then, lo and behold, footage emerges where they can be clearly identified, but it can all be covered up for a modest sum. Only it never is, and the demands keep increasing. Looks like you've landed the jackpot here, Ted, for your first foray into the murky world of Drugs,' Bradley said.

'You're going to want to round up all your cuckoos as soon as possible, no doubt. But let me just say now that we wouldn't want every single one of them pulled in before they can lead us to the source. We'd want at least one left loose.'

'We've got some serious abuse going on ...'

Ted started to speak but Bradley cut him short. 'But if we don't cut off this supply chain, with shit like this on the market, we could be looking at any number of deaths.'

He looked across at Jim Baker as he said, 'No point me and you playing case poker, Ted. It's something our gaffers will need to argue over.

'Now tell us about this famous blind dwarf of yours. I must admit us two thought you might be sampling the goods when we heard that story.'

'Let me start with a question,' Ted replied, addressing everyone. 'And this isn't a criticism. How do we know our person of short stature is blind?'

There was a brief silence, into which Ted went on. 'Precisely. We don't. Any of us could carry a white stick and wear dark glasses. It's a perfect distraction technique and we all so nearly fell for it. So now can we please concentrate on the main thing about this character which would be much more difficult to fake. And that is their short stature.'

Chapter Nineteen

'I thought I'd better wake you up before I go out. I know you're not programmed for getting up on Saturdays. I've brought you some tea and toast,' Ted told his partner, putting the tray down on the floor, then rearranging cats to make room for it on the bed.

Trev made a groaning sound and pulled the duvet up over his head. His voice was muffled as he said, 'I've decided I don't want to be an adult today.'

'It's a hard life, being a business tycoon.'

One arm appeared slowly, pushing the duvet back to reveal Trev's tousled black curls and sleepy blue eyes. Ted lifted up the mug of tea and put it in his hand.

'Are you going in again tomorrow, to keep on top of the books?'

Trev took a grateful swallow of the tea. 'No, I've changed my mind. I've decided six days of being a grown-up is enough in one week. And I think the takings are pretty much okay for now. I'll go in next Sunday, though, just to make sure.'

'We're still flat out, but at least we now know that both bodies belong to the same case. I'll have to go in tomorrow morning, to keep on top of things. But if you're not going to work tomorrow, I thought I could leave it to Jo in the afternoon and we could maybe go out somewhere. Take the bike up to the Peaks, perhaps? Whatever you fancy.'

Ted had put the tray up on the bed now and Trev took a bite out of the toast before he answered.

'Is this going to be another of your broken promises, though? I'll get all dressed up and ready to go, then you'll either forget entirely or phone me up at the last minute full of excuses and promising to make it up to me.'

'No, I'll make sure Jo knows I'm off for a few hours. And before you ask, I've already told him the same for Monday, when you speak to Jono. I'm picking him up from the station to bring him here, and I'll stay with you as long as it takes. I'll even switch my mobile off, then you know I can't get called away. I promised to support you if you agreed to testify, and I will do.

'I've no idea what time I'll finish tonight, but you decide where you want to go tomorrow and I'll take you.'

Ted was first in the office. The phone in the main office rang early, before Mike, Virgil, or Sal, who was covering for Jezza, had arrived.

'Serious Crime, DCI Darling.'

'Morning sir, it's PC Harris from the safe house, with Ronnie. I was hoping to speak to Maurice, please.'

'He's on a day off today, Cathy. Can I help?'

'You really put the wind up Ronnie when you visited. She now wants to talk. She's begging to talk. She says she's thought of some things which would be useful. And she's lowered her sights considerably from South America. Apparently she's got family in Southampton and she's happy to go there.'

'She can't go anywhere she has family or any other connections. She needs to understand that. If these drugs people are as bad as she thinks, that would be too easy for them. But we can find her somewhere to start out with a new identity. As long as she comes up with the goods.

'Speaking of which, at some point someone is going to have to explain to her that for her new identity, she'll really need to ditch the fake tans. Go back to whatever colour she is underneath. It's too much of a trademark. Makes her too easy to spot. Perhaps you could start to float that idea past her. You'll certainly do it more tactfully than I could.

'Has she been kept away from the news? She still doesn't know about the second body?'

'CBeebies is stretching her, intellectually. She's not interested in news or current affairs or anything. Mind you, she likes the old cop shows, especially the American ones, and she's come up with her very own brilliant sting operation, as she calls it. Or so she thinks. To draw out the other cuckoos for us to round up and arrest.'

'If she'd told us who they are we could have done that by now. But I'm prepared to come and listen to what she has to propose and see where we go from there. Certainly in the absence of much else to go on for now. Is she up and about yet?'

'That's an indicator of how rattled she is after your visit. She doesn't usually surface until dinnertime but she was up bright and early, wanting to tell me all about her idea. I told her it was down to you for anything like that. She's asked me at least a dozen times so far today to phone you.'

'I'll come over in an hour or so. I have stuff to do here first, and I don't want Zofia to start thinking she just has to snap her fingers and we'll jump to it.

'I got this idea, right.'

Ronnie started talking as soon as Ted walked through the door. She was sitting up on the sofa this time and even turned the TV off herself when she heard him at the door. 'So you can get the others an' then you can fix up for me to go somewhere safe.'

'I told you before, Zofia, that's not quite how it works. I need to listen to what you're offering in exchange and evaluate its usefulness to us before I can agree anything for you.'

She scowled at him, looking like a petulant child. 'How do

I know I can trust you?'

'You don't,' Ted told her candidly. 'So what you need to decide is whether you trust me more than you trust this Big Man, whoever he is.'

He sat down in the armchair opposite her, motioning to PC Harris to take a seat. Like any officer coming and going from the safe house she was out of uniform. No marked cars, no uniforms anywhere near the place in an attempt to keep it anonymous.

Ted got his phone out and put it on the table again to record as he said, 'But I need you to understand, Zofia, you have to make that decision soon. I can't go on supporting you staying here in return for nothing at all.'

'You want to get the others, right? The ones from Abi's flat. I don't know all their names. Just nicknames and first names, mostly. But I got this idea of how to fix up a meet wi'them all.'

'Go on,' Ted prompted her, when she stopped again.

'Data's the brainy one. He has all the ideas. He's the newest, too. Only turned up about four months ago. Summat like that. Kane's the one who always goes and gets the gear. We all sell a bit here and there. Data sells the good stuff. In the posh clubs an' that. That's new. We never got that stuff before Data turned up.

'An' we got this code, like. For if we need to meet up away from the flat. We always meet up in a park. Nowt unusual, seeing a bunch o'teens hanging round in a park. Data checks where there's no cameras and we meet there.

'We use about six o'them. Parks. They all got a number. Like, Hollywood is number one. We met there last time I seen 'em all. So next time will be number two. That's Shaw Heath Rec. So we don't need to say where we're meeting, in case anyone else sees the text. Everyone will know.

'If you give us me phone back, I can text all the others and fix up a meet. Then they'll all be in the same place at the same time. Up to you to round 'em all up then.'

'You can't use your own phone, Zofia,' Ted explained patiently. 'I told you we were taking it to see if there was a trace on it, and there was. I can get you a new pay-as-you-go, unused, and you can try from that. There's always a risk that the others won't read texts from a number they don't recognise. There may be a workaround for that, but I'd have to check with the technical members of my team.'

'I don't know none of the numbers, though. Not without my phone.'

'There's no problem with that. We can easily transfer your contacts from your own phone to the new one. I'll do that and bring it round later today, so you can put the message in. The same way you'd always message them. I'll send it later, from somewhere well away from here. Just in case they're clever enough to trace where it's been sent from. Now, I'm going to need a list from you of all of the parks, in numerical order.'

She seemed to take him at his word about the risk of being traced unless she used a clean phone, although he knew he was probably spouting nonsense. But she looked suspicious, instantly on the defensive, when he asked for the list.

'Why? I already told you where the next meet needs to be.'

Ted's tone was patient as he explained to her. 'If this Data is as smart as you say, he's going to be suspicious. He's not heard from you all week and suddenly you want to meet up. Don't forget the others might have been meeting while you've been out of circulation, so you won't know which is the right place to ask for the meeting.

'Even if they haven't met and you're right about Shaw Heath, I still need time to check out all the possible locations in case someone decides to change places at the last moment. We'll only get one chance at doing this, so it has to work. For your sake, as much as ours. Because if this goes wrong for any reason, your friends will know you've been talking.'

'Yeah, but I'll be safe, won't I? Witness protection and

that? You said I'd be protected if I helped you, and I am doing.'

'You've made a start, Zofia. But I have to show results for what it's costing me. You need to work with me. So give me all the names of all of the parks, in the right order. I'll get them checked out, then I'll come back later today with a new phone for you and we'll see first of all if you can set up the meeting. Then we can take it from there.'

Ted had parked a couple of streets away so as not to draw too much attention to the safe house, with a lot of different vehicles coming and going. As he walked back to the car, he made a quick call.

'I shouldn't be too late home tonight so I wondered if you fancied eating out somewhere? If we can book anywhere decent at short notice.'

'Hmm, that sounds nice, but it also sounds like you're softening me up to say you can't, after all, take the afternoon off tomorrow,' Trev replied.

'You know me too well. There's a chance I may not get away as early as I hoped tomorrow. There's a biggish op I need to run. I'd rather do it tomorrow then it's sorted and I don't have to worry about it on Monday. I want to give you all my time and attention then.'

Trev sounded slightly mollified as he said, 'It may mean somewhere outrageously expensive, in that case. As you said, as long as we can get in at short notice. But money always talks. Leave it to me.'

'At least it looks like Zofia's trying to tell us factual info now,' Ted told the team when they caught up over takeaways and sandwiches at lunchtime. 'She's no way of knowing the rest of them have already met up at Shaw Heath. But we know that from our eye witness, who found the piece of tongue. Which means that the next meet-up should, in theory, be Alexandra Park.'

'Isn't it going to make her suspicious, if you change the venue from where she thinks it ought to be?' Mike asked, emptying two more sachets of brown sauce onto his bacon sandwich, which was already swimming in it.

'I'll tell her I've done a recce of the sites she told me about and this one would be the easiest one for us, operationally speaking. I'm having to be a bit inventive and bend the truth somewhat in what I'm telling her, which I don't really like doing.

'But it goes without saying, this is likely to be our one chance to get the stragglers. Zofia doesn't know there's only three left unaccounted for – Data, Sarwar and Lauren – so she'll want to message all of them. That's where there's a risk this could rebound on us, as we don't know where Kane Lomax's phone is. If it's in the hands of whoever killed him and they read the message, they might also turn up.'

'But if the location is coded, would they know where to go?' Mike asked.

'Don't forget how extensively he was tortured before they killed him, Mike. I'm betting he would have told them everything he knew and more besides, hoping to save himself. I expect they know considerably more than we do at this stage. We need to find a way to get Zofia to message all the others except Kane, if anyone has an idea how we do that.'

Sal spoke up. Working Fraud, as he now did, he was probably the most switched on to mobile phones and their secrets of any of them present.

'Boss, if you're really not that bothered about bending the facts to Zofia, there's a couple of things I would suggest. The first and most obvious is to spin her a yarn that she can't actually send the message herself because it might give away the location of the safe house. So she could enter the message and then give you the phone to send it from a more secure location. That way we could simply delete the text to Kane's number.'

'I already mentioned something like that, although I wasn't sure if it sounded feasible. She was a bit suspicious, so if there's another option, let's hear it, Sal.'

'The second thing would be to spin her some technical explanation that as Kane was the go-between with the Big Man, they would have put some sort of a device on his phone as a precaution before they let him take any of the gear away. So if she sends a text to his phone, she risks alerting the gang as to where she is, through that device.

'Of course either of those would only work if she's neither bright enough nor techie enough to realise it's implausible.

'Well, I can certainly tell her that with a clear conscience. Most of this is beyond me so it all sounds plausible enough to me, and hopefully will to her, too.

'Right, the thing we need to talk about next is who's in on this op. I know there's only three of them likely to turn up, as far as we know, but it's essential we don't let any of them get away. Although I need to flag up here that there's just a possibility that Drugs will want one of them left untouched.'

As various team members started to speak, Ted cut them short.

'I know, but that decision will be taken at a much higher level and won;t be up for debate. And there could be more of the gang that we don't yet know about, of course. We need to lift the ones we can, for their own safety, as much as anything else. So I might need to bring you all back in tomorrow, and I'm sorry if that spoils anyone's plans. It may well be overkill, but I don't want to run any risk of losing them. Not unless I'm ordered to.

'It's likely to be lunchtime because according to Zofia, they like to pick a time of day when there's not all that many people around. It's still a bit chilly for people to be having a picnic, so on a Sunday, it should be on the quiet side.

'We need enough of us to be within reasonable distance to cover each entrance point and we need not to stick out like coppers on a stake-out. Ideas, anyone, please?'

'Boss, they have a basketball area there. Believe it or not, when I'm not pumping iron, I've been known to shoot a few hoops,' Virgil told him. 'I've even met up with Jo and his sons to do it on a weekend, before now. Perhaps he could even bring them along for this.'

Ted shook his head. 'I'd rather not run any risks at all with this one, while we don't really know who we're up against. But the two of you playing together shouldn't look that unusual. I can put my running gear on and do a few laps round the park while we're watching for them. I'm not a sprinter, when it comes to chasing anyone, but I run distance, so I can keep it up for as long as necessary.

'We'll need someone to control things from a car nearby. To coordinate and, if necessary, go after any of them who slip past those of us on the ground. Mike, do you fancy that?'

'I'm never going to live it down, am I? Nearly letting Ronnie slip away. But yes, on that form, it's probably as well not to rely on me for the catching, unless all else fails.'

'Sal, I'll put you in another car on the other side. That leaves us Rob, Maurice and Steve to dot about the place. Surely, between us, we should be able to grab them all, without wanting to tempt fate. The one I'm most sceptical about is Data. If he's the brainy one, as Zofia seems to think, there's a good chance he'll be watching very carefully before he shows his face. Bearing in mind we have no clear visuals on him, nothing on record and all Zofia's told us is that he's mixed race. Even that might not be accurate.

'Zofia, of course, will need to be there or there's a risk none of them will show. But she could be wired and I'll tell her exactly what she can and can't say. Plus she'll have her babysitter from the safe house to keep an extra eye on her. So fingers crossed.'

'This looks nice,' Ted said as he stood aside to let Trev go into the restaurant first.

'Is that your euphemism for expensive?' Trev laughed. 'And is that whimpering sound coming from your credit card, Mr Scrooge? You told me money was no object. It took all my considerable charm, plus speaking Italian, to get us in here. So now I'm going to enjoy the food, and spending some time with my husband. Listening to him grovelling about having to stand me up tomorrow after he promised to take me out, for which this meal is only a down payment. The rest will be extracted when we get home.'

Chapter Twenty

'Right, Zofia, here's your new phone back, and you've had a couple of replies. Have a look at them now, please, and confirm that they're from Sarwar and Lauren,' Ted told her, handing it to her. 'Remember, don't reply. You don't want to give away this location. Then we need to go over a few details about how today is going to proceed. It's important that you listen carefully, remember what I tell you, and follow instructions at all times. Not only for your own safety but for that of my officers.'

The phone which Ted gave her was the one on which she'd entered the message, under his watchful eye, the day before. Once he'd taken it back to the station, he'd deleted the text to Kane's phone. If she was sharp enough to check the circulation list when she looked at it, she would spot straight away that his name was missing. He'd left the others. Latte's phone was turned off and in a police evidence bag. Those belonging to Bethany Hayes and Reece Williams had been taken from them when they were arrested. Ted doubted Zofia was bright enough to think of checking, but he wasn't taking any chances on this one.

'As you know, Sharon will be taking you to the park in plenty of time for the meet-up, then she'll be staying nearby to keep an eye on you. There will be other officers about, some of whom you may recognise. Do not react in any way to any of them, please. That's very important.'

'I'm not thick, you know,' she told him, her tone sullen. 'I watch this stuff on the telly all the time, so I know what happens.'

'I'm not implying that you are. This is standard procedure. I'm briefing you in exactly the same way that I will brief anyone involved in this operation. That's to reduce the risk of anything going wrong as much as I possibly can.

'First of all, do any of the others drive? Are any of them likely to turn up at the park in a vehicle of any sort? Car, bike, motorbike? It's essential I know such details so I can cover all options.'

She shook her head. 'None of 'em has a car. They wouldn't risk nickin' one for summat like this either. We don't take no risks of gettin' chased by the feds when we have more important stuff to talk about.'

'Good, thank you. Now, apart from Abigail's flat, do you have any other premises where you stash things? Like drugs, for instance. Another flat? A lock-up? Anything. Or have you ever been to any other property where one of the others might be living, or staying occasionally?''

A non-committal shrug.

'But you must have other premises where you can safely store things. Especially anything of any value. Not just the drugs but personal effects. Things like camera equipment, perhaps.'

He saw her eyes widen slightly at that.

'Because we know about the porn films that were being made at Abigail's flat. We haven't yet found the camera used to make them and we're very keen to get our hands on it for evidence. So perhaps you can help us with where to look for it.'

She shrugged. 'Dunno anything about no porn.'

'Oh, but I think you do, Zofia. The trouble with pixelating faces out and thinking that means job done is that there are other identifying marks which show up on film.'

She instinctively tugged down the sleeves of the hoody she

was wearing as Ted went on, 'It's not just the butterfly on your wrist, though, is it, Zofia? You have some quite impressive tattoos elsewhere. And they show up all too clearly on the footage.'

'What, you've been lookin' at porn stuff? What are you, some kind of perv? It were nowt. Just some messin'. Nowt illegal.'

'I'm a police officer. Investigating serious crime. And we both know that what went on in Abigail's flat with the camera running went well beyond "messing". If you're expecting me to see you're protected and no action is taken against you, you need to be fully honest with me, Zofia. It's not just about rounding up the rest of your friends. It's about making sure that I have the evidence to get some convictions. And in particular, I want to get to the people behind all of this. The drug suppliers, as well as those dealing with the serious porn, if they're different people.

'If anything should go wrong with this operation today and anyone gets away, I need to know where to start looking for them. You'll be perfectly safe. You have nothing to worry about. Officers will protect you as a priority. But I want to know where any of your friends might head for, if they give us the slip. I need to know all of the other places you've been using. Call it a show of faith, if you like. And I need to know that now, before we even think of carrying on with this operation.'

'Are you sure we aren't going to need Firearms back-up on this one, boss?' Mike asked at the start of the team briefing before the planned operation.

It was the first question Jim Baker had asked Ted when he'd phoned him to go over the plans. Ted gave the same answer he'd given earlier to Big Jim.

'It would be a logistical nightmare to even contemplate for a public park, on a Sunday, when we have no real grounds to suspect anyone present will be carrying firearms. We'll be in place early. The slightest sign of anything which presents a risk – and I do mean anything – we abort. All we're interested in for now is to pull in Sarwar, Lauren and, hopefully, Data.

'Zofia's given us some more places to look. Squats, mostly. The thought that I knew where the rest of her tattoos were made her uncomfortable enough to be more cooperative. So if any of them do give us the slip, we at least know other boltholes they might head for.

'So, Mike, you in a car on Edgeley Road, please. Hopefully somewhere you can keep an eye on both entrances. Sal, you take Edgeley Fold, and the same thing applies. Maurice, you get Dale Street. Steve, Cheadle Old Road end. Sykes Meadow entrance. Jo, that leaves you, me, Virgil and Rob on foot in the park.

'Thanks to talk of the porn films having loosened Zofia's tongue a bit, we know roughly whereabouts they usually meet up and it's not that far from the basketball area. Sharon – PC Andrews, for those who don't know her – is bringing Zofia, again fairly early on, then she's also going to be running as her cover, so she's an extra reliable pair of hands. And she's a sprinter, too, so that could be useful.

'We all need to stay in constant touch. Keep our eyes open for anything at all out of the ordinary. Above all, no heroics. From anyone. Is that clear?'

There were nods and murmurs of assent. Virgil was the one who risked replying. He still had vivid memories of having to grab hold of the boss on top of a church tower to stop him from falling.

'Same goes for you, boss. No heroics this time.'

PC Sharon Andrews let Ronnie out of her car near to one of the entrances, then went to park her vehicle. She knew the chances of her trying to make a run for it were slim, knowing as she did that officers were watching every entrance into the park, as well as being dotted around inside it.

Ronnie had been thrilled to find she would be wearing a wire. She didn't know that there would only be contact between her and Ted. She would be on a different channel to the rest of the operation. The many television programmes she watched had given her a somewhat unrealistic idea of what her role was going to be. They couldn't risk her saying the wrong thing at the wrong time and blowing the whole operation.

Sharon had been impressed with how patient the DCI had been in explaining to Ronnie that he didn't want to do anything which might put her in danger. He'd gone over and over her cover story with her to make sure she wasn't likely to say anything to give the game away.

'Whatever else you do, Zofia, trust me, please. We have to make it look realistic out there in order to protect you. Which means that you'll also be arrested, along with anyone else who turns up. You'll be taken back to the station and processed just like everyone else. Charged and interviewed. But while they'll be remanded in police custody, you'll be slipped quietly out of the back door when all's clear and taken back to the safe house for now.'

'Ain't I going to Southampton?' she demanded.

Hats off to the DCI that he didn't show in his face or his voice what a stupid question it was. He just carried on in the same even tone.

'Your new destination is a long way down the road yet, I'm afraid. There are legal processes which have to be gone through before we can arrange anything at all. As I told you, you will have to testify but you will be protected and your identity can be concealed if necessary for your safety.

'Just remember, don't do anything at all to draw suspicion to yourself. Behave as you normally would if you were being arrested. But please remember, you can trust me.'

As Ted started his slow, steady circuits round the park, he hoped Zofia would trust him and wouldn't blow the whole thing by her reactions. He was taking a big gamble with her and he knew it. But it was still their best chance of finding any of the others.

The one thing Ted hadn't yet told her was that Kane was dead. If she'd known about his death, especially if she'd got wind of how he died, there would have been no chance of her agreeing to any of this.

Ted watched as Zofia walked to the bench where she told them they usually met up. There was no one occupying it. She slouched on the seat, mouth open, chewing gum, hands thrust deep into the pockets of the jacket she was wearing against the stiff breeze.

She and Ted didn't so much as look at one another as he lapped her for the first time. Sharon Andrews was also running circuits but in the opposite direction. Going much faster than he was. Ted wondered how long she could keep that pace up. They exchanged the complicit smiles of two athletes training. Nothing in that to arouse anyone's suspicions.

Next he passed Virgil and Jo, shooting some hoops. Jo was surprisingly good. Having six children, several of them sporty, clearly kept him on his toes. They were enjoying themselves. Laughing and joking. Anyone watching would see two friends letting their hair down together, mucking about, being kids again.

Rob was sitting on a bench not far away, eyes glued to his mobile phone. He looked up occasionally, as if waiting for someone. To a casual onlooker he looked like someone whose date was either running late or had stood him up.

'Looks like Sarwar and Lauren are just turning into the entrance now.' Mike's voice through one of the earpieces Ted was wearing. They were all in constant contact. 'No signs of anyone with them who could be Data. Just the two of them. Positive ID on Sarwar. The girl looks like the one from the stills at the flat.'

'Let them come in,' Ted told them. 'They're not that late and we don't want to show our hand too early. We want to give Data time to turn up, if he's coming. Anyone got eyes on a possible for him?'

'Sir, I've got a single male youth approaching Sykes Meadow along Cheadle Old Road from the direction of Mountfield Road. A possible for Data but cannot confirm at the moment.'

'Keep us posted, Steve. I have a possible person of interest.'

Ted had spotted a man walking his dog. Nothing unusual about that. But there was something about the way the man moved and held himself which had caught Ted's attention. In his Specialist Firearms days, he'd done a lot of training alongside military personnel. His main trainer, Mr Green, had been ex-Army. Special Forces. The man he could see ahead of him, walking a large dog towards him on a tight lead, moved in a specific way which instantly caught his attention.

He was wearing black combat trousers with a matching field jacket. Black military boots. He could have been an off-duty police officer or fire officer with a service dog, giving it a quiet weekend walk. The way the brute lunged towards Ted as he ran past immediately told him he wasn't. The dog would have failed the temperament test. The handler jerked it back to heel with such force that it yelped and cringed. The man spoke harshly to it in a language Ted didn't recognise. Then he went back to talking through his mobile phone headset, seemingly in the same language.

Ted sidestepped as the dog reacted. Made a pretence of stumbling to give himself some time to observe. The man merely lifted a hand in apology but carried on walking and talking. Ted turned to check his line of sight. The man's eyes were fixed on the bench where Zofia was sitting waiting, looking up now as she'd caught sight of Lauren and Sarwar, heading her way.

'Steve. Update, please. Is it Data? Where is he?'

'Still walking towards the Sykes Meadow entrance, sir. I still can't say definitely if it's Data or not. Oh, hang on a minute. There's a black 4x4 just coming up behind him. It's slowing down near him.'

There was a pause then, 'Shit! Whoever it was has got in it and the 4x4 is driving off at speed.'

'Get the number, Steve, and go after them, but stay well back. Mike, you go too. I want to know where that vehicle goes, but do not put yourselves at risk.

'Rob, you follow the bloke in black, with the big dog, who's just gone past me. Same thing. See where he goes but don't get too close. The dog's nasty. If he gets in a vehicle, get the number but don't try to follow, unless it's anywhere near where your car is parked.

'Sal, Maurice, get round to Edgeley Road. Make sure Lauren and Sarwar don't make a run for it. Sharon, Zofia's your responsibility. Keep your eyes on her. Don't let her slip away. Jo, Virgil, with me. Let's lift Lauren and Sarwar while we have them in our sights. I'll arrest Zofia, so we don't blow her cover. I still have eyes on her and the other two have just joined her. Go!'

In the few short moments between the other two walking up to her and Ted's team hitting them, it was clear from Ronnie's behaviour that they had told her immediately that Kane was dead. Probably even something about the way in which he had died.

Virgil made straight for Sarwar Dabiri. The lad was neither large nor very bold. He didn't even try to run as he saw Virgil's big black bulk bearing down on him. He stood petrified, like a rabbit caught in a car's headlights, as Virgil arrested and handcuffed him.

Lauren, the as yet unknown one, at least put up something of a fight, kicking, clawing and swearing like a fishwife as Jo tried to get a hold on her without getting himself injured.

Ronnie rounded on Ted as soon as she saw him approaching her, no doubt feeling betrayed.

'You lying bastard ...' she spat.

Ted barked, 'Shut up!' at her then, as he forced her arms none too gently behind her and reached for his cuffs, he put his mouth close to her ear and breathed, 'Shut up and trust me.'

Steve was driving as fast as he dared after the 4x4. Sundays were not a good day for a car chase. All the older weekend drivers seemed to be out and about in force. Driving slowly and sedately in the middle of the road, making it impossible to pass. Creeping timidly out of side turnings then stopping in their uncertainty. Steve was having to do a lot of swerving and was also doing more swearing than was normal for him.

He was on the radio to the station, giving details of the vehicle he was pursuing, and the direction it was travelling in, and asking, more in hope than anticipation, for any available units to assist. He wasn't surprised to hear there was currently little chance. Nor that the registration number he'd quoted didn't fit the model of vehicle he was pursuing. They were cloned.

Mike was liaising with him, trying his best to find a route to get ahead of the fleeing 4x4, so far without success.

It was clear to both of them that the vehicle was being driven by someone who knew what they were doing and knew every inch of the backstreets into which it kept disappearing from their sight.

They had to abandon pursuit when Mike almost pulled out of a side-street into Steve's path, both of them hitting the brakes so hard they left marks on the road.

They both got out of their vehicles at the same time, Mike looking in surprise as Steve kicked viciously at one of his car's front tyres and swore again.

'The boss isn't going to be pleased I lost them,' Steve said, his expression glum.

'We've lost them for now, Steve. That's all. The description's being circulated. Someone will spot them sooner or later. It's not the end of the world. Come on, we best head back to the station and see if the others at least rounded up the two stragglers, even if Data's given us the slip for now.'

Chapter Twenty-one

Data was walking along Cheadle Old Road, heading for one of the entrances to the park. Head down, hood up, hands deep in his pockets. Despite appearances, he was alert and watchful.

It had been a surprise to get the sudden contact from Ronnie after more than a week of radio silence from her. She must have had his text to arrange the last meeting because her message gave the number of the next park on the list. It could be that she'd simply been too scared to show up. Maybe she'd had the feds on her tail and had been clever enough to steer clear until the heat died down. He doubted it, though. He'd never had her down for the sharpest knife in the drawer. Lauren was the clever one amongst them. She was as bad as any of them – worse than some – yet she'd always managed to stay one step ahead of the law so she didn't yet have a record.

He wasn't planning to go straight to their usual bench. He wanted to have a good look round before he went anywhere near, to check for anyone watching. He hadn't passed any suspicious-looking vehicles on the way, but he didn't plan on taking any chances.

He was instantly wary when a black 4x4 came purring up from behind and slowed to a crawl next to him. His first instinct was to run for it, suspecting it was an unmarked police vehicle. Despite himself, he had to turn his head and look. The rear nearside window was gliding down and Data found himself looking at the dwarf in the mirrored glasses who'd confronted them in the park a few days ago.

All his flight and survival instincts were screaming at him to run. But Data's eyes were transfixed by the menacing black eye of a pistol in the small man's hand, pointing unwaveringly straight at him.

The dwarf's voice was almost pleasant as he said, 'Get in, Data. There's a police reception committee waiting for you, in force. And the Big Man doesn't want you falling into their hands. Get in. Now.'

Data's hand was trembling as he reached out to open the door. As soon as he slid on to the leather seat and pulled the door shut behind him with a soft clunk, he heard the unmistakable sound of the central locking being applied. He knew instinctively that there would be no way he could open the side door from inside the vehicle, which was now speeding away.

'You made the right decision, Data,' the short man told him. The gun was still in his right hand but he now laid it casually across his leg so it was no longer pointing straight at Data. The sinister white stick, with its deadly blade inside, which Data had seen on their last encounter, was propped up against the seat.

Up close, Data could see that the man's torso was of average size, but all four limbs were disproportionately short. So much so that his legs stuck out in front of him, his thighs not long enough for him to be able to bend his legs at the knee where the seat ended.

'Very soon, I expect us to pick up a trail by the filth. But don't concern yourself about that. Igor here is very good at his job. He can lose any tail, anywhere. And don't worry, we can talk freely in front of him. He doesn't speak English. His name's not Igor, either. That's just my little joke.'

The short man laughed at his own humour. 'So relax, young Data. You're in good hands. Our orders are to keep you safe at all times. Because you have unfinished business with the Big Man, don't you?' There was a sudden note of menace in the way he said it.

'We couldn't get the gear back from the flat. We tried, but the feds were all over the place.'

Data was ashamed to hear how wobbly and whiny his voice sounded, even to his own ears. 'But I've got some money for the Big Man. Safely stashed. From stuff I sold in the clubs. Only I didn't know how to get it to him, with Kane gone. He was our only link.'

'Good boy. That's what we like to hear. That's why the Big Man wanted you kept safe from the police's little trap. You're not as clever as you think you are with your silly amateur tracking devices. But you're still a valuable asset. Kane and any of the other lame-brains are good enough for selling a bit of skunk on street corners.

'But you, Data, with your looks and the way you speak. You can get into the posh places, to push the good stuff. And that makes you priceless. That and your performance in the films. Especially swinging both ways at will. You look like you'd happily fuck a corpse when you're hyped up like that. He likes that. He even thinks it would add a little something to a future film. Snuff movies make seriously big money.'

The man's arms were so short he had to lean sideways to run the back of his hand suggestively down the side of Data's face. The gesture sent a chill through his whole body. He instinctively clutched himself with a desperate hand, convinced he was about to piss his pants in fear. The man saw the reaction and laughed.

'Calm down, little Data. My brief is to deliver you safely, and I'm going to do that. As we get nearer to where we're going I'm going to have to do the boring thing of getting you to lie on the floor while I put a bag over your head. Don't be afraid. I'm not going to hurt you. The rule always is, the less you know, the safer you are. So at the moment you can relax. I promise you, you're safe. For now.'

The team were all back in the main office, heading gratefully to make hot drinks. They were in generally high spirits. Apart from Steve, who was quieter even than usual and looking like a whipped puppy. Ted found time to go over to him and have a quiet word.

'Don't worry about it, Steve. We weren't geared up for a car chase. My fault. I took Zofia at her word that none of them would come by vehicle. I should have considered the possibility that someone else might be transporting them. Drugs may very well be pleased we let one go.

'Do you think it was Data, from the stills? The one who got into the vehicle.'

'I wish I could say for sure, sir. I didn't really get much of a look at him before he got in the vehicle. And I'm really sorry I lost him.'

'Seriously, not your fault. We weren't prepared for high-speed pursuit so it was a lost cause. Get your notes written up and make sure you include every detail you can think of about the lad who might have been Data. And of anyone in the vehicle. What can you tell me about that?'

'Male driver, and it looked like a single male passenger in the back seat. Data, if it was him, got in the back, too. It all happened very quickly.'

'Got in voluntarily?'

'It seemed that way, sir. No one got out to force him in or anything. But like I say, it was very fast. Sorry.'

Ted's plan was to let some of the team go, as soon as they'd written up their notes. For once, he was including himself in those taking some time off. Jo would be in charge for the rest of the day so he went to discuss things with him.

'A partial success at least. I'd have liked to get Data, of course, but we still might. Unless Drugs decide otherwise.

'Keep an eye on Steve, won't you? He's beating himself up about it, as usual, and it's not his fault. At least now that we have the elusive Lauren we can get her prints and run those against the ones found in Abigail's flat. If we can place her inside there, we've got something to charge her with, at least.

'I'm intending to knock off as soon as I've finished speaking to Zofia. I did promise Trev I'd try to get home at a decent time.'

'Why don't you get off now? One of us can talk to her easily enough. There's four of us on the rota and only two of them who need interviewing. We'll question them at length then stick them with a holding charge and remand them in police custody overnight, as we discussed. Is that still the plan?'

'I should talk to her myself,' Ted told him, nodding in response to his query. 'I know she feels I let her down by not telling her about Kane. I'd better quickly build some bridges. Then I'll happily hand her over to someone else to interview at length before we send her back to the safe house.'

Ted found Zofia sitting, with a furious look on her face, in an interview room. Despite the recording, he asked PC Andrews to stay with them. He didn't trust Zofia further than he could throw her and the feeling was mutual. He wanted the extra safeguard of a witness.

'You lied to me, you bastard. You never told me about Kane.'

'I didn't lie to you,' Ted told her patiently. 'I chose not to tell you about Kane because I knew it would worry you. I promised you that you wouldn't be in any danger and you weren't.'

'But Sarwar said some fucking midget chucked half a tongue at them and said it were Kane's ...'

'Does that mean anything to you? Someone of short stature? A dwarf, perhaps? Have you ever heard any of your friends mention such a person before?'

'I don't know. It were always Kane who met with the Big Man and he never said much about how it went or who was there. He were scared shitless of him, but he pretended not to be. And look where he ended up. If I knew owt about some midget I wouldn't tell you.'

'You'll be safe, Zofia, I've already promised you that.'

'Yeah, but that were before I knew about Kane. I ain't saying no more now.'

'Let me clarify this with you then, Zofia, so we are in absolutely no doubt. You now wish to withdraw your cooperation in this case and therefore to rule yourself out of the witness protection scheme. Is that what you mean?'

She sat bolt upright at that, looking panic-stricken. 'No! I want protecting. I told you stuff already. I helped you get Sarwar an' Lauren. It weren't my fault Data didn't turn up.'

'But I've made it clear to you all along that witness protection will depend on you cooperating fully and testifying. I've repeated that to you several times, always in front of witnesses. Like Sharon. Can you confirm that, for the recording, PC Andrews, please?'

'I can, sir. I confirm that you have explained fully to Zofia, in my presence, that her protection was dependent on her full cooperation and testimony.'

'Thank you. So, Zofia, if you've decided against that, there's nothing further to be said,' Ted made a show of gathering his things together and standing up. 'I have somewhere else to be so I'll send another officer in. You'll be charged with several offences and remanded in police custody for now. Tomorrow morning you'll appear before the magistrates for a further remand in custody.'

'Hold on a minute,' Ronnie almost shouted as Ted turned and made for the door. 'You can't do that. I need protecting.'

Ted turned back towards her but made no move to sit back down.

'So give me something that's worth the trouble and cost of keeping you on the scheme. You're holding back, Zofia. We both know that.'

'There's another place,' she blurted. 'Another lock-up.

Data keeps stuff there. I been with him one time. It's like a big old place, like a factory or summat. With all, like, small rooms, cabins, that sort of thing, where you can lock stuff away. There's a lift you go up if you ain't got a car. That's well creepy. It got stuck one time when we was coming down. Data's mad. He wanted us to do it while we were stuck there.'

Ted sat back down, facing her.

'By "do it", you mean he wanted to have sex with you? In the lift? Wasn't he sleeping with Abigail?'

'Fuck, man, Data would shag anything with a pulse. He'd knob a dog if he were randy enough and there were nowt else. Not just girls, either. Lads too. Anything. That's why he likes doing the porno films.'

Ted was so glad he hadn't already sent Trev a text to say he would be home early. He knew he could easily hand over to Jo at this point, but he wanted to see it through a bit further himself. Another half hour, he promised himself, then he'd go home. They'd still have enough time to go out for a walk or a spin on the bike somewhere. Maybe another meal out, by way of grovelling apology.

'Sorry, sorry, I meant it to be earlier than this, honestly,' Ted was already apologising before he'd got much further than the front door. 'I just had a bit of a breakthrough with a witness and I didn't want to leave it there.'

Trev was lying on the sofa, accompanied by all the cats, watching a film. His new resolution about drinking less had clearly been a victim of his disappointment at Ted being later back than he'd promised, judging by the nearly empty bottle of red wine next to him.

Ted bent down to kiss him and to stroke the cats. 'We could still go out somewhere,' he said optimistically. 'I'll drive, of course. Anywhere you fancy. And don't worry about tomorrow. That's a definite promise. Jo knows. He's under orders to arrest me if I'm even a minute late leaving to pick up

Jono. Although he doesn't actually know where I'm going or why it's so important.'

He perched carefully on the edge of the sofa, being careful not to disturb any of its occupants. Trev's look was not particularly welcoming.

'I really should have learned by now not to get my hopes up. But I do. I did. It was a nice day. I was having visions of a spin out somewhere, with a bite to eat in a country pub. Sometimes I honestly think I should have married a boring accountant or someone else a bit more reliable.'

'I really am sorry. I should never have said anything. Just turned up early to surprise you.'

'One day you might do that and find I've finally decided to get myself a nice bit on the side. You might come in and catch me in the act of having a passionate romp on the sofa with some fit and faithful man who's anything but a policeman.'

'You could always try a romp on the sofa with your totally unreliable policeman husband,' Ted suggested. 'Who's pretty fit for a boring middle-aged copper. And who is currently desperate and willing to do anything – anything at all – to get back in your good books.'

He was slipping out of his jacket as he spoke, kicking off his shoes, and lifting protesting cats onto the floor out of his way.

Chapter Twenty-two

Ted was in early on Monday morning, determined to get on top of work before he went to pick Jono up from the station. They'd spoken at length by phone but it would be the first time he'd met DI Jonathan Moore in the flesh.

Sal Ahmed was already in, working away at Jezza's desk, in her absence. He looked up as Ted entered the office.

'Morning, boss. Following on from what Ronnie told you about the lock-up, I thought I'd make a start on looking at Abi's financial situation, now we've got the bank statements from her mother. They show that Abi has been paying a monthly fee for a storage unit. And it seems to be in the same building as the one Ronnie mentioned. Coincidence?'

'Which you know I don't like. We need to take a look inside that unit. I have to be out for part of today, but I'll sort out a warrant to search it before I go. Can I safely leave that one to you, Sal? Ask Inspector Turner for someone from Uniform to go with you.

'Is there anything else coming to light on the financial side of things?'

'Well, I'm trying not to be judgemental of the parents, but I do wonder why the father, in particular, doesn't seem to have queried the amount of money she was going through. He's a businessman, so he must know his way round the financial side of things. But he just seems to top the account up at the end of every month, presumably without querying anything. And it's often right up to the generous overdraft limit.'

'That's pretty much what Mrs Buller told me. Guilt money, it seems.'

'I can understand that, boss. But surely things like the storage unit should ring alarm bells? Why would he think his daughter needed one of those? I'm taking it she doesn't drive, to take anything which she needed to store there?'

'We haven't specifically checked. We rather made an assumption,which we shouldn't have done. But I would think it highly unlikely. Get someone to double-check that, though, please. And perhaps when you visit the place, find out about who goes there and how they take stuff in and out. If there is a vehicle going to any lock-up, they usually have to sign in at reception, I think, so there should be a written record, as well as CCTV.

'I want to know what's inside that unit as soon as possible. With any luck, it's the missing camera, for one thing, and that could be very useful to us. Especially if there's footage on it which we haven't yet found online.'

'There's another thing. Her bank card has been used to withdraw the maximum cash amount daily on a number of occasions. Even that doesn't seem to have rung any bells with the father. What does he think she's spending that kind of money on?'

'So the cuckoos have been making good use of her money for their own ends. The chances of us getting Abigail to trial, never mind getting a conviction, on this one are slipping further away with each new revelation. The porn footage we have already is a gift to the defence, and it sounds like there's even worse still to emerge.

'Good work, Sal, thank you. Keep at it.'

'Any news on when Jezza is back? Only I'll no doubt be summoned back to the Fraud fold fairly soon. It's the same story there. Too many cases and not enough of us to go round at the best of times. Although it is nice being back with old friends, I must say.'

'I've not heard from her yet, and I'm trying not to press her. I don't want her rushing back before she's fully fit. I'll try giving her a call at some point today, though. I'd hate her to think we'd forgotten about her.'

There was at least a bit more promising news at the morning briefing.

'Boss, Sarwar is definitely the weak link,' Rob began. 'He was falling over himself to tell me anything he could, to get himself a lighter sentence. He's already had a brief taste of life inside, as a young offender, and I gather it didn't go well. He's desperate enough to want to avoid repeating the experience in an adult prison. I think he's dreading his first shower; a small, good-looking lad like him.

'The trouble is, he doesn't have a lot to bargain with. He doesn't know much. He's a bit at the bottom of the food chain. He swears blind he doesn't know who the Big Man is and that it was only ever Kane who had direct contact with him. He does say that Kane mentioned the dwarf on a couple of occasions. He said he was there to protect the Big Man's identity, but the others always thought he was just joking. Some bogeyman Kane had dreamed up to keep them all in line. It has to be said that if we didn't have that reliable witness to him, we might be tempted to think the same.'

'So what can he give us that Zofia hasn't already? Now she's finally understood that her only chance of a fresh start is to tell us absolutely everything she knows.'

'Sarwar's the quiet one. On the fringe of the group. He hangs around with them because otherwise he'd be homeless and penniless. He comes from a decent family, though not well off. Ultra-religious, he said. But he had a big falling out with them over something, he won't say what, and walked out. He's not seen them since. But he's observant. He sees details others might miss. For example, he's said Data is definitely Asian, not mixed race. He thinks British Pakistani. Now I know that doesn't narrow it down all that much, but it's a start.

'I started interviewing him and we seem to have made a connection of sorts, so I was going to carry on with him for now.'

'One thing you could try,' Ted suggested, 'is show him some of the milder film footage. Let's see if we can get a definite ID on which one is Data from Sarwar. Then we could take a closer look to see if any distinguishing features show up that we're not yet aware of.'

'The main one seems to be that he's randy as a billy goat on Viagra, which is pretty much what Ronnie told you, boss.'

'Right, Jo, you have the conn today, Mr Sulu. Once I've sorted this warrant to search the lock-up, I'm unavailable for a chunk of the day.'

Ted went back to his office. The warrant arranged, he phoned Jezza. He'd been trying to hit the right balance between concern for her welfare and not wanting to be intrusive into her private life.

Her voice sounded sleepy so he began with an apology.

'Sorry, Jezza, I didn't mean to wake you. That was thoughtless of me. I just didn't want you to think we'd all forgotten about you.'

'Oh, I never thought that for a minute, boss. Not after the lovely flowers. I'm guessing Maurice had a hand in that. Anyway, I was going to phone you today. I've seen my doctor and she says I can come back to work tomorrow, but would need to take it easy for a few days. No chasing around after the baddies. But if you need another pair of desk-bound hands, that could be me.'

'Just don't rush it, Jezza. We'd be thrilled to see you back, of course, and we do need extra help. But only when you feel you're up to it.'

Urban legend has it that one copper can always recognise another in a crowd. Although Ted had never met Jono, he'd looked him up online and had an idea of who to look out for getting off the London train. He suspected Jono had done the same.

Ted clocked him early on, more from his copper's sixth sense than anything. Medium height, shoulders like a rugby player, and black. He saw from Jono's face that he'd been recognised at almost the same time. Ted stepped forward to shake Jono's outstretched hand.'

'Ted, is it? I'm Jono. Good to meet you, at last. I wasn't sure whether I'd need my passport up here. This is the furthest north I've ever been.'

'I hate to break it to you, Jono, but there's another country above us before you hit the North Sea. They call it Scotland.'

Jono laughed as the two men walked out onto the station approach, turning up coat collars against the persistent wind-driven drizzle which was making the temperature feel lower than it was.

'Now you wouldn't be making fun of an inner-city London boy, would you, Ted?'

'Perish the thought. The car's just down here. I hope it's okay with you, but we're going to my house. I don't usually like taking work home but Trev didn't want to do the interview at the station. He's well known there.'

Seeing Jono's look, he hurried on, 'No, I don't mean he has a record. He does a lot of socialising, with some of my team, for one thing. He didn't want tongues to wag. This is really quite a big thing for him to be doing, so he wants it on a strictly need to know basis. If you're okay with that?'

'Absolutely fine by me, mate. You know the rule on cases like this. Whatever makes the witness happiest is how we like to do it.'

'Great, thanks. Trev will have to get straight back to work when we've finished, but I picked up a few rolls that I thought you and I could tackle over a brew afterwards, before I drop you back at the station. I didn't know what your taste was, so I got a bit of everything, including some veggie ones.'

Jono made a face as they reached the car and got in. 'I'll pass on the rabbit food, if that's all right. Strictly a meat and two veg caveman type, me.'

'I told Trev what time I expected us to be there so I hope he won't keep us waiting long. It has to be said that I didn't marry him for his timekeeping.'

Trev had been under strict instructions not just to be on time, but to confine the cats to the kitchen before he went out that morning. Ted had no idea whether or not Jono was an animal lover. Even if he was, Brian, in particular, had a habit of vomiting up partially digested wildlife all over the floor. It wouldn't appeal to everyone and Ted wanted to try to keep this interview on a professional level.

'What does Trevor do for a living?' Jono asked, while they waited.

'He's a partner in a motorbike dealership. Bikes are his thing. Speaking of which ...' he stood up and looked out of the window at the familiar roar of Trev's red Bonneville coming down the road.

Ted went to meet him at the door and exchange a hug.

'Are you all right with this?' he checked, as Trev peeled off his leathers and left them where they fell, heading for the living room. Ted automatically picked them off the floor and hung them up before following him.

'Jono? Hi, I'm Trevor. Nice to meet you.'

Trev said it as if welcoming a valued guest for a social event, instead of preparing to talk to a police officer about one of the darkest periods of his life. One which had caused an irrevocable split between him and his parents. As well as deep, emotional scars which showed no signs of healing.

Jono asked permission to record the interview, then let Trev begin, in his own words and his own time. Occasionally Jono would make a note of something to come back to. He only interrupted to go over something for clarity. To ask pertinent questions, skilfully phrased, when he needed more detail. He mostly sat quietly and let Trev talk.

Ted had brought water and glasses from the kitchen, deftly fending off cats determined to find out the reason for their incarceration, while he did so. Trev took frequent sips of his. Once he'd stopped talking, of his own volition, and Jono had asked all the outstanding questions he had, Jono thanked him for his time and stood up to shake his hand.

Ted walked back to the hallway with Trev and handed him his leathers, scanning his face anxiously. He'd warned him that Jono was obliged to ask him some graphically detailed questions as part of the interview, and he had done. Trev seemed as upbeat as ever, despite it.

'Are you all right?' Ted asked him, giving him another hug. 'Drive carefully, and I'll try to be back at a decent time this evening, if you want to talk about it. What are we doing about supper?'

'I made something yesterday, when you stood me up. Before I opened the wine. So we're sorted. And yes, I'm fine. He's nice. Sympathetic. Not judgemental. Easier to talk to than I imagined. Right, I'd better get back to the helm. See you later.'

He planted a kiss on Ted's cheek, then he was gone.

'I'll put the kettle on, then we can eat something. But first I need to let the cats out.'

'You have cats?'

'Seven,' Ted told him, going through to the kitchen and shooing them all outside.

'I've got a little dog. One of those silly French things. White and fluffy. A Bichon. It was the wife's pride and joy. Trixie, she called it. Bloody silly name for a bloody silly dog. Then she went and met a Mr Much More Right than a copper on low pay and long hours. So she buggered off with him and left the little yapper with me because the new man didn't approve. It's company, of a sort. But I have to pay a bloody dog walker to take it out when I'm at work all day.'

They were making inconsequential small talk. Going all round the houses to avoid the matter they were clearly both avoiding being the first to bring up. They both knew it. But neither of them wanted to broach the subject.

Ted put sandwiches on the dining table in the living room. Made coffee for Jono, tea for himself. Let the cats back into the kitchen but shut them securely in there while he went to eat.

It was Ted who broke the silence first, after they'd both made a start on their food.

'He's not going to make a good witness, is he? CPS aren't going to like their chances of putting him forward.'

'Bloody hell, Ted, I'm glad you mentioned it first. I've been turning myself inside out here wondering how to bring it up tactfully with you, when we've only just met.'

'Pretend it's just another case conference. I'm just another copper you're working with. No connection between me and your witness at all. Then tell me your thoughts.'

'Okay, then. On the plus side, he was under age at the time, so it's a criminal offence. Without a shadow of a doubt about it. On the other hand, he comes across as ...'

'Glib. Flippant. Making light of it. Showing too much affection for his supposed abuser. Still convinced he was in love with Warboys at the time it happened.

'That's the public face he shows to people he doesn't know. I know the private face. I've seen first-hand what it's done to him. He's never forgiven his parents for believing Warboys over him. For throwing him out of the house, which meant he lost the horse and the life he loved, amongst other things. He didn't even know he had a sister until she was a teenager. That's the Trev I know.'

'And that's what the court needs to see. Could you talk to him, Ted? Explain things.'

'Coach a witness? I couldn't do that.'

'Well, could you at least find someone who would talk to

him. It's up to CPS at the end of the day, whether or not they want to put him on the stand. But I can see them having some serious concerns when they hear this recording. You know how paranoid they are about witness credibility these days.'

'I used to go out with a Crown Prosecutor. Before I met Trev.'

'Well, could he help, then? Just a friendly chat and a bit of general advice. You know as well as I do that the defence are going to bring in their biggest guns for someone of Warboys' standing. And I don't want to go down in history as the SIO of a big and costly case which collapsed over witness credibility issues.'

'He died. The prosecutor,' Ted said shortly, waving away Jono's apologies and condolences. 'I'll see if I can think of anyone who could help. But first, the hardest bit is going to be for me to explain to Trev why we need to do something like that. It took a lot of time and patience to persuade him to even consider testifying. I'm just worried this is going to feel like another type of betrayal to him.'

Chapter Twenty-three

The search warrant for the storage unit had come through swiftly. Superintendent Debra Caldwell had a way of moving things along at a good pace when she wanted something.

Sal was on his own for now, driving to the lock-up with the warrant in his pocket. He hadn't found anyone spare at short notice. He'd decided to at least go and see what was needed, then call for an extra pair of hands if necessary. There might, after all, be very little of interest there and he didn't want to waste scarce resources.

For the same reason, he didn't bother driving his car up the many ramps to get to the unit in question on an upper floor. No point, unless and until he knew if there was anything for him to seize from inside it. He had evidence bags in his pocket. If it was just a camera or two, he could carry that back down in the lift.

The man on duty at the entrance hadn't done more than glance at the warrant Sal stuck in front of him before handing over the keys. He was clearly keen to avoid any trouble.

'I'll go up and take a look inside but I'm going to need a list of anyone who's visited recently, certainly in, say, the last two weeks to start with. Perhaps you could be putting something together for me, while I'm up there? And we're also going to need any and all security camera footage you've got.'

The man sighed and put down the magazine he'd been looking at.

'I can look at sign-ins but I'm going to have to get

permission to get you the footage. We don't keep it all that long, either.'

'Get the permission, then. Hopefully you can give me an update when I come back down after taking an initial look. Or better still, give me the footage.'

Sal took the lift up to the appropriate floor and found the unit halfway along one aisle. He wasn't sure what he was going to find as he fitted the key to the lock then raised the door.

It was like stepping into Aladdin's cave. Three walls were lined with all kinds of electrical goods and other merchandise, some new and still in packaging, others not in boxes but still looking in good condition. Sal thought he'd found a plausible explanation for where at least some of Abigail's money had been going.

He put gloves and shoe covers on before he stepped inside to take a closer look. The first box he looked at confirmed his suspicions. A lot of the goods were cheap rip-off copies of expensive branded goods. Another lucrative sideline for the cuckoos. And far too much of it to store in Abigail's flat.

He started by photographing everything exactly as it was. It was going to be a big job to sort through what was in there. But Sal had spotted something which was hopefully going to be of immediate interest and use to the enquiry. An expensive-looking camcorder, sitting on top of cardboard cartons in one corner of the unit. A collapsed and partially telescoped tripod was leaning up against the wall next to it.

Sal walked over to the camera. Picked it up carefully. Switched it on, hoping there was still some battery life left. That way he could at least see if there was anything relevant to the case. If there was, he'd take it straight back to the station for further examination.

It sprang into life when he switched it on. The battery indicator showed less than half-full, but that was more than enough for him to start looking at playback.

He managed less than a couple of minutes before he

switched it off in disgust. Viewing it would be a job for someone with a stronger stomach than his. He put it carefully into a bag and did the same with the mains lead he found with it.

The tripod could be collected later, once the detailed search of the unit contents was under way. There was a good chance that forensic tests could place it directly in Abigail's flat from fibres on the feet matching the carpet there. A small enough detail but one more to add to the slowly mounting pile of evidence against the cuckoos.

Ted was still wondering how he was going to handle the situation with Trev as he drove back to the nick from dropping Jono off for his train.

Jono had given him a firm handshake and a sympathetic, 'Good luck with it all, Ted,' as he'd got out of the car and headed for the southbound platform.

Ted knew several barristers through the CPS. A couple were still decidedly cool towards him because of his break-up with their colleague. It was years ago now but it had destroyed Philip, although that had never been Ted's intention, and he had died a broken man. Albeit with Ted at his bedside as he'd requested. It meant that Ted wouldn't feel comfortable talking to anyone from that circle about his current problem.

He arrived back at the nick just as Sal was talking to Jo about his findings at the lock-up. The camera was on Jo's desk, still in the evidence bag, when Ted walked in for an update.

Sal gave him a quick recap and said, 'The stuff I had a very quick look at is hard core. It was also recorded more than a week before Latte's body was found in the flat. I haven't yet got all the information from the storage place about who might have put it there and when, but it looks as if no more footage was shot after Latte was killed. Presumably that meant that none of them could get access to the flat and to Abigail, their star turn. And that they didn't know Latte was dead inside.

'It's an expensive piece of kit so they wouldn't want to risk losing it. They possibly thought it was safer and more accessible to them in the lock-up. I'll go back to Abi's financial records now because I suspect there's a good chance it was bought with her money. And the tripod for it is at the lock-up, so I would imagine that can be tested for fibres to place it in the flat, beyond reasonable doubt.'

'Some more results from Forensics, too, boss,' Jo told him. 'They were able to lift DNA from some of the semen stains on the sheets on Abi's bed. We've got a positive match for Kane and for Latte, but that's all. It probably means nothing more than that not all of them were going bareback. Oh, and there were significant traces of Abi's blood there, too, which suggests it got pretty rough sometimes.'

'I couldn't face much of it, but I can confirm that,' Sal told them both. 'Definitely violent. Strangely Abi seems completely passive throughout. They must surely have been giving her something to keep her like that. I know the reports say she's always been placid and easily manipulated, but it goes way beyond that. Jo, can I leave it to you to view this latest lot, while I go back to the figures? I'm better with that than having to watch any more of the films.'

'Can you sort out a full search of the lock-up, please, Sal?' Ted asked him. 'Chase up the tapes, and let's try to get a drugs dog in there before we start moving anything, in case some of it needs to go straight to Drugs.'

After Sal left them, Jo said, 'I've been thinking we should speak to Her Majesty about another public appeal on this one, but from a different angle. Abigail could very well not be the only victim of the cuckoos on our patch. It's possible that our delightful bunch were doing the same to someone else as well at the same time. Maybe more than one person. It could be much more widespread than we know so far.

'So I'm wondering if we should be asking people to keep an eye on any vulnerable family members or neighbours, perhaps? To see if they're getting more frequent visits than usual, especially from significant numbers of strangers.'

Ted hesitated. 'Would that be opening up a can of worms, though? Planting the idea? If people started looking out for the vulnerable members of society, might that not serve to emphasise there's a lot of at risk people out there who are easy to exploit?'

'Don't you ever get tired of thinking like a cynical copper, Ted?' Jo asked him. 'I do. We think up something which should be simply decent human behaviour and straight away we see it as another way the lowlife types can exploit it.'

'I do, too. Often. But the day we stop thinking like they do and acting accordingly is the day we lose the battle against crime, I reckon.'

Ted's mobile phone rang in his pocket. He checked the number. Gina Shaw. One of the two undercover Drugs officers.

'I need to take this, Jo. I'll put your idea to both bosses, though.'

He answered the call as he went out of the door and headed for his own office.

'DCI Darling.'

'Hello, Ted, it's Gina, from Drugs. Are you happy for me to call you Ted? Only I know some senior officers are a bit anal about rank, and I noticed most of your team call you "boss".'

'It's fine, Gina. What can I do for you?'

'I've been doing some digging around, with my contacts. I'd like to discuss a few things with you. I'd prefer to do it in person, but not at your nick. Not that you weren't hospitable, but trips to a police station are always risky when you're working under cover. We'd never go back to the same one too soon after the first visit, by choice.

'I wondered if you could come up to Manchester this evening. Say around eight. There's a wine bar I use.'

She mentioned an address to which Ted replied, 'I know of

it. And yes, I could do that.'

'Great. It should be fine because you really don't look much like most people's idea of a copper. No disrespect intended. Just don't be worried by the mwah-mwah greeting you'll get from me. It's my cover. PR and marketing. So it will be me schmoozing a potential client over a glass of wine. It doesn't mean I fancy you.'

Ted laughed at her directness. 'Just as well. My partner might get jealous and he's a martial arts expert.'

It was her turn to laugh. 'It will be a very chaste mwah-mwah, in that case. I'll see you later.'

Ted hesitated with his phone in his hand after she rang off. He should phone Trev, to let him know he'd be late. Part of him was relieved at having an excuse to put off the conversation they needed to have. He was still no nearer to a solution.

'Hey, you,' Trev greeted him. 'Let me guess. You're phoning to say you're going to be late because something came up at work and that I should go ahead and eat without you. Am I right? Is that a good bit of detection?'

'It's worse than that. I have a hot date with a woman in a wine bar. Sorry.'

'And you're going to try to convince me that's work?' Trev asked, but he was laughing. 'Honestly, Ted, it's a good job I know the one thing I can totally trust you about is women.'

'You can trust me on most things,' Ted told him, trying to sound indignant.

'Except reliability, keeping promises about when you'll be home, standing me up at the last minute … shall I go on?'

'You'd better not. Sorry. I've no idea what time I'll get back. Don't wait up if it gets very late.'

Ted was punctual as ever but Gina was already at a table, talking animatedly into the mobile phone in one hand, tablet open on the table in front of her. He'd never been in the bar. It looked like the sort of pretentious place he would normally avoid like the plague.

Gina saw Ted as he walked through the door, raised her free hand to wave to him, calling out, with no apparent trace of irony, 'Eddie! Over here, darling.'

As he reached her table, he heard her say, 'I have to go, Tristram, sweetie. My next client's here. Love you lots, speak soon.'

Then she stood up to gave Ted the promised air kiss to each side, saying under her breath as she did so, 'I can't stand the twat but you have to play the role.'

She picked up an open bottle of red wine from the table and waggled it in Ted's direction. There was a spare glass there ready.

'I don't drink,' he told her. 'I'll just get a mineral water from the bar.'

'Oh, we don't do that here. I'm well known. Just watch this. Do you want some food? Or even some tapas? It all goes on my expenses tab, so why not? And it needs to look authentic.'

She raised an imperious hand and waved it towards one of the people working behind the bar. A young man came over to the table almost immediately.

'Some decent mineral water for my client, Raoul, please. Sparkling, so I know it's not from the tap. And some of your finest tapas.' She looked toward Ted as she asked, 'Ice and a slice?'

As the waiter walked away to bring their order, she turned the tablet towards Ted and said quietly, 'Sorry about the Eddie. I thought it would work better than Ted in this scenario.

'Now, for the sake of my cover, you need to look at this as if it remotely interests you. Perhaps shake your head a bit and point at the screen once or twice. Make some suitable comments. How are your acting skills?'

'I'm about to find out,' he told her, as he looked at the

screen. Some sort of a mock-up of an advertising layout. As the waiter came back with his drink and the tapas and started to put them on the table, Ted waved a dismissive hand towards the screen and said, 'It doesn't jump off the page at me. And I hate those muted colours. They don't fit the brand image at all. I need it to pop. To grab the reader by the throat. The basic idea is there, but it's too tame. I want it bolder.'

Once they were alone again, Gina smiled at him as she said, 'The boss done good. That sounded just like some of my real clients.'

It was noisy enough in the bar that they could talk quietly, without fear of being overheard by anyone.

'You do this for real, then?'

'Oh yes. The best cover is always as close to the truth as you can get. And I studied graphic design. Anyway, back to the reason for our meeting. Ian's off the radar for the foreseeable. He's gone in deep, so I'll hear from him only as and when he can make contact. He's working his own cases, but he's also seeing what he can find out that might be of use to you. I'm doing the same.

'I've been asking around and letting it be known I'm in the market for top quality stuff. Better than I've been finding lately. A couple of people I've spoken to have mentioned a young lad called Data who's been hanging around the clubs a lot lately and has some of the best stuff on the market.

'I haven't wanted to seem too eager or it will set alarm bells going, but I asked how I could find him, and I've been given a few possible leads. I asked what he looks like. I was told he's late teens, early twenties. Asian or mixed race. Medium height, slim. Well-spoken and very good looking. That's why he blends in at the sort of places where he hangs out. I've not seen him yet, but does that description help you at all?'

'It matches what we have so far, so yes, it does. Thank you.'

'I've also let it be known, in view of what else we know about your case, that I'm in the market for something really out of the ordinary for my boyfriend for his birthday. I've been careful not to say too much too soon but I've dropped broad hints about it being a very open relationship. We're up for experimenting. Three in a bed is so last year, and so on.

'But for now, I'd better be going. It will look too suspicious to anyone who knows me if I spend more time with you than I usually do with any of my clients. I'll be in touch. You stay and enjoy the tapas. They're usually very good here.'

She stood up, gathering her things, putting the tablet away in a smart briefcase, raising her voice slightly so she could be heard.

'I'll go away and rework it for you. You want pop? When I've finished with it, it will pop your eyeballs.'

Trev was in his customary place in front of the television with the cats when Ted got back. He stretched lazily, reached for the remote and paused whatever it was he was watching.

'Hey you, how was your hot date with a woman?'

'Interesting. And hopefully productive.'

'Are you hungry? Do you want me to make you something?'

'I pigged out on tapas, which were very good, so I'm fine, thank you. How are you?'

'I'm fine, too. It wasn't as gruelling as I thought it might be. Was it all right?'

The question Ted had been dreading. He wouldn't willingly lie to Trev. But it was not a conversation he wanted to have now. He wanted to have a plan in mind of a way through it all before he broached the subject. First he needed to think of someone Trev might be happy to talk to, without feeling he'd been let down. He opted for a distraction technique.

'I bet you're pleased that part is over. What are you

watching? I could do with something mindless after today.'

'*Beaches*,' Trev told him. 'Bette Midler.'

'Again? How many times is that? And you always cry when you watch it.'

'I know. It's so beautiful. Watch it with me, Ted. And you can sing the song to me, while I cry buckets.'

Ted smiled indulgently in relief. There couldn't be a better distraction.

Chapter Twenty-four

The main office door opened just as morning briefing was about to start and Jezza walked in. She looked pale and tired, dark rings under her eyes, but she was smiling round at the team, clearly glad to be back.

Maurice was the first on his feet to welcome her back with a gentle hug. He was tactful enough not to ask any questions.

Ted decided to say nothing, knowing Jezza would want as little fuss as possible. He'd no idea what, if anything, she'd told the others about her absence. If she'd told anyone what had happened, it would have been Maurice. He instead launched straight into an update about his meeting with Gina from Drugs and her possible links to Data. He repeated the information she'd given him about Data's physical appearance. The team would have to do some more digging to see if they could find anyone resembling him, even if that person didn't yet have a record.

'Whatever money the cuckoos are making from drug sales and porn films, we don't yet know where it's going, boss,' Sal told him. 'Data, or whoever's been in charge of their finances, certainly wasn't stupid enough to launder any money through Abigail's account. He must have known, or at least guessed, that her parents would monitor it.

'Unless Kane was delivering all the money in cash to the Big Man straight away, then giving the others their cut, also in cash, they must be keeping any money they made somewhere else. I imagine they would have to turn the takings in fairly swiftly, so it is just possible that Kane was delivering the last lot when he was killed. Once they couldn't get back in Abi's flat, they would have had nothing left to sell. Not from that source, at any rate.'

'What's the latest from the lock-up?' Ted asked him.

'The sniffer dog didn't find anything of interest, so all the contents have now been recovered and brought back here to be gone through and listed. I've got the security camera footage, too, so all that will need looking at. I could definitely do with a hand on that.'

'Boss, what's the priority for today?' Jo asked. 'Before we decide who needs to be working on what.'

'A bit of an unusual departure for us. I've got a meeting late afternoon with both Supers and another case conference with CPS to sort out what we do about Abigail. We really need to decide before much longer if we can proceed with any kind of a charge against her. From what we have so far, I'd say it's unlikely. So I need a bit of devil's advocate work from you all. We need to go over every scrap of evidence we have and see if we could make a case against her. Or not.

'Maurice, go and talk to Zofia again. Ask her in particular about Abigail's relationship with Latte – Giorgio Mantone. Was she afraid of him in particular?'

'He's certainly one of the more brutal little shits in the filming,' Jo put in. 'I've gone through all of that now so I'll write up the salient points from it. He's into partial strangulation during sex, for one thing. I can pull off some stills of that.'

'Jezza, can you finish putting together your report based on what the school said about her. Any and all details which might be relevant. At some point we need to show Abigail some shots from the security cameras in the flats to get her to identify people by name. Or at least the names she knew them by.'

'So she's moving from suspect to witness, then, hopefully, to victim?' Jezza queried.

'Let's not jump the gun. We need to do a thorough job and let CPS decide. And we need to find Data. Virgil, without stepping on Drugs' toes, can you try any of your contacts?'

'I can, boss, but they're not really your "posh clubs and bars in Manchester" crowd. I have been asking around about the dwarf. I've just been laughed at so far.'

'You're definitely leaning towards there being no case against Abigail?' Jo asked, seeking clarification of the way the boss was thinking.

'Let's try hard to make one. If we can't, then yes, I think that's what CPS will say today. And I'd guess that when it gets to the inquest, there's a strong chance of it being ruled a lawful killing. Self-defence. It would be hard to show any hint of pre-meditation, I think, with Abigail. I'm fully expecting to be told it's not in the public interest to proceed and to drop all charges.'

'Nearly there, young Data. Then I'll be able to take your hood off. Until then, just hold on tight to my arm and trust me to guide you. It really is the blind leading the blind.' The short man laughed at his own joke again as he said it, then warned Data of three steps up as he did so.

'This way, now. Once we're inside, you can start to relax a bit. I can even arrange a cup of tea for you. How civilised is that?'

Data wasn't sure what he was expecting to see when the rough fabric of the bag was finally removed from his head. Some sort of empty warehouse, perhaps. Maybe with a noose hanging from a beam, all ready for him. Instead he found himself in a spacious and pleasant dining room. A big picture window looked through a conservatory to a large, well-maintained garden, surrounded by high brick walls and dotted with mature trees and shrubs.

A woman came into the room from a doorway at the sound of their arrival. Data could see a bright, well-appointed kitchen beyond. She was dark-haired, darker eyed, stony-faced, wearing a black blouse and skirt with a white apron. She said something in a language Data couldn't identify.

'Ah, this is Olga. Mrs Igor. Of course that isn't her real name, either. And she doesn't speak English, any more than Igor does. Now, what would you like? Some coffee? Tea? A soft drink? We have some excellent *chai*.'

'Are you going to kill me?' Data couldn't stop himself from blurting.

'Kill you? Good heavens no. Not here, at any rate. Olga would never forgive me if I got blood all over her nice clean carpets. Let's have some *masala chai*, then. Please, sit down. No, not there, imagine blood on that lovely chair. Sit there instead.'

Then he threw back his head and laughed loudly. 'I'm joking, Data. You'll get used to my warped sense of humour. We're going to have a nice long chat over some tea. With any luck, Olga may have baked something for us.'

'Am I going to meet the Big Man?' Data asked, trying to keep his nerves from betraying him through his tone of voice. 'Like I said, I've been carrying on selling stuff and I have the money safe for him. I just didn't know how to get it to him.'

'Not today, I'm afraid. You're going to be having a long chat with me. But don't worry, the Big Man will be aware of everything you say. Every little gesture you make.'

Data looked up, instinctively scanning the room for cameras. There was one high up in one corner, pointing directly at the chair he'd been skilfully manoeuvred into taking. The short man seemed to follow his look and smiled.

'Smart boy, Data. You don't miss much. We like that. Try to relax now.'

'But I know what you did to Kane. You told us. You threw a piece of his tongue at us.'

'Oh, Kane,' he waved a small hand in a gesture of dismissal. 'He was useless. Worse than useless. He was taking too many risks and costing us money. He wasn't a leader. But you, Data, you have potential. We need to start again, from scratch. And you are the Chosen One. We've lost a lot of money in this mess. We need someone with more brains. As well as the looks and the style to get in anywhere. Which you've already proved you can do. With you in overall charge of your end of the operation, we could really be back in business, in a big way.'

This time Tony Alleyne from the CPS was attending in person for the case conference. Jim Baker was also there, as overall Head of Serious Crime.

Ted had brought his full file to date and handed round copies of the salient parts.

'It's rare for me to be sitting here making a case not to go ahead with a murder charge. But I honestly think, from the evidence we have so far, we stand virtually zero chance of getting a conviction on this one. I'm prepared to be guided by you, though, Tony.'

'It's my job, as ever, to consider the worst case scenario. Here we have a young woman with, what's the correct phrase nowadays? Learning disabled? Moderate to severe learning difficulties? Is that right? Who has no previous form for violence of any sort.'

He looked at Ted as he asked, 'I take it you have checked that out thoroughly? Not just relied on her having no convictions? I apologise for the egg-sucking lesson, Ted, but you know it's my job to cover all bases. Truly to play devil's advocate.'

'No record, nothing at all in her school reports about violence. Quite the reverse, in fact. She's always shown herself to be passive. A natural target for bullies because she has never even shown an inclination to defend herself, never mind go on the aggressive.

'The parents apparently tried starting her off in mainstream education, after she'd recovered from the measles which left her as she is now. The father's idea, no doubt. Part of his total denial about how disabled she is. It was disastrous and she only lasted a term before they got her into special education. Even there she was always the one who was bullied.

'Similar story even when they'd got her into the private sector. All her school reports say that although they have a very strong anti-bullying policy, Abigail was easily led astray and was always the scapegoat for anything anyone else got up to.

'We also have to consider the fact that Abigail is pregnant. We're fairly sure she had no idea that she was, but no doubt the defence will latch onto that and make a big thing of it. So we'd have a vulnerable young woman, fighting to defend not just her own life but that of her unborn child. And I'd hazard a guess that one or both parents would be prepared to perjure themselves and say Abigail had already told them about the baby before the killing. I think they would be capable of saying anything to keep her out of prison.'

'Right, so let's suppose that we decide it is not in the public interest to proceed with a murder charge against this vulnerable young woman, so we drop all charges. Then the next time someone decides to bully her, she grabs a weapon and does the same thing. Where does that leave all of us, here in this office, who were instrumental in putting that decision forward?'

'Out on our ears, with our pensions tantalisingly in our sight, for some of us,' Jim Baker said, his tone glum.

'The good news, of course, is that the decision is not mine alone. It will have to go much higher. My recommendation, however, based on everything your team has sent through, Ted, and confirmed by what you've said today, is that we immediately drop the murder charge against Abigail. I don't see how there is any chance of getting anywhere with that. It's up to you when you tell her, but I would make it sooner rather than later.'

'I'll do it tomorrow morning, when she comes in to sign as

part of her bail conditions. She tends to come with her mother, so that will make it easier for all concerned. I'll need to book the Makaton interpreter though, if she's free, to be absolutely sure Abigail understands everything.'

'Good. If at some future stage we decide there is a case to be made for a lesser charge, we could still, theoretically, proceed. But I imagine the inquest is going to result in a lawful killing verdict. I don't see what else it could be.

'We just have to hope and pray that once we let the young lady loose on society, she doesn't decide, the next time anyone does anything to her against her will, that the best solution is to grab the nearest pointy thing and stick it in them.'

Jim Baker stayed to talk divisional finances with Debra Caldwell after Alleyne left, but he'd already suggested to Ted that as soon as they were both done for the day, they should adjourn to The Grapes together. Ted suspected it would be about Jim and Bella's wedding, the date of which was creeping rapidly closer. Ted had allowed himself to be coerced into being the best man. Much as he liked Jim and considered him a friend outside work, he was never wild about dressing up in a suit away from the office, or making speeches.

He decided to give Trev a quick ring, in case Jim wanted to make it a long session. Knowing how much he was worrying about getting every single detail right on the big day, it might take some time to go through it all.

'Let me guess. You're going to be late. Again. You don't know what time you'll be back. Again. I should have another lonely TV supper. Again. Is that about right?'

'You know me too well. But in my own defence, Big Jim wants to talk, away from the nick. So I imagine it's to go over the wedding arrangements. Again. And to ask me about my speech. Again. And so on.

'And speaking of the wedding, he'll no doubt want you to help him with his famous first dance at least once more before then. He was talking about going to do it at the venue, for one thing. It has to be said that doing a turn or two around our living room with me isn't going to be quite the same as the big dance-floor where the reception is.

'Sorry, I've got to go, my desk phone is ringing. I'll be back as soon as I can, but don't wait to eat.'

He ended the call to Trev as he picked up his desk phone, saying, 'DCI Darling.'

'Sir, there's a Mr Lloyd asking to speak to you personally. No one else.'

Ted almost groaned aloud. The only Mr Lloyd he could think of who would phone and ask to speak to him by name was Trev's father, Sir Gethin Lloyd Armstrong. Possibly the last person he wanted to speak to right now while still undecided about how to talk to Trev about his interview.

'Sir? Shall I put him through?'

'Yes. Thank you. Put him through.'

'Ted? Thank you for taking my call, and apologies for the very unsubtle subterfuge.'

'If this is work, I'll talk to you. If not ...'

'It is. In a sense, it is. I told you when we last met that I'm now involved with other families whose sons were also victims of Warboys. As was Trevor Patrick. I know now that some of those victims have already been interviewed by the police and I wondered if perhaps Trevor has, or if he is still waiting for that?'

'I've told you before. I'm not prepared to discuss Trev or anything about him with you, behind his back.'

'I understand and respect that. I just wanted to let you know. Now we're a group, a collective, or whatever you want to call it, we have strength in numbers. We're doing everything in our power to right old wrongs. Especially those of us who behaved abominably at the time.

'We're establishing quite a support network. We have counsellors. We also have a retired judge who's been helping by going over with the victims how the trial process will go and what they might expect when being cross-examined by the defence. Now, I know you are well placed to help Trevor with such things ...'

'I would never coach a witness. Not even Trev.'

'Yes, of course, excuse me. I'm making a mess of this. I just wanted you to know that there is help and support available, should Trevor need it. I know he would never accept anything from me by way of help or advice. But perhaps you could let him know that there is a network open to him, should he feel the need.

'Most of it is London and Home Counties based, inevitably. But if he needed to talk to someone impartial, with expert knowledge ... He would, of course, always be welcome to use our London home, if he wanted to. And I would ensure that neither myself nor Lady Armstrong was there at the time because I know he wouldn't entertain the idea otherwise.

'Please could you let him know all of that, Ted? I'm sorry once again to put you in a compromising position, but I understand there is no way he would ever speak to me in person. Just please tell him there is help for him if he wants it. And that there is genuinely no hidden agenda. Thank you for your time.'

Ted had conflicting thoughts as he hung up. The prospect of someone impartial and expert to talk to Trev would be a weight off his mind. The downside to it was that in order to bring the subject up in the first place, he was going to have to admit to Trev that he'd spoken to his father again. And that would be seen as the biggest betrayal of all.

Chapter Twenty-five

'Have you time for a hotpot or something?' Jim asked Ted as they ordered drinks at the bar. 'I'm avoiding Bella a bit at the moment. If she shows me one more wedding outfit, you might have to come and arrest me.'

'You sound like Kev, trying to avoid the cruise his wife wanted. He got lucky on that, though. Apparently one of her friends, who'd been raving about how wonderful a holiday it was, happened to be on a ship where there was a sudden and very bad outbreak of food poisoning. It seems that's rather changed Sheila's mind for her, so Kev is off the hook.

'So go on, then. I already warned Trev I might be late home. It's going to cost me a fortune in dinners out, making it all up to him. Which means that the hotpots are on you.'

Jim did want to talk about the wedding. A lot. He was putting as much care and thought into it as he would in preparing a case file. It meant that Ted was even later home than he'd hoped to be.

Trev was in the kitchen, rinsing crockery and shoving it haphazardly into the dishwasher. Ted tried not to wince too visibly at the sight. Instead he went to rearrange it discreetly as they spoke.

'I was right. Major wedding nerves. And he would like you to have a practice dance with him at the venue, if you don't mind. I've got some dates he suggested, when he's available and the venue could let him have access for an hour or so.'

'Oh, bless him. He is so sweet about the whole thing. So

anxious to get it right. It must be love. Have you eaten? Do you want a brew? I was just putting the kettle on. Oh, by the way, your mother phoned, as usual. Dropping broad hints that she never hears from you. And I rang Eirian to find out what she's up to these days. She's decided she has such bad luck with men that she must be a lesbian, so she's going to put that theory to the test.'

Ted smiled at that. Trev's capricious sister could be amusing, as well as a source of concern, with her latest antics. He still wasn't entirely used to Trev calling her by her second name,Eirian, her latest choice, rather than Siobhan.

'Tea would be good, thanks. I've eaten, with Jim. We had hotpot. How was your day? How's the book-keeping going?'

He was buying time. Making small-talk. Before the inevitable explosion when he told Trev he had been speaking to his father.

'I think I'll be able to catch up with everything on Sunday. That's the plan, anyway.'

Trev made the drinks; put Ted's mug of green tea in his hand.

'Sir Gethin phoned me again today,' Ted began cautiously. He knew better than ever to refer to the man as Trev's father.

Trev's whole posture changed in an instant. His face turned to stone as he said, 'And you hung up on him, of course.'

'Well, no ...'

'Ted, we've talked about this before.' Trev's tone was icy. 'I don't like you speaking to that man.'

'I know, and I'm sorry. He was phoning to update me. To say that there's now a network in place for anyone testifying in the case against Warboys. Counselling, if they need it. The chance to talk to someone, a retired judge, about what to expect under cross-examination. That sort of thing. I thought perhaps you might find that helpful.'

'I was rather hoping you would do that for me. There have to be some benefits to being married to a policeman, after all.

Reliability certainly isn't one of them.'

He banged an oven dish down on top of the items Ted had carefully arranged, making some of them fall over. Ted decided it was probably wise to leave it like that. A broken pot or two was a risk worth taking to avoid a potential explosion.

Ted made an apologetic face. 'I can't really coach a witness ...'

'A witness?' Trev raised his voice sharply, at which Barcelona, the nervous black cat, leapt off her chair and shot into the other room to take refuge behind the sofa. 'Is that what I am to you? A bloody witness? How about your husband?'

Ted stopped fiddling with the dishwasher and tried to put his arms round a clearly furious Trev, apologising again as he did so. His partner pushed him roughly away.

'Why do I need coaching? What's wrong with what I said to Jono? It was the truth. Isn't that what you're supposed to say in court?'

He'd stepped back, leaning against the cooker, arms folded. Deliberately putting distance between himself and Ted. More of the cats were becoming restless now. They weren't used to discord between their two humans. Adam started his habitual climb up Ted's trouser leg.

'Yes, of course, and you spoke frankly. It's just that ... things can be a bit different in court. Sometimes a ruthless defence lawyer will try to shift some of the blame onto the victim. Jono and I talked about perhaps suggesting you might like to talk to someone independently ...'

'So you discussed me with Jono, as well as that man? Ted, how could you? And now I've become a victim, not even a witness. I never wanted to get involved in this whole mess but I let you persuade me. Do you know how hurt I feel now? What a sense of betrayal?'

Ted tried again to move closer to him but Trev raised an arm sharply in a defensive gesture and spat, 'And don't bloody say sorry again. It's just a meaningless word.'

'I don't know what else I can say. Yes, I did a debrief with Jono as I would after any interview. I was honestly going to talk to you about it. I was just trying to find the right moment. And the right words. So I didn't make a total bollocks of the whole thing. Which I have done.'

Adam had climbed high enough for Ted to scoop him up in his arms and hold him there. He had no idea what to say or do next to try to undo the damage done.

Trev had also gone quiet. Eventually, he said, 'I was going to ask you if you could be sure to be on time for self-defence tomorrow. And if just for once, you could keep your promise, if so. I'm seeing a potential client in the afternoon and there's just a chance I might be delayed.'

'I will. Of course I will. I'll make sure Jo and the team know I'm going to be leaving early, come what may.'

'Good. Now I'm going to bed. Alone. Apart from the cats. You can sleep down here. Or in the spare room. I don't care which. But you need to take some time to think about which is more important to you. Being my husband. Or being a policeman.'

He turned to go, most of the cats following him. Then he turned back and looked at Adam.

'Are you coming, Adam?'

The little cat snuggled down further into Ted's arms, making no move to go with the others. Trev said nothing else. He simply turned and left the room.

Ted stood for a moment, listening to the sound of Adam's contented purring. Then he looked down at the cat.

'Looks like it's you and me on our own, then, kid.'

Ted and Jezza were waiting downstairs for Abigail and her mother when they came in to answer to Abigail's bail conditions. Their signer, Emma, was also with them. Ted had taken Jezza aside in his office to ask her if she was happy to talk to Abi.

'Because she's still happily pregnant and blooming and I'm not? Boss, on all the many courses you've been on, at university and beyond, wasn't there a single one on tact and diplomacy?'

His expression immediately turned so glum Jezza had to suppress an overwhelming urge to hug him.

'Sorry, Jezza, I seem to make a habit of putting my foot in it. Especially recently.'

'It's fine, boss. Seriously. I'm happy to talk to Abi and I'm pleased for her, if she's going to get to keep her baby. Are you all right, though? If ever you need to talk ...'

She could almost see the shutters come down. He was such a private man and his boundaries so firmly drawn. At least she'd made the offer, even if she'd known he would never take her up on it.

'Thank you for that, DC Vine,' Ted told her, his tone and formality making it clear the subject was closed. 'Now shall we go and give Abigail and her mother the good news?'

Abigail's mother was instantly on the defensive when she saw Ted and Jezza waiting.

'Do I need to call our lawyer? Or my husband?'

'No, not at all. In fact, I have good news for you both. Which is why I asked Emma to join us, so that we can be sure that Abigail understands what I'm about to tell you. Shall we go to the witness room?'

Ted spoke slowly and carefully, looking directly at Abigail, to tell her that the charges against her were being dropped. After that, her mother asked to have a private word with him. They left Abigail happily beaming from Jezza to Emma and back while the two of them went over everything again with her. Ted had also been able to tell them that the forensics team had finished with the flat so Abigail could move back there, if and when she wanted to.

Ted found an empty witness room and stood aside to let Mrs Buller go in first.

'Thank you, inspector. Thank you for all your kindness and compassion towards Abi. You've treated the whole situation with great sensitivity, and it hasn't been easy for any of us. You included, I imagine.

'I wanted to tell you that now we're being allowed access to the flat once more, I'll be sending in professional cleaners to make it spotless in order to sell it. Clearly Abi can't possibly go back there after all that's happened. Instead I'm going to choose another flat for her from my husband's property portfolio. And I'm moving in with her.'

Seeing his surprised look, she stretched the corners of her mouth in what might have been a smile. 'That's right, I'm leaving my husband. It's about time. I'm going to live with Abi, and the baby, and look after them both.

'I've promised to spare my husband the ignominy of a public divorce, as long as he agrees to leave us both alone and to carry on paying the bills. Which I expect will be substantial, since I'm determined to spoil my daughter and my grandchild rotten to make up for letting Abi down so badly. So thank you once again, for all your kindness.'

'At some point in the future, it is possible that we might need Abigail to testify as a witness against the gang who were living in her flat. I should warn you that she has been subjected to some fairly horrific abuse and assault, so it's not going to be pleasant.'

'We should never have left her alone. She was always vulnerable. So passive. I somehow managed to convince myself that she was managing. But things are going to be very different from now on. Abigail is going to be fine.'

Ted asked for a mid-afternoon catch-up with all of the team. As he told Jo, he was determined to get away at a decent time to go and open up for the children arriving for their self-defence class. He had a lot of making up to do with Trev and this was going to be the start of it. Keeping a promise, and being on time.

'From the interviews with the others, it seems that Kane was the only one who ever dealt with the Big Man face to face,' Jo began the summing up. 'He would never say much about him, except that he was dangerous.'

'According to Ronnie, Kane was always scared witless when he needed to meet him and hand over any money. He never trusted him,' Maurice put in. He was back from the safe house, after a morning of talking to Zofia.

'With good cause, it seems,' Jo replied. 'Did he ever say where he went to meet him?'

'Nothing. Kane only ever knew a day and an approximate time and place. He'd be picked up by a vehicle being driven by what he always called "a foreign bloke". There was always a second person in the back. Often the dwarf, sometimes another "foreign bloke". He always had a bag put over his head so he never saw the route. All he ever said to the others was that he was taken to a big posh house to hand over the cash and stuff like the films, and to pick up fresh supplies for them to sell. And whenever he got back he was always white and nervous and wouldn't say very much. He'd get drunk or off his face or both, and if they did any filming after that, he was always more violent than usual.'

'Pretty much the same story from all of the others, boss,' Mike told him. He'd been collating information as it came in from the rest of the team interviewing the other cuckoos. 'They all confirm that no one except Kane ever had direct dealings with the Big Man, and he wouldn't say much about him. The others aren't stupid, though. The fact that we're asking so many questions about Data now and none of them know where he is makes them suspect the Big Man has him. And that's scaring them into not wanting to say anything at all.'

'Jo, have we got anything at all we can charge any of the others with? Anything concrete?'

'We're close to having enough for some serious assault

charges arising out of the films. Except for the thorny question, which any defence lawyer is sure to raise. How can we tell whether or not Abigail consented to what was happening to her?'

'That's one for CPS to sort out ultimately. But let's try and put together enough from what we have got to get them charged and remanded. Now we can safely forget about Abigail, until the inquest, at least, let's concentrate all our efforts on the cuckoos. And finding Data.'

The youngsters from the self-defence club were surprised to see Ted there to welcome them at the start of the session. His number one fan, Flip, was delighted.

Ted hoped that Trev would turn up. He wouldn't proceed without another adult present. It was always running a risk to do so. Worst case scenario, Bernard didn't live far away and would come if he was called.

He instructed the juniors to go and get changed while he did the same, then he hung about anxiously in the corridor outside the gym they used. He had a view of the car park. To his relief, he saw Trev's bike turn in and his partner park it not all that far from where Ted's Renault was standing.

Ted scanned Trev's face anxiously as he strode in, still in his leathers, with his kit bag slung over one shoulder. There was no sign of the familiar warmth in his expression, but Ted knew he would be professional enough not to show anything in front of the children.

'Hi, are you okay? I made it on time, as promised.'

'Good. You made the effort. That's something. But how am I? Still furious. Still feeling totally betrayed. Don't worry, though, the kids aren't going to know anything of that. It will be situation normal, as far as they'll be aware.

'I'm not staying for judo afterwards, though. I'm going out with friends for a meal and probably rather a lot to drink. Oh, and I won't be home tonight, either.'

Chapter Twenty-six

Trev was true to his word. The self-defence club went on as it always did. It was fast and fun. The youngsters were totally engaged for the whole session. There was no way the children, or the watching parents, could have detected any difference in the way Ted and Trev were together. Only Ted, up close and personal, was aware of the coldness in his partner's eyes.

Young Flip excelled himself. Now he was learning judo as well as self-defence, he was quick on his feet, picking up any new moves in an instant. He visibly swelled with pride when Trev singled him out to demonstrate something.

Both his adoptive parents were there to watch him. His mother always came with him but his father wasn't usually there. Once the session had finished, they both stood up to move towards him as he rushed over to them. Ted was watching, smiling to himself. He saw a lot of himself, as a boy, in young Flip.

'Fantastic job, Philip, you were terrific,' his father told him. 'Well done, Big Man.'

Ted, about to go over to them, stopped dead in his tracks.

How could he have been so stupid?

If he'd been near enough to the wall, he'd have banged his head against it.

He was always going on to his team about hiding in plain sight. Yet he'd overlooked the most obvious answer, which had been staring him in the face all along.

Flip was small for his age, as Ted had always been. The

nickname was clearly his father's way of helping to boost his self-esteem. To let him know that height wasn't everything. It was a name which could as easily apply to status as to physical size.

Ted turned back to Trev. He was itching now to get back to the nick and start looking in the direction he should have gone in much sooner, but anxious first to have one more try at building bridges.

'Have a good time this evening. Will I see you tomorrow at some time? Shall I pick up a meal for us?'

'I'm going out again after karate tomorrow. And staying out.'

'Apart from me behaving like a complete pillock, yet again, is there something else wrong?' Ted asked him, looking at him shrewdly. 'I knew you'd be angry, but this ...'

'You really don't get it, do you? Have you thought about how you would have felt if I'd been in touch with your mother, after she abandoned you, and before you'd made things up? Give it some thought. Because that's how I feel, Ted.'

They were both speaking quietly, keeping their expressions neutral, anxious not to be having such a discussion where the youngsters could overhear them.

'Look, this isn't the time or the place to discuss it. But please can we talk? Soon?'

'I told you, I'm going out tonight and tomorrow night. So make sure you see to the cats,' Trev told him, then turned and walked away, heading for the changing room.

Ted would have to follow him, if only to retrieve his own clothes. He decided the diplomatic move would be to put on his coat and shoes but otherwise drive home as he was. He didn't fancy a public scene in the changing room, not with the youngsters present. Perhaps it would be better to give Trev some space for a day or two in the hopes that he might calm down.

He waited just long enough to make his excuses to Bernard

when he arrived. He'd decided not to stay for judo either. It wasn't the same without Trev there, and now he'd had something of a lightbulb moment, he wanted to make the most of the inspiration.

He went home to shower and change, and to make sure the cats were all right. He was planning to make a night of it.

'I'll leave the telly on for you, but I don't know how late I'll be,' he told them, as he grabbed his car keys and went back out.

He knew he was in for a long session. As long as it took to get over the hump they seemed to be stuck on. He was going to do what he should have been on top of all along. Oversee the operation, rather than trying to do too much of the groundwork himself. That was what his role was meant to be. To use his experience to spot things that had slipped past his team members. It was why he held the senior rank.

And now the germ of an idea was planted in his brain, he had a feeling they had all been taking too much at face value.

He stopped to pick up a hot meat pie on his way. Ate it quickly in his car on the station car park, so he didn't risk dripping gravy all over his office after Mrs Skinner had cleaned it. She'd have been in and done her work by that time of night, so he should be able to work through without being disturbed for as long as it took him to make some sort of progress.

He and the team had so nearly fallen for accepting that the person of short stature they'd heard about was blind, because of the dark glasses and white stick. Now he realised they'd also dismissed him out of hand as being the Big Man in person, without even considering him as a possible.

Hearing the way Flip's father had used the term in praise of him achieving great things made Ted realise that they'd all been taking it too literally. It was a common enough phrase for a person in charge. Perhaps they'd thought the short man was too obvious. He fervently hoped they hadn't subconsciously dismissed him simply because of his size. That was the sort of prejudiced judgement he despised.

Somewhere in all of the statements so far, which Ted was starting to wade through, there was a reference to the Big Man being capable of slitting someone like a kipper if crossed. Kane's tongue had been cut out by a razor-sharp implement. And their eye witness in the park had seen the small man pointing a stick towards the cuckoos there, shortly before he threw the severed tongue at them.

But what if it hadn't been simply a white stick? What if there had been a blade attached to it? Or a knife in his hand? Something the cuckoos could see but that the woman who'd witnessed the incident, standing further away, couldn't?

Ted knew the team had been working hard to try to find any mention on file of a person of short stature involved in drugs or other crimes. So far without success. He intended to spend time running it through the system again on the off chance, but he doubted that the man would be brazen enough to be appearing in public if he had a record of any sort. If he really was the boss of a sophisticated drugs operation, he would have known there was a risk the police were watching his sellers.

The next route would normally be a public appeal based on what little information they had to date. It would be hard to produce an artist's impression from witness statements. The dark glasses were a perfect disguise. They would have to appear on any sketch but it was likely they were nothing but a prop, worn to distract.

Next there was the "foreign bloke" Kane had spoken of to Ronnie. The one who was present in the car when he was taken to visit the Big Man. Ted was thinking of the man he'd seen in the park, with the dog, when they'd been rounding up the rest of the youths who'd been squatting in Abigail's flat. The man's presence there could have been coincidental. It was possible that he was simply someone exercising his dog. But he was there, and on his phone just before Data was picked up and spirited away. There had been something about him that had raised Ted's suspicions. He may have been there to keep an eye out for any signs of a trap waiting to be sprung. He could easily have been phoning through to tip off other members of the gang if something had alerted him.

He'd been rather overlooked once the team realised Data was getting away and had concentrated on trying to find him and to arrest the others.

All of which suggested that it may well have been the Big Man himself, with one of his "foreign blokes", who had spirited Data away.

Ted could provide a reasonably accurate description of the dog walker's clothing and appearance. It would help if he could identify what language he had spoken to the dog in. It certainly hadn't been English. Ted was no linguist. He'd learned some Welsh from his mother as a small child, but that was as far as it went. He could make a stab at repeating the sound of what the man had said. Logically it must have been a command to his dog, which was making a lunge at Ted as he ran past. Something like 'heel' or 'leave it', most likely.

If Trev hadn't been currently too furious to speak to him in any language, Ted could simply have had a go at repeating the sounds he remembered and Trev would at least have found a way of identifying the language for him. Or narrowing it down to a few, or even to a region of the world.

The one resource Ted wasn't short of was time. There was no one to hurry home to. Even the cats would be fast asleep on the sofa, no doubt. He opened a translation app on his computer and, more in hope than anticipation, started entering the likely phrases, obtaining the translations in different languages, and playing the recording of how they were pronounced. Sooner or later, he might hear one which sounded something like what he thought he remembered.

It was gone two by the time Ted had got home but he was still back in before the rest of the team in the morning. He wanted to lay out his theories to them to see if they sounded even more far-fetched in morning light than they had to him alone in his office the night before.

He set out his new theory and what had prompted it, then went on, 'So we need to find this person of small stature, as a matter of urgency now. But we also need to keep in mind that he might just possibly be the boss, rather than simply a messenger.'

'Sir, I've been trawling the system for short people with a record. I've printed off some shots of anyone in roughly the right height range who I've not been able to rule out. And that would be because they're dead, back inside, or definitely known to be out of the country.'

'Good work, Steve, thank you. Let's get the last of them carefully checked out. But my gut feeling is that he won't have a record. I think he's probably too clever and hides behind the men he has working for them. I suspect they're the muscle of the outfit. Possibly ex-military, maybe ex-Special Forces. I know lots of people wear army boots, which could account for the footprints where Kane's body was found. But the man with the dog I saw in the park on Sunday also looked like a former Special, and I've seen plenty of those.'

Jezza was frowning at him. 'Hang on, boss, rewind. What military man in the park with a dog? While I'm desk-bound, I'm collating on this case, remember, and I haven't seen any mention of some army type in the park at the time of pulling in the others. With or without a dog'

There was an awkward silence for a brief moment. Then Ted said, 'Sorry, Jezza. My fault entirely. I clearly forgot to mention that in my report and I should have done, of course. I'll write it up and let you have it.'

'Boss, excuse me for speaking frankly, but there does seem to be a bit of a lack of communication thing going on here,' Jezza pressed on. 'Because now you actually mention your dog man, I remember seeing one near to Abi's flat when you and I first went there. When we got the first shout. It was when I took Abi out to the car but I was standing outside it because the smell was clinging to her clothes and it was a bit overpowering.'

'What kind of a dog did your man have?'

'I don't know much about dog breeds. One of those shepherd types. Like a German Shepherd, only not as hairy. The Dog Section has some of them.'

'A Belgian Shepherd? Malinois?' Jezza's fingers were flying over her phone as she spoke. She found what she was looking for and held it up. Ted went across to look at it and nodded.

'Yes, that's the sort of thing. Not very friendly. It lunged at me as I ran past. That's what made me notice it, and the handler, in particular.'

'Sorry to bang on, boss, but that makes it slightly worse. That's the breed of dog I saw the man walking, near to Abi's flat. I didn't know, at that point, that we were looking for military types with a dog. The only reason I noticed at all was that the man looked like a bit of a hard case, and so did the dog. But the man was carrying one of those dispensers hanging from his belt with poo bags in it, and it was pink. So were the bags. It just struck me as incongruous and a bit funny.'

'Five eight, five nine, solidly built. Black hair, regulation short back and sides, black stubble. Black cargo pants, black jacket and black military boots?' Ted asked her.

'The same. Looks like we missed a trick there, boss.'

'Entirely my fault, everyone, and I can only apologise. Jezza, you're absolutely right. No reason for you to have mentioned the first sighting, but if I'd mentioned the one in the park in my report, we'd have been onto that connection much sooner.

'We're all busy working on our own and the left hand isn't keeping track of what the right hand is doing.

'But back to our Man with Dog. Clearly, we need to find

him, if only to eliminate him from our enquiries. Although I think it's a coincidence too far that he was seen near to Abigail's as well as in the park on Sunday.

'When his dog had a go at me, he said something to it in a foreign language. I'm not good at languages. No idea what it was. But I spent a bit of time last night trying to work out what it might be. I looked for phrases like "Leave it" in different ones then listened to them online. Not very scientific, but it was the best I could think of at the time.

'The trouble is, I found quite a few where the translation sounded similar to me. About seven in all, including Bosnian, Croatian, Macedonian and Serbian. So it doesn't advance us all that much. Unless we hit a miracle and Forensics can pin down the tread on the military boots from the last murder scene to the forces of one of those countries. Because I'd put money on the man I saw being ex-military.'

'I'd agree with that, boss,' Jezza confirmed. 'There was something about the way he carried himself that said military. Or police, of course, from a specialist unit.'

'Are we going public with this now, boss?' Jo asked him. 'Get some details and artists' impressions out, of him and the short Big Man?'

'They'll go to ground, as soon as we do,' Ted told him. 'We ideally need to try to find them without letting them know we're getting closer. Save the images as a last resort if we can't find them the old-fashioned way, with a bit of legwork.

'But that's not to say we shouldn't be showing the images around to people we talk to. Just not yet making them fully public. I'll talk to Uniform to see if we can get some help with it.

'Steve, is there any way someone more skilled than I am might be able to pin down that language more accurately than I could with my efforts?'

'Océane will know, if anyone does. If I can record you saying it, as close as you can get, she might be able to identify it for us. Or someone else at Central Park might know.'

'Good, now we're getting somewhere. Apologies again, everyone. If anyone needs me, I'll be in my office, giving myself a good kicking and possibly murdering the waste-paper basket.'

Jo followed on his heels as the boss headed for his own space.

'Are you all right, Ted?' he asked him, pushing the door to behind them. 'It's so out of character for you to slip up like that.'

'I have no excuse, Jo. I let myself get distracted by other stuff and I shouldn't have done. But so I can deal with that other stuff to stop it from getting in the way of work, come what may, I'm going to be off on Sunday. All day. Off. Invisible. Not to be contacted. And so on. Can I count on you? If things go according to plan then, I might report back for duty on Monday morning with something resembling a working brain. One worthy of a Serious Crime SIO.'

Chapter Twenty-seven

It was late afternoon when Ted's mobile rang. The display showed him it was Gina Shaw calling him, from Drugs.

She was clearly somewhere she was sure of not being overheard because her voice had none of the false bonhomie of her PR persona.

'Hello, Ted, Gina here. I have some updates for you so can we meet up again? The same place would be fine, but could we make it later this time? Say nine o'clock? If that doesn't totally ruin your family or social life.'

He wasn't about to admit that both of his were currently in tatters, so he simply agreed.

'I've seen your acting skills, which were not bad at all, considering I caught you on the hop. So, what's your quick change routine like? I've heard from Ian and he needs to speak to you. Don't get too excited. Neither of us has an oven-ready result for you, but we have made some progress. Only Ian is still in deep so you won't be able to use your businessman talking to PR consultant cover to see him.'

'What do you suggest? If it helps, I go running sometimes. Roads, parks, that sort of thing.'

She hesitated. 'The kind of places Ian hangs out generally might be a bit of a risk for a lone jogger, especially after dark.'

'I'll probably be all right. I can run quite fast when I have to.' Ted made light of it.

'D'you smoke?'

'Not at all. Never have.'

'Well, make sure you have some ciggies and a lighter in your pocket. It's how Ian will make contact with you. I'll get him to set up a suitable place not far from where we're meeting, you and I. You'll need to do your costume change in your car, probably. But it's also up to him to do the risk assessment, so he'll only accept your idea if he's sure it will be safe enough.'

Ted said nothing to that. He knew it was the correct procedure and he wasn't about to query it. Nor to mention his SFO days which had seen him facing potential danger on a regular basis.

'I'll call you later when I've spoken to Ian, but you knowing the venue for your meeting with him is likely to be a bit last-minute. I've told you before he's paranoid about his cover, so it may even change several times until he's happy.

'I'll see you in the bar at nine and I'll have a really eye-popping pitch to show you.'

Bearing in mind Jezza's valid points about lack of communication, Ted called the team together before they finished for the day, to update them on his plans for the evening.

'Run that by us again, would you, boss,' Jo told him. 'Meeting Gina in a wine bar is one thing. Anyone else around would only cramp your style. But going jogging by yourself in the sort of location undercover Drugs officers are likely to favour isn't going to be sensible. You surely wouldn't get either of the bosses to sign off on it, for one thing.'

He saw Ted's expression and went on, 'Tell me you weren't going to go maverick on this one, boss, and not tell them?'

'Ahh,' Ted began, before Jezza joined in, eyes flashing angrily.

'Boss, no way are you going on your own without any kind of back-up. The Drugs officers are used to this kind of shit. You're not, lately.'

'It'll be fine, Jezza, the risk is minimal ...'

Well, that's going to make a bloody marvellous epitaph for you. "The risk was minimal". It's not that long ago that you and I went on the same risk assessment and management course. I must have slept through the module where they said it was perfectly fine to go into a park where drug dealers hang about without any form of back up. And not even carrying a side arm or wearing a stab vest. Which clearly you aren't planning to do if you're using running as your cover.'

'She has a point, boss,' Jo told him.

Most of the team members were also nodding their heads in agreement.

'It's up to Ian how the meeting goes. I can't risk his cover by having back-up that could be spotted.'

'Boss, my own family don't recognise me if I get the bling on and my pimp's threads,' Virgil told him. 'Mike, you've seen me in the role and you can confirm that. In a setting like that, no one takes any notice of me, because I is black.'

'What if me and Virgil happened to be sitting in a car, near where you're meeting Ian, having a burger or something?' Rob suggested. 'Then at least there's someone close by if anything should kick off.'

'It's not on our patch, for one thing ...' Ted tried again, to a loud scoff this time from Jezza.

'What, we suddenly have to go through customs and passport control to go up to Manchester for a burger these days, do we?'

'Boss, they do have a point,' Jo tried again. 'Ian's on his home turf. Doing what he's trained for and does all the time. With the greatest respect, if you've done undercover in the past, it was quite some time ago. You're the SIO. Meetings in dark and potentially dangerous parks isn't really part of your remit, is it?'

Ted looked round at them all. He wasn't going to win this one. Pointless even to try.

'All right. Here's the deal. And it's subject to Ian's approval. If he says no, it's no. Rob and Virgil, in a car, not too close, and eating a takeaway to make it look authentic. I'll keep my phone on and connected to you. You make a move only on my instruction. Is that clear?'

'Thank god you saw sense, boss,' Jezza told him. 'It's not just that we're all quite fond of you, although we are. It's basically that we're all too scared of facing your Trev if we let you do something really stupid and get yourself injured. Or worse.'

'Hi, Eddie, over here!'

Gina was on her feet and waving to Ted from a different table to the last time when he walked into the crowded and noisy wine bar.

This time he'd ditched his work suit and gone for casual; jeans, a polo shirt and a jacket. It would make it easier for him to change into his running gear in the car, once he had final confirmation from Ian where they were going to meet.

Gina greeted him with the same double air kiss as before. Ted saw that she'd already ordered a bottle of mineral water and an extra glass, which sat on the table ready for him.

'I took you at your word about not drinking. I hope that's all right? Do you want tapas again, or something more substantial?'

'Neither, thank you. I'm going running afterwards and I prefer to do that on an empty stomach.'

If anything, it was even noisier than their last meeting. Gina was having to lean closer to hear Ted, whose voice was quiet.

'I'm just waiting for final confirmation of the location,' Ted told her.

He'd spoken to Ian by phone on his drive up to Manchester. He'd explained to him his team's insistence on him having back-up not too far away just in case.

The Drugs officer was resistant at first, not wanting anything which anyone could interpret as a police presence to blow his carefully created cover. It was only when Ted assured him that Virgil was big, black, in a flashy black motor, and on his own admission, looked like most people's idea of a pimp, that he relaxed enough to give the green light.

He gave Ted a rough location to start from, so he could at least ensure that Virgil and Rob were not all that far away, and promised to confirm it nearer the time.

'Now, you wanted eye-popping, sweetie,' Gina told him, slipping straight back into her role and lifting the lid of her laptop, like a magician about to reveal the secrets of the locked trunk. 'This will hopefully blow your mind.'

Ted looked at the screen. She was good. If he'd really been looking for an advertising campaign, and had wanted bold colours and a strong message, her work would have fit the bill perfectly.

He realised he wasn't sure if he was meant to accept it or not, or how their scenario was meant to unfold from here. He'd have to wing it.

'That's more like it. I'm happy to sign off on that. Have your people contact my people.'

He saw the fleeting amusement on Gina's face at his improvisation and hoped he'd not gone over the top. Not that it mattered much. Most people around them were reduced to shouting at one another to make themselves heard over all the talk and the background music.

'Too much?' he asked her.

'Perfect! You must have watched a lot of *Ab Fab*.

'Now, an update of what I've found for you so far about Data. I'm afraid the answer is still not a lot. In fact, there's now allegedly a new young man doing the clubs and selling the very good stuff. No one's seen Data for a few days.

'Except that, if I were you, I wouldn't take that as gospel. I'm hearing that Data Mark II is young, slim, very good looking, well-spoken, brown-skinned, possibly mixed race.'

'So you're thinking it could simply be Data himself with a bit of a makeover?'

'Well, I know it's not something you're probably familiar with, but I wonder just how much notice anyone takes of their dealer. Change of hairstyle, different clothes, I wonder if anyone would seriously notice if it was actually the same person. It could simply be a big and bold bluff.

'I've been asking in particular about the porn stuff, as that seems to be Data's speciality. I've been told there's been a temporary disruption in supply, but it's hopefully going to be sorted soon. So far, not much to help you.'

'Does any of it go on in here?' Ted asked her, glancing round.

'Oh, heavens no. This place is strictly legit. It's too obvious. It's where initial contacts are made, but nothing ever changes hands in here. Not even in the loos. That's the unwritten law.'

'Speaking of hiding in plain sight,' Ted began, not wanting to delay her unnecessarily and compromise her cover, so only briefly filling her in about the latest theory on the Big Man.

'Interesting, and plausible. I'll try asking around again but phrasing my questions differently. Now I'm going to have to throw you out once more before it looks suspicious.'

As they exchanged air kisses once more, she said quietly into his ear, 'Good luck with Ian.'

Ted had already run two laps of the park, passing Ian on both occasions, before the undercover officer made any contact. He was clearly being careful, which Ted respected. Despite the late evening hour, there were still a few people passing through the park who looked to be there for things other than trying to score drugs.

Two older people, with a large golden retriever on an extending lead, were walking towards them as Ian unfolded his long, lanky frame from the bench where he'd been sitting and addressed Ted.

'You got a fag, mate? Or the price of some?'

Ted decided to give his acting skills another go, for the benefit of the couple.

'Why don't you get yourself a job, then you could buy your own?'

The man and woman nodded agreement and tutted, going on their way. Ted heard the man's parting shot of, 'Probably getting benefits and spending them all on drugs.'

'I don't smoke,' Ted told him, still playing the role in case they were being watched. 'Runners don't. But you're in luck. I confiscated my dad's before I came out. I keep telling him he's smoking himself to death, and he can't get out by himself to get more.'

Ian gave him an appreciative grin for his performance. Ted took a lighter and cigarettes out of his pocket and held them out to him.

'I'll just take one, if you can light it for me, then put them all back in your pocket. It would look wrong if I suddenly had fags to flash around.'

He took a cigarette from the packet with a hand which shook, then had to bend down to cup both hands around the lighter Ted held for him.

'Is it going to look strange, us standing talking?' Ted asked him.

'Not really. If anyone else comes near, we can start an argument about social injustice. Or you can try to persuade me that if I only went clean and got god, my life would be transformed.

'Is your back-up in place?'

'They are. Are you expecting trouble?'

'No reason to. But the problem with drugs and users is they tend to be unpredictable. Things can kick off at any moment for no real reason. It's quiet enough just now, but you can never tell how the night will end up.'

'Have you found anything out?'

'Yes and no.' Ian paused to take a long drag on his cigarette, which produced a few coughs, before he continued. 'Your Big Man is definitely new on the patch. We knew that by the quality of the stuff he's supplying. He's running the risk of turf wars with some of the existing dealers. But the word on the street is that he's well hidden and well protected by some seriously hard types.'

'We now think the Big Man might actually be our person of short stature. We've been thinking of them as two people, but that might be a red herring. There's a chance that his hard types could come from somewhere like Bosnia, Serbia. South Eastern Europe. But that's just a theory at the moment, based on something someone said to a dog.'

Ian smiled at that. 'That's an interesting method of detection, Ted. One I've not come across before. But you could be on to something there. Did you know that Albania is a bit of a mover and shaker on the international drugs scene? And they've been closing in big time on the UK market recently. Geography's not my strong point, but I think they're all in that sort of area.'

He was suddenly wary. His peripheral vision had caught sight of three young males walking down the path towards them. Two blacks, one Asian.

Ian spoke again, raising his voice.

'Look, mate, you gave me a fag and that's great. It doesn't give you the fucking right to tell me how I should live my life. You've got no idea about me ...'

'I know there are jobs out there, if you'd get off your arse and go and look for them, instead of hanging round in a park begging for a smoke,' Ted countered, his voice louder than it usually was, trying to hit the right note of self-righteous hectoring.

Ian started to poke him in the chest as he ranted on, 'You

ever been homeless, mate? Ever tried to get yourself a job when you've no address? No bank account for your pay?'

The young men had drawn level with them now and were laughing.

'You tell 'im, bro. You all right, Ian? Need a hand telling him his fortune?' one of them asked.

'Nar, mate, you're all right, I got this.'

They went on their way, still laughing.

'Nice one, Ted. Now, where were we?'

'Albania, I think. By way of Bosnia.'

'The pieces are starting to fit together. It's getting harder to get drugs into the country directly from source, so some of it is tending to come in from Eastern Europe.

'Where your dwarf comes from, or where he fits into any of this, I don't yet know. But having Bosnian or Serb protectors makes sense, and it gives me another direction to look in.

'Now you'd better piss off before it looks too suspicious, us talking too long. For one thing, my young friends who just went past will be looking to score and they won't risk it if they see a face they don't know.'

'You supply them?'

Ian smiled at him and tapped his nose. 'There are things about the kind of work I do that it's best decent people like you don't know about, Ted.'

Trev had clearly been in the house at some point. The cats' dishes had been topped up, the litter trays cleaned. Plus there was a tell-tale trail of dirty clothing in the bedroom, which hadn't made it to the laundry basket.

Ted was hungry by the time he got back, though not in the mood to cook anything. He put a ready meal in the microwave while he gathered up Trev's clothes and some of his own to put a wash on.

He almost took his phone out to at least text Trev, to make

sure he was all right, but then decided against it. If he'd gone out after karate and was planning to stay out, he'd probably be with his friend Mark. If there was no news by tomorrow, Ted would give Mark a call.

Otherwise, he was pinning all his hopes on his plans for Sunday helping to heal what was clearly a serious rift in their relationship.

Chapter Twenty-eight

'Today I'd like your help. I need to see a man about a dog.'

Ted was standing at the front of the room with Kevin Turner, having once more asked if he could attend his briefing of the officers coming on shift. Some of Ted's team were with him, to save repeating everything.

He waited until Kevin had finished his piece before he spoke to them.

A ripple of amusement ran round the room at the DCI's attempt at humour. Ted was generally well liked and respected by Uniform officers because he acknowledged the work they did and never forgot his own time as one of them.

'We all like you well enough, guv,' one of the older sergeants told him, 'but probably not enough to take you to the little boys' room.'

Ted wasn't keen on guv. It's why his team called him boss. But down here, he was on Uniform territory and quite happy to abide by their rules, their traditions.

'The dog in question is a Malinois. Belgian Shepherd. I think,' he went on, once the amusement had abated. 'The man is a possible witness to both our murder at the flats and the disappearance of a key witness we've been trying to find. The young man we so far know only as Data.

'I saw him in the park when we went to arrest the remaining members of the cuckoo gang last Sunday. DC Vine had also seen him near to the flats when we first got the shout about a body. Two weeks ago. The connection between the two sightings has only just been made and that is entirely my fault, for which I apologise.

Another reason Ted was popular. He owned up to his own errors instead of trying to blame anyone else.

'We really need to speak to that man. As a matter of some urgency.'

'Why am I sensing a but?' Kevin Turner asked him.

'There is a but. The dog is possibly nasty. It went for me when I was running past it. Now, most people know I'm not good with dogs, especially big ones, so it may just have smelled my fear and reacted to it. But the second point is the man himself. Both Jezza and I agree that he has the look of someone who knows how to handle himself. Ex-Forces, ex-Police, perhaps Specials. Something like that, is what struck both of us about him. About the way he carried himself, and the way he handled the dog.'

'So are we looking at making an arrest or simply issuing a polite invitation to come in for questioning?' Kevin asked.

'Neither, please. This is strictly a spot and report request. Do not approach. We're likely to have to jump through all sorts of risk assessment hoops on this one.'

'Are you expecting him to be armed?'

'It's quite possible. Even if he's not, we all need to remember that Kane Lomax was killed not by the torture he endured but by having his neck cleanly and professionally snapped. By someone who knew exactly what they were doing. Another reason I suspect special forces training.

'Added to that, I have a gut feeling that the dog is trained to attack on command. So unless any of you knows the Serbian for sit and stay, because the man appears to speak something like that to it, it's definitely keep clear and report in only, please.'

'Firearms, then?' Kevin asked.

'I'd prefer to do it with Tasers and minimum attention if we can. I've spoken to someone in the dog section. Apparently we can safely Taser the dog, as well as the man. I was worried that might be too much for it and kill it. I don't want that kind of bad PR. You know what the public are like about animals getting killed.'

'They don't care if any of us are, though,' one of the older officers grumbled. Ted ignored him and carried on.

'If any of you happen to see them anywhere,' he repeated the description of the man and gave a rough one of the dog, 'call it in immediately. Observe and don't approach until we get there.

'Inspector Turner, we'll need at least two Taser-trained officers, when we go in, please. One for the man, the other to concentrate on the dog. We'll need both of them, man and dog, taking down fast, before we can judge it safe to approach. I'll get someone from the Dog Section to attend. Even when the dog is down and hopefully out of it, we'll need it making safe. They have electric shields and catching poles to deal with that sort of situation. Then they can take it away and hold it safely until we've talked to the man.

'Any questions, anyone?'

'Guv, do we know if this bloke speaks any English or just Serbian, or whatever?' one of the Uniform officers asked. 'Only it could all get a bit nasty if we're just politely asking for a chat and he doesn't understand. It could kick off in a big way because of lack of communication.'

'Yeah, and what does the dog speak? Is it only Serbian, or whatever they speak in Belgium as well?' another asked.

There was always some humour in these shift briefings, no matter how serious the situation.

'French and Flemish,' Jezza supplied helpfully.

Ted would have pulled his team up at this point. But these were Kevin's officers. He left it to him.

'All right, you bunch of comedians. If you don't want me to resort to speaking some Anglo-Saxon, just take on board what the DCI has told us. It's clear enough. If you see this Man with Dog of his, do not approach. Do not even speak. Call it in and keep obs, without putting yourself in danger, until back-up arrives.'

'Any idea where he may turn up next, guv?' one of the sergeants asked him.

'None at all, at the moment. Sorry,' Ted told her candidly. 'As I said, he was spotted at the flat, which suggests he was aware of where the cuckoos were staying, or possibly where they'd stashed stuff. He must have known they were no longer able to gain access because sales had dried up.

'We know from Zofia – or Ronnie, as most of you will know her – about the meeting places in parks, so they were probably keeping those under observation. It's highly probable Kane would have told them everything under torture. It's likely they've realised by now that we have everyone except Data, so it's guesswork where they'll be watching next.

'And if they have got Data, that will largely depend on what he's told them, I imagine.'

'Boss, what about the lock-up?'

Sal Ahmed was still with them, despite Jezza's return. Ted had managed to negotiate with Fraud to keep him a few days longer as he'd been doing invaluable work for them on Abigail's finances. Steve might have got there in the end, but Sal could do it in a fraction of the time, so it represented a big saving.

'That's worth a shot, Sal,' Ted told him. 'Kane will have told them about it, no doubt. They may think it's worth keeping an eye on, just in case any of the others turn up there trying to get their hands on the stuff inside. They might even watch to see if it's safe to take Data back there to recover things. Assuming they have got him.

'You've made contact there already, so give them a ring. You've already asked them to report any suspicious people hanging around, but make sure they also let us know immediately if they see our Man with Dog anywhere nearby. A random dog-walker might not immediately attract their attention. Just make sure they understand not to approach them, at any cost.'

'Same goes for all of you. Stay away from them until they're out of action, even if you do come across them anywhere. And never mind worrying about the dog. If any of you messes this one up by not following instructions, I might need Tasering and muzzling myself. We can't afford to screw up because I'm guessing that if we blow our first chance, we're unlikely to get a second one,' Kevin Turner warned them all.

'So it's a bit of a waiting game. Uniform are keeping an eye out for our man, and whenever any of my team are out and about, they're doing the same. Kevin's sorting two Taser officers on standby for us and I've got the Dog Section ready to take over with the dog at fairly short notice.'

Ted was in the Ice Queen's office, summing up the plans. They were on a conference call with Jim Baker, in his own office.

'And you're going to be coordinating all this from the nick, aren't you?' Big Jim asked him pointedly.

'Well, no, I was going to be there in person. Only Jezza and I have seen the man so far and she's on desk duties. So I felt I ought to go out if we get a potential sighting to confirm it's the right person, before we start Tasering innocent men walking their dogs.'

The Ice Queen's expression was sceptical but it was Jim who spoke first.

'Because the streets of Stockport are full of ex-special forces with killer dogs, wandering round speaking Serbo-bloody-Croat, or whatever you said you thought it was.'

'It would be cheaper on the budget though, Jim,' Ted tried to persuade him. 'With my SFO skills, I could assess the situation quickly and hopefully accurately, without you having to bring anyone else in from outside.'

'The "hopefully" isn't filling me with confidence, Ted, it has to be said,' Debra Caldwell told him. 'Whether or not you're going to be there in person, how safe is this operation going to be? We'll need a full, watertight risk assessment not only for our officers, but for the public as well.'

'Whatever you do, if any members of the public watching have got their mobiles out and pointing at the action, don't let anyone hurt the bloody dog,' Jim told him. 'You know what the public are like with animal casualties. We'll never hear the end of it if there are pictures of it twitching and whimpering all over social media.

'Get the bloke, by any legal means. He's our main hope of finding the Big Man and the rest of them. But don't hurt the woofer.'

Sometimes, no amount of good, solid police work brought the desired results. But then occasionally, though not often enough, a bit of sheer good luck moved a case on fast to its conclusion.

Or the gods he didn't believe in were smiling down on Ted.

Today was one of those days.

They'd had a few false starts. Jezza was fielding calls of possible sightings, trying to keep her patience when Chinese whispers seemed to be at work with the description.

'No, Maurice, bonny lad. Brown with a short coat. Black and long-haired is a *Groenendael. Similar breed, different colour. ... I don't care if the man's all in black and looks tough, it's the wrong type of dog.'

'No, sarge, our man is definitely five eight, five nine with black hair. Not older, shorter and with white hair.'

She was doing a lot of eye-rolling and at one point commented aloud to no one in particular, 'Is there some kind of Belgian Shepherd convention in Stockport today? I never knew there were so many around.'

Ted had made the time to write everything up and pass his report to Jezza. She was right. He hadn't been on top of things so far.

He was standing next to her desk when the main office phone rang and Mike answered it. Jezza was still on her phone, repeating yet again the description of the right dog.

'Boss, a sighting that sounds hopeful, at last,' he told Ted, a note of excitement in his voice.

Ted crossed the office and took the call.

'An area car has spotted a possible for your dog man, Ted,' Kevin Turner told him. 'He was walking north on the A6 then turned off to the right. It's just possible he's heading for Heaton Norris Park. At least that's not too populated an area to try to apprehend him. I've told my officers to stay close by but to keep a low profile. It's all the back-up I can spare you for now.'

'It's a big open space to lose him in, though. Right, we're on our way. Can you send our Taser officers soon as, please.

'Jo, you go with Virgil. Rob, you drive for me, so I can phone coordinate on the way. Vests on, everyone.'

'Have fun, boys. Don't get shot or bitten. Think of the paperwork for us poor sods left behind,' Jezza called after them as they hurried out of the door. There was a wistful note to her voice. She always liked to be in the thick of the action.

Ted spent the whole of the short drive glued to his phone. He needed everyone to be in the right place at the right time if this was going to go the way he wanted it to. To result in the safe apprehension of a potential witness or suspect, without serious injury to anyone involved.

He would have liked longer to set things up. To check there was no way the man could leave the park by a different entrance. Above all, to make sure there weren't too many members of the public around who could be put at risk.

It was just possible the man was looking for stragglers from the cuckoo gang. Ones Ted and his team didn't yet know about. Which would mean more than one arrest to be made. He was crossing his fingers that it was just their man on his own, exercising his dog.

He was relieved to hear one of the Taser officers on their way was PC Susan Heap. He knew she was reliable. Accurate. He thought it was a racing certainty they'd have to stop the man by force, if he was all the things Ted thought he was. But he was equally as anxious to stop the dog. A specialist officer was on his way, with the means to control the brute whether or not they managed to drop it.

Ted would have loved to have had the resources at his disposal to form a cordon round the park. But he didn't. All they could do was wait and go over what they planned to do.

Virgil went for a walk round inside the park, to see what he could see. As usual, he offered himself as the least cop-looking one of them all. Luckily, the way the dog man had gone meant he wouldn't have a clear view of the road to see any vehicles arriving.

Susan Heap and the second Taser officer turned up not long after the others, leaving their vehicle a short way back so it was less obvious. The dog van wasn't long after them and parked behind.

'He's let the dog off to do its stuff, boss. He's even picked up after it and put it in the bin, like a good citizen,' Virgil told him via his mobile. 'He's clearly not planning on staying long, though. He's called it back and put it back on the lead. Now heading back in your direction.'

'Is it the right person? Does he match the description?' Ted asked him. 'We don't want to finish up Tasering some innocent dog walker.'

Virgil repeated back Ted's earlier description and added, 'Let's just say there's something about the two of them that makes me want to give them a wide berth. I won't follow him straight away. I get the feeling he's observant enough to spot anything like that.'

Then he laughed loudly, a rich dark chuckle, and said, 'You too, honey. I'll be home as soon as I can.'

He rang off. Ted assumed he'd seen or felt the man's eyes on him and was trying to make it look innocent enough. A man calling his wife or girlfriend before setting off for home, after pausing for a driving break and a leg-stretch.

Ted spent a moment talking to Susan Heap and Laurie Bailey, the other Taser officer. Checking Taser range. Making sure his own timing was spot on in manoeuvring the man into exactly the place where he wanted to have a confrontation, if one was coming. Part of him hoping this was just an average dog walker. The other part was praying they'd get their man in the slim hope he might give them more information about the Big Man.

Then the man came into view, holding the dog on a short lead, walking briskly. Ted stepped forward, holding up his ID as he said, 'Excuse me, please. Police. I wonder if I could have a quick word with you?'

The man's reflexes were as fast as Ted had imagined them to be. His left hand slid down the lead to release the catch, while his right one reached round behind his back.

Susan and Laurie moved as one, Tasers raised, both shouting a clear warning.

'Taser! Taser! Taser!'

As the dog bounded forward, bunching its muscles ready to spring at Ted, Laurie's shot hit it smack in the chest. It half flipped in the air with a terrible yelp, before thumping to the ground, hard, where it lay twitching and trembling.

Susan's reactions were as fast and her aim as good. The man's hand hadn't had time to reappear before her shot took him down. Before he'd gathered his forces enough to do anything, both she and Laurie were on him, pinning his arms behind him and cuffing them, using a foot to clear the handgun which had clearly been in the rear waistband of his trousers.

The dog handler let them get clear before rushing over with his catch pole to make sure the dog was under control well before it started to regain its senses.

'Can I have your name, please, sir?' Ted asked the man, his tone civil.

All he got was a vitriolic outburst in a language which meant nothing to him. But everything was being recorded on both Susan and Laurie's bodycams, so with luck they could find a translator to watch the footage and tell them what it meant.

'I have to tell you that you're being arrested for possession of a firearm with intent to endanger life,' he cautioned him, then went on, 'You'll now be taken to the station where you will have the chance to consult with a solicitor. Do you understand what I've told you, sir?'

He didn't understand a word of what the man spat at him. But he could make an educated guess at its meaning.

Chapter Twenty-nine

Ted insisted on travelling back in the area car with Susan and Laurie. He'd had the man they'd arrested installed in the rear seat, hands cuffed behind him, seatbelt securely on, and Ted sitting next to him. He instructed Jo and Virgil to drive directly in front, Rob to bring up the rear.

Now that he'd seen the man close to, he was convinced his theory about special forces was right. He knew all too well, from his training with Mr Green, that such a man could kill with his bare hands even when handcuffed from the front. It would be much harder with his hands behind him, but still theoretically possible.

Ted also knew that the man would be trained to escape at any cost, including his own life, and that would be his primary objective now.

The weapon they'd recovered at the scene was a Beretta Px4 Storm, now in an evidence bag and firmly locked in the boot of the area car. It was a semi-automatic pistol, in wide use by law enforcement units, the military and special forces.

Ted tried again to ascertain whether or not the man spoke any English. He didn't get an answer in any language. He didn't expect to. If anything, the man looked faintly amused by the whole thing.

Once they arrived at the station, Ted took the unusual step of having the man locked in a cell immediately, rather than put into an interview room. He also had the handcuffs left on for now.

He went straight to the Ice Queen's office. He'd have to square any and all such departure from procedure with her. Luckily, she'd also done a couple of training courses with Mr Green in her own Firearms days, so she was unlikely to go against Ted's evaluation of the risks surrounding their suspect. She'd want to know his reasoning, clearly, but he was fairly sure she'd trust his judgement.

'He obligingly gave us a reason to have him remanded in custody. But I'd like a Firearms watch on him throughout while he's our responsibility,' he told her, after he'd outlined the arrest. 'Preferably two officers at all times.'

'You really rate him as dangerous as that?'

'I do. We were very lucky with the arrest. He clearly wasn't expecting us to turn up Taser-ready. If we hadn't, there would probably have been fatalities on our side. And the reason I want him keeping cuffed, if we can, is that he won't need a weapon to kill someone. We can't take that risk.'

'How are you going to proceed if you don't know if he can understand what's being said to him? We have to be so careful with this one. To draw the fine line between avoiding risks and not breaching his rights.'

'We'll try a translation app with him to see if we can at least find what language he does speak, then try to get an interpreter. But I'm serious, Debs. I want an armed presence while he's interviewed. Can I have one?'

'Leave it with me.'

He went next to stick his head round Kevin's door.

'Bloody hell, Ted, that was a close call. What if he'd had time to get his gun out?' He'd clearly already heard all about it.

'I know. But Susan and Laurie were excellent. I've just been to see Her Majesty to get Firearms in while we interview him. Can you please make sure everyone knows that this bloke can kill with his bare hands as easily as with that Beretta. I don't want anyone forgetting that or underestimating him.

'If we get done at a halfway decent time tonight we'll

probably go for a bevvy to celebrate getting him, if you want to join us. I'd personally like to buy Susan and Laurie one, if they're free.'

He was feeling pleased, though aware there was still a long way to go. He took the stairs two at a time to go up to the main office. His team members were visibly buzzing. They were possibly one step closer to tracking down the drugs gang, and the elusive Big Man.

'A swift one, after work, if we get finished in time. My shout,' he told them. 'Meanwhile I'm waiting on Firearms before we even attempt to interview our man. He's to be considered as high risk at all times, even when cuffed.

'The first priority, once the AFOs arrive, is to establish what languages he speaks and find a way to caution him. I'm going to conduct the interviews myself. Steve, I'd like you with me on this one. You're probably the fastest on your phone looking things up. I'd narrowed down half a dozen languages which sounded about right for what he said to the dog. We also need to factor in Albanian, from what Ian told me, although what I heard didn't sound like what the translation into Albanian came out as when I was looking. It's probable he speaks more than one language.

'Once we're ready to go, you and I will have a very quick briefing. I'm not putting you at any risk, but it is important that, more than ever, in a situation like we'll be facing, you do exactly as you're told at all times. Forget rank. With something like this, the AFOs have the final say on everything, even over me as SIO.'

He went back to his office while he waited. He wanted to start by up looking which military forces used the Beretta model the man had been carrying. That might help to narrow down his country of origin.

Anyone being arrested would normally be required to turn out their pockets while they were being booked in. On Ted's instructions, they hadn't even followed that procedure yet. Ted didn't want him fishing in his pockets without an armed presence. It meant they had no ID for him. No driving licence, passport, nothing. So no clue as to his identity, nor his nationality.

The first user country listed for the gun model was Albania. The information under that entry worried him. 'Albanian army and special forces.'

He searched a bit further and found *Batalioni i Operacioneve Speciale,* or BOS. Nicknamed 'The Unit'. Their motto, 'We better die for something than live for nothing', sent a chill through him.

On a total whim, he took his phone out, made a call and, more in hope than anticipation, left a message on the answering service which picked it up.

He didn't expect an answer so he went back to his own research. He was surprised when he was interrupted, not five minutes later, by a call from a masked number.

'What the bloody hell are you doing bothering me, Gayboy?' Green's voice snapped at him. 'What part of retired do you not understand?'

'Sorry, Mr Green,' Ted tried to sound suitably contrite. 'Thanks for calling back, though. I just needed some info and I thought you'd know. Can you tell me anything about the Albanian special forces?'

'The Unit? Steer clear, Gayboy. Punching way above your weight there. You thought The Regiment were bad? That lot are worse.'

The Regiment was the SAS. Green's old army unit. They had a formidable reputation. If he was saying the BOS were worse, then Ted hadn't overreacted with his precautions.

Ted heard a small but insistent voice in the background over the phone.

'Poppo? Are you coming back to play now?'

'I'm coming in just a minute,' Green's tone changed beyond recognition as he responded to the child, then he barked back at Ted, 'Now piss off and let me get on with enjoying my retirement. And don't call again unless it's urgent. Haven't you heard of Google?'

While he had his phone in his hand, Ted tried another call. He wasn't in the least surprised when it went straight to voicemail.

'Hi, it's Ted.' Then he groaned inwardly. Trev would know exactly who was calling him, which was probably why he wasn't answering. He pressed hurriedly on. 'Will you be back today? Only I may be a bit late. I've got a tricky interview coming up, then I want to take the team for a quick one. They've played a blinder today.'

For a moment, he couldn't think how best to end the call. He didn't want to gush or sound desperate. He settled for, 'Hope to see you later. Take care.'

It was a bit lame, as bridge-building went, but it would have to do for now.

'I'm not trying to tell you how to do your job. I've done it, and I never appreciated that,' Ted told the two AFOs who been assigned to watching their suspect. 'But I have good reason to believe this man is special forces. Which means that even without a visible weapon, he is to be treated as a serious risk and a threat to life.

'We haven't even searched him yet as I judged the risk to be unacceptably high to do so without armed back-up. We'll do it now you're here, then we can crack on.'

The two officers were young. Ted didn't know them by sight. There was no reason for them to know he was an ex-SFO. The way they were looking at him said they didn't. But he knew they were up against a dangerous and sophisticated gang and he wanted to raise their awareness of the risk.

He'd had a call from the dog handler shortly before he came downstairs to start the intervew. He told him the dog had been scanned and didn't have a microchip, as was required by law. But its collar was fitted with a GPS tracker. Which meant that its owner, or anyone else with access to the system, would know where the dog was at any given moment. So they might well know by now that it was in the hands of the police.

Steve was next to Ted, standing close, as the man was brought from the holding cells to be booked in and empty his pockets. Ted had been fairly sure he wouldn't be carrying anything which could identify him and he was right. All he had was a simple pay-as-you-go burner phone, no doubt with no stored numbers, which was unlikely to tell them much.

Ted was as vigilant as either of the AFOs as the man carefully and slowly emptied his pockets. He was no fool, although he showed no real concern. He must have known that the wrong move could get him shot.

Because he was being arrested for the firearms offence they would take his fingerprints and DNA, although there was a strong chance they wouldn't find him on record. If the Big Man was new to the area, it was likely his men were, too, and possibly even from abroad.

There was not a lot of space in the interview room so Ted asked for one of the AFOs to stand inside, with clear line of sight to the suspect the whole time and the other to stand in the open doorway. He didn't want to take any chances at all.

'I'm DCI Darling, this is DC Ellis. Do you speak English?'

No response.

Steve was working alphabetically through the possible languages. He found the translations on his tablet, starting with Albanian, and playing the audio.

'*A flisni anglisht?*'

The man did no more than lift an eyebrow and smile.

'*Govoriš li engleski?*' produced much the same reaction.

They could be in for a long and frustrating session, but there was no way Ted could charge him until he was convinced the man understood what was being said to him. He needed to offer him a solicitor and, if necessary, provide a translator.

The man let Steve work his way through most of the countries of southern and eastern Europe. When he got to Slovenia, he said, 'Yes, I speak English. No, I want no solicitor. No, I make no comment.'

'Can you please confirm for me that you understand the reason for your arrest? And that you understand you are going to be charged with possession of a firearm with intent to endanger life?'

Ted cautioned him again to have it on the recording, then asked the man his name.

'I understand the charge. I make no comments,' was all he could get out of him.

Jim Baker had come in for this one and was watching over the monitors. Ted took a short break to check with him that he was happy on procedure. He hoped the two AFOs really had taken on board his warning about the man and the danger he presented.

'No ID on him?' Jim asked, as soon as Ted walked into the room.

'None, but I didn't really expect there to be. His sort often don't carry anything which might identify them.'

'With any luck he'll be an illegal and we can just hand him over to the Home Office lot to send home. Will he talk, if you press him?'

'Not a hope in hell, I would say. You've seen him, Jim. He's a pro. He knows he risks nothing worse than being sent back to his own country, which probably suits him. I'll try, if you like, but I don't see any reason why he would tell us anything. We've nothing to bargain with.'

'I agree. We need to get him remanded in custody as soon as possible. And keep the armed guard on him until we can hand him over.'

'I'm going for a drink with the team, once all the paperwork is sorted. Are you up for that?'

Jim shook his head. 'I daren't, Ted. Bella will go off the

deep end if I'm not straight back. Who knew a wedding took so much planning, eh? And speaking of that, would your Trevor be free on Monday after work, by any chance? To practise this bloody dance? Only it's the hotel's quiet day, so they could let us in. And Bella's going to her sister's to talk clothes, or flowers, or goodness knows what she still has left to fuss over.

'She still doesn't know what I've got planned and I want to keep it that way. To make it a real surprise for her.'

'I'm not sure,' Ted replied. Jim was his friend, but he wasn't about to tell him the current situation between him and Trev. 'He's working all hours at the bike shop at the moment. His business partner's in hospital for an operation.'

'Serious?'

'We're not sure. Neither of us dares ask in case it's anything intimate or embarrassing. But I'll find out and one of us will let you know.'

Ted had asked Susan and Laurie to join them for drinks. He felt he owed them both one for their work, which had undoubtedly stopped him either being attacked by around thirty kilos of snarling dog, or getting himself shot. Kevin Turner was there too. Once Ted had sorted the drinks, he went and sat with him at a quiet table while the team let their hair down.

'Good result today, Ted. But here's to food poisoning, eh?' Kevin said as he raised his glass. 'You heard, I take it? I'm off the hook where the cruise is concerned. Stories of people puking up all over everywhere put the wife right off the idea.'

'Are you sure you didn't arrange it?' Ted asked him with a grin. 'So where are you going instead?'

Kevin made a face. 'Still abroad. Some place in Minorca that she's found. It looks quiet enough, though. I should be able to cope.'

Ted's mobile phone was ringing. He reached for it, hoping it might be Trev. The screen showed him it was his mother, Annie.

'I better take this, Kev,' he excused himself and went to find a corner away from the noise.

'*Helo*, Teddy *bach*, it's your mam. I hope I'm not disturbing you?'

'*Helo, mam*,' Ted tried to pronounce it the Welsh way as she had, to please her. 'I'm in the pub, just having a drink with the team.'

'Oh, sorry, *bach*. I just wanted to make sure you were all right.'

'You've spoken to Trev, then?'

'You know he phones me almost every day. He said you'd had a bit of a falling out but nothing more. I hope it's not serious?'

'We'll get through it,' Ted tried to sound confident. He didn't want his mother to be worrying. 'Look, mam, I have to go. I'll try and get down to see you, as soon as I can get a bit of time off. We both will,' he added hastily, in case it made it sound as if the rift was likely to be long-term.

'I'll look forward to that, *bach*. *Nos da*, Teddy.'

'*Nos da*, mam.'

Somehow, talking to his mother made him want to go home. Even if he knew there was no guarantee that Trev would be there. The team were all fine. Kevin was now deep in conversation with Jo and wouldn't miss him.

Ted went to put money behind the bar for drinks and asked Dave, the landlord, if there was any chance of a hotpot to take out. He didn't feel like cooking and he knew he should eat something.

'You'll get me into trouble, officer. I'm not supposed to be a takeaway. But I can help out a good customer now and again, so it's on the house. Just bring the dish back at some point.'

The house was in darkness and unwelcoming when he got home. Once again the cats had all been seen to, so Trev must have been in at some point during the day.

Ted would have a good few hours of paperwork the

following day. They were going to have some good results, with charges against four of the cuckoos, and now a possible member of the drugs gang in custody.

But then it was Sunday. And come what may, no matter how many Albanian drug barons popped out of the woodwork, he was going to hand over all responsibility to Jo and sort his home life out.

Chapter Thirty

Sunday morning. Ted was on a stakeout.

Alone. Sitting in his own car. Munching his way through a hot bacon barm, sipping tea from his travel mug.

He'd been there since first thing, so far with no sign of his target.

Trev never usually went to work on a Sunday, but with Geoff away, he had said he would be in to sort the books out. And if there was one thing Ted was good at, it was paperwork and organisation. If he could persuade Trev to let him help for the day, it might go some way to showing that he was at least trying to be as much of a husband as a police officer.

He still hadn't heard anything from him. He'd left a few messages, trying not to overdo it. He'd phoned Trev's friend Mark, from the karate club, guessing that's where he would be staying. Mark hadn't answered. He'd tried phoning the bike shop the previous day, to be told by Neville that Trev was with a customer and couldn't currently be disturbed.

In desperation, he'd phoned their mutual friend Willow, with a pang of guilt when he realised he had no idea how far on in her pregnancy she was now, so didn't know if his call would be intrusive.

'Ted! How lovely to hear from you.' Her tone, at least, was warm and welcoming.

'I'm sorry to bother you, Willow, I just wondered if by any chance you'd seen Trev recently? Or if he might possibly be staying with you?'

'Oh no, have you two had a falling out? I'm sorry. But no, sweetie, he's not at ours. Not unless he's broken in, that is. Rupe and I are currently in the south of France on a shoot.'

'I'm sorry to have called you, then. I didn't realise you were still working.'

'Good heavens, yes, there's an obscene amount of work for glamour maternity wear. So I'm getting paid oodles of money to lie about on a beach, looking serene and blooming. It's rather marvellous. I hope you track him down soon. I don't like to think of you two being at odds. And if he happens to call me, which he does from time to time, I'll tell him to phone you, at least.'

It was gone ten before Trev turned his bike onto the forecourt of the dealership and switched it off. As he was removing his helmet, Ted crossed the road and held out a paper bag from the bakery.

'Peace offering. Almond croissants. Your favourite. I remembered you were coming in to do the books, so I thought I might be able to help. I've booked the day off. Strictly Do Not Disturb.'

Trev's face remained stony at his words so Ted asked anxiously, 'If that would be any help?'

Ever-present good manners got the better of Trev as he said, 'Thank you. It's a kind offer, which I won't refuse.'

He unlocked the front door, stood aside for Ted to go in first, then turned off the alarm before locking up securely once more. The showroom contained thousands of pounds worth of stock in the shape of bikes and expensive accessories. They'd been lucky so far in never having had a break-in.

Everywhere was spotless and orderly, laid out for maximum sales potential and pulling power.

Not risking saying too much too soon, Ted followed his partner in silence through the sales area and along a corridor to the office, which was usually Geoff's domain. Trev's speciality was front of house. Out there charming the customers into parting with their cash. Or going out to drum up service contracts and replacement bike sales.

Ted was used to a certain amount of chaos, living with Trev. His partner always laughed off Ted's attempts to domesticate him and blamed it all on his privileged upbringing, with staff to clear up behind him.

Even so, Ted was shocked by the state of the office. Papers were strewn all over the desk and had overflowed into heaps on the floor. There were several dirty mugs, some with cold, untouched tea in them, dotted about. Some had left tell-tale rings on the papers on which they sat.

Trev saw his look and said, with a note of guilt, 'I know it looks a bit chaotic, but I didn't get as much office time as I'd hoped for, which is why I came in today. I did get us some new contracts, though, which Geoff will be pleased about.'

'It's fine,' Ted said, with more optimism than he felt. He didn't dare ask if Trev had been seeing any of the potential clients in the office. He hoped he'd always gone to them. 'It won't take long to get on top of this. Why don't I make a start in here? Are you going to do a stock-take?'

Trev frowned. 'I wasn't going to. It's not long since we did the last one. Do you think I should?'

Ted had taken off his leather jacket and hung it on the back of the door. He began by gathering up the mugs and heading towards the small kitchen to do the washing up.

'It might be a good idea. It would help with getting the books straight. Why don't you start on that, since you know what you're doing on that score? I'll get some sort of a system going in here. I'll give you a shout if there's anything I can't fathom out.'

It took Ted some time to sort things into some sort of logical order so he could work on them. Once he'd done that, he was starting to make some degree of progress when Trev came back into the office, looking concerned.

'Have you got anything on the sales sheets for a set of

leathers? An expensive one? Around fifteen hundred. Only I can't find it and I'm sure Nev or one of the others would have told me if they'd sold it, because that would be a good sale.'

Ted looked through the paperwork, now neatly sorted and in separate piles on the desk.

'Nothing here that I can see so far. Do you have some sort of a system in place, other than the till, to note what's sold? Or a way to sign out spare parts from stock so they get onto the right invoice? I don't know much about the spares side of things, but it does look from a first glance that quite a few have been used this past couple of weeks.

'You're sure the leathers haven't simply been tidied away somewhere? It sounds daft but could someone have put them out on display and because it's so obvious, you've not noticed?'

Trev shook his head. 'I've looked in all the likely and unlikely places. Ted, it's all getting a bit worrying now. What if I've had my eye so far off the ball that someone's nicked them?'

'They have security tags on, presumably?'

'Yes, of course. But there are tags there, in the shop which could have come off them. The leathers aren't there.'

'So if they have been taken, it's not an outside job, I'm presuming. It would have to be one of the staff, surely?'

After all his determination to be a husband rather than a police officer for the day, Ted found himself in familiar work mode once more.

Trev sat down opposite him.

'That makes it even worse. If one of the lads has taken them, that means they know I'm so useless at the management side of things that they're prepared to take the piss by stealing right under my nose. Not quite the situation I hoped to create for Geoff when he gets back.'

He looked and sounded miserable now. Ted put down his

pen and looked at him.

'Perhaps we can fix it, before he gets back. If it was someone who works here, who would you suspect, if you had to put your money somewhere?'

'Neville,' Trev said, without hesitation. 'Don't get me wrong. He's a nice bloke. Very loyal. Good, too. He can fix any bike. If he can't, it can't be fixed. He's taught me so much. He's been with Geoff for years. But he doesn't earn a huge amount. And he has a son. Keir. Nearly twenty now, I think. He's into bikes in a big way, but he doesn't earn much, either. We help out, with spares at cost price. But it's probably not enough.'

'So an expensive pair of good leathers, plus the odd spare part as needed, might possibly be a temptation too far?' Ted asked, standing up and getting his jacket. 'Right, come on, there's only one way to find out.'

'We're going round there? Ted, if you arrest him, think what that's going to do to the business. And what Geoff's going to say about it all.'

Ted smiled at him. 'I'm not going to arrest him. I'm not a policeman today. I'm your husband. Helping you out and putting you first. That's what you wanted, isn't it? Are you coming?'

As soon as Neville opened the door to them, it was clear that Trev was the last person he expected to see on his doorstep on a Sunday morning. Especially in the company of Ted, who Nev knew full well was a police officer.

'Hi, Nev,' Trev greeted him. 'Sorry to call unannounced on a Sunday morning. You remember Ted, of course. He's been helping me with the books and paperwork this morning. I wondered if we could come in for a moment? There's something you could perhaps help with.'

Ted knew, straight away. He'd interviewed too many guilty – and innocent – people not to be able to spot the difference a mile off.

Neville showed them into the front room but didn't invite them to sit down. Ted noticed that his hand was shaking when he closed the door behind him. He'd never noticed a tremor when he'd met him previously.

'I've been doing a bit of a stock-take this morning, while Ted went over the books. Only I can't find that good set of leathers anywhere. The one Geoff said might take a while to sell because they were a bit pricey. Perhaps they've been moved somewhere.'

Neville's eyes were darting from one to another of them, panic plain to see on his face. Then Ted spoke. Quietly, as ever.

'I had a thought, though. I have that sort of a suspicious copper's brain. I thought that perhaps, someone like yourself, Neville, with a young lad, into bikes – Keir, isn't it? – might want to get him something really good. Like those leathers. Maybe for a birthday or something. So that person might just take them home for their son to try on. Just to see if he liked them. Then he could take them back to work straight away and ask about a trade discount. And easy payment stages.

'Now if that person had forgotten to talk to anyone about the idea, or forgotten to put a note somewhere, saying that's what they were doing, it could be open to misinterpretation.'

Trev was staring at him in evident surprise. Neville was still looking from one to another, clearly wondering what on earth was going on. Ted carried on speaking in the same reasonable manner.

'It's quite likely that such a person wouldn't know that for a charge of theft, the prosecution has to show intention to permanently deprive the owner of the goods in question. Which would make the difference between a bit of a telling off and a prison sentence of up to ten years. Although that wouldn't be very likely for a first offence. But still. A big fine, and almost certainly being sacked from their work place.'

Neville's eyes had widened at the mere mention of a prison sentence.

'Of course, on the one hand, removing an article's security tags would tend to suggest theft. But then it would avoid the full-scale panic of setting the alarms off. And if the person had the intention of re-tagging them once they'd been tried on, say when they took them back to sort out a proper written agreement on payment terms ...'

He left the sentence hanging and looked at Trev. 'When are you expecting Geoff back?'

'Wednesday, unless anything changes with his treatment plan or whatever.'

'Good. Then I think you'll find that the missing leathers will be accounted for by then and all the necessary paperwork done. Sorry to have bothered you, Neville. I was sure there would be a perfectly simple explanation for it all.'

Neville didn't say a word as he showed them out. He wasn't sure he could trust his voice not to wobble. Trev was quiet. He didn't say anything either. Not until they were in the car and driving back towards the bike shop.

'I can't believe you just did that.'

'You wanted me to put you first. Above being a copper. That was me trying to do that. Being your husband rather than a police officer.'

'Can you do that, though? Shouldn't you have arrested him? Or got someone from the local force to arrest him?'

'He's a good worker, isn't he? You always seem to be singing his praises. He did something really stupid, but probably for a decent enough reason. What do you think are the chances of him doing anything like it again?'

'Zero, I would think. I thought he was going to wet himself when he saw you on the doorstep.'

'So it's sorted, then. Make sure you do get the paperwork in place. And try and give him a decent discount. I actually felt quite sorry for the bloke.'

Trev put his hand on Ted's thigh and gave it an affectionate squeeze.

'Thank you for that.'

'I know it doesn't completely make up for me being a total pillock. But it's a start. And in my defence, that's why I felt sorry for him. I was doing the wrong thing, but for what I thought was the right reason.'

'I'm sorry I behaved like a spoilt brat about it all.'

There was a pause, then Trev spoke again.

'I'll come home tonight. We need to talk. Get things sorted once and for all. We both made mistakes. And I want to talk to you about me going down to London. To talk to these other people, in the same situation as me. Possibly even this retired judge, if he's not a friend of Sir Gethin. I might as well make use of The Olds' modest pad to visit. And I'll see if Eirian fancies coming up to join me. I can perhaps help with her current sexual identity crisis.'

'That would be nice. Will you see the housekeeper again? Mrs Payne, was it? The one you were fond of? We saw her when you took me riding.'

Trev laughed, sounding much more like his old self.

'Oh, dear, Ted, we do come from different backgrounds. One doesn't have the same housekeeper for one's townhouse as one's country estate. It's someone new, I believe.'

The familiar note of teasing, and of fondness, was back in his voice. And his eyes.

'Right, let's go and get the rest of the work done and go home. We have a lot of catching up to do.'

Chapter Thirty-one

'For goodness sake stop wriggling, Ted. How am I ever going to tie this thing if you don't keep still long enough?' Trev said, exasperated.

'I feel a total prat,' Ted grumbled. 'A tie would have been bad enough, but a bloody cravat? I wouldn't even know how to tie one, without you helping me.'

'Well, I do know how to tie one, but I think it would be easier to do with one of the cats than you when you're squirming about like this. Right. There, that's done. You look utterly gorgeous, of course. I'd marry you myself if I wasn't already married.'

'You may well mock. If I think I look stupid now, I'm going to look even more ridiculous very shortly, standing next to Big Jim waiting for the blushing bride to arrive.'

'Have you got the rings?'

Ted patted the pocket of his waistcoat, something else he'd been complaining about.

'Ring. Jim refuses to wear one. But yes.'

'So let's go and do this. I'll drive there, then you can concentrate on your speech or whatever you want to stress about next. But you are definitely driving back, because when I see my *protégé* taking his new bride around the dance floor, much to her astonishment, I shall be in floods. The only way for me to recover will be copious quantities of champagne.'

The ceremony passed off without a hitch. Ted acquitted himself well at the reception with his speech. Short, respectful, and with a suitable touch of humour.

True to his word, Trev stood with tears unashamedly running down his face once the room was readied for dancing. Bella clearly had absolutely no idea what Jim had planned for her. Her face was a picture as he went and stood in front of her, large hand outstretched, and said, 'Mrs Baker, may I please have the honour of the first dance?'

For a fleeting moment, Ted had a mental image of a large grizzly bear, folding its big paws carefully round a delicate fawn, looking at the height difference between the happy couple. But they did look happy. Blissfully so. He could never remember such a tender expression on the face of his boss and good friend with the first Mrs Baker.

Once other couples began to join in, Trev dragged Ted up and whirled him around in flashy fashion. As they drew level with Jim and Bella, now doing little more than holding onto one another and moving their feet slowly, Jim reached out and tapped Trev on the shoulder.

'Trev, take my lady wife for a proper spin round the floor, please. You know my limits, and at least I know you'll behave like a gentleman.'

Laughing his delight, Trev swept Bella off to take centre stage. Jim looked at Ted and chuckled.

'Don't look so worried, Ted, I didn't cut in so I could dance with you. Let's go and find a quiet corner so I can rest my feet. These shoes are pinching a bit, and I could murder a beer after all that champagne.'

They got drinks and sat down, Jim surreptitiously slipping his feet half out of his shoes.

'You know I'm not good at all this stuff, Ted. No man hugs or anything. But I wanted to tell you that you've been a good friend to me, for a good few years. I appreciate all you've done for me, although it may not always have seemed like it at the time. And you've played an absolute blinder today. You and your Trev. Thank you.

'I wanted to tell you this myself, before you hear it on the gossip mill. And it may surprise you. I'm retiring shortly. I can finally get at my pension, so I might as well.

'But you haven't seen the last of me. I've been told I can continue in a civilian consultancy role. So I could still be SIO on some cases, for instance. But on a strictly as and when basis, rather than on constant call.

'That heart attack I had really scared me. As much as it did Bella. For a moment I thought I was really going to cark it. Then I thought of all the things I could be doing if I had more time, instead of endless meetings and number crunching. Spending some time with my grandson and that daughter of mine, for one thing. Not to mention with the new Mrs Baker.

'So I'm taking the chance.'

Ted raised his Gunner towards him and said, 'Congrats, Jim. I'm pleased for you. And I'm sure Bella will be thrilled. I'll miss you, though. If you're not going to be full-time, do you know who's taking over from you?'

'I was just coming to that. You've got a good record, Ted. This latest case has been complex and a PR disaster waiting to happen, but you've handled it well. Definitely the right outcome for Abigail. You've got four of the cuckoos arrested and you've plenty to charge them with. Including serious assault and probably even rape, too.

'We've agreed you can probably close the case on your Body in the Bowl. It's a racing certainty your unnamed Albanian was behind that, with his skills. It would have been nice to bring him to justice here, but far safer all round just to deport him back to where he came from.'

Ted took a sip at his drink. On the dance-floor, Trev and Bella were now jiving with no inhibitions. She was laughing at the way he was sliding her about with ease.

'I would have liked to get nearer to the Big Man. I'm worried he'll simply have moved somewhere else and will start again. The same for Data.'

'Even if you found your dwarf, I think we both know full well he will be squeaky clean. No record, cast iron alibis for any times of interest to us. And above all, any business interests he has will be as pure as the driven snow.

'Drugs might still succeed in getting him. They know what they're doing and they're tenacious. It might not be your collar at the end but I know you're not bothered about the glory. As long as we get the bad guys.'

He took a long pull at his sleever of bitter. Smacked his lips in appreciation and smiled at the sight of his new bride, clearly having the time of her life.

'So not surprisingly, when I was asked to suggest a successor in my role, I gave your name. You know the Chief and the ACC would both back you like a shot.'

Ted opened his mouth to start to say something but Jim waved him to silence.

'Before you get too excited, the top brass have made it clear that as part of the cuts, they're looking to fill the post with an experienced DCI, not a Det Sup, to save money. So there'd be no promotion or associated pay rise. Just a bloody lot more work for no more money. You'd have to be mad to want it.

'Plus the catchment area is growing all the bloody time, as you well know. You probably heard we had to send some officers to the back of beyond in North Wales a couple of weeks ago. Something serious and only a local bobby and a couple of sheep there to deal with it.

'So it would bring you more work. Less time with your Trev,' he was looking at the way Ted's eyes were glued on his partner, enjoying himself on the dance-floor. 'Probably ulcers to match Kevin's and no more money for your pains.

'But DCI Darling, Head of Serious Crime, has a certain ring to it, eh?

'What do you think, Ted? At least talk to your Trev about the idea. And give it some serious thought.'

She walked out of the shop and bumped straight into the young man who was hurrying in. Her bag fell from her grasp to the pavement, items spilling out and rolling about.

'Oh, gosh, I'm so sorry. How clumsy of me. That was entirely my fault,' he said hastily, already crouching down and trying to grab the packet of biscuits which was rolling determinedly towards the curb and the road beyond.

'That's all right,' she told him. 'It was an accident.'

He looked up at her and gave her the full force of his smile. Down's Syndrome, he thought to himself as he looked at her. Although that wasn't what they called such people on the porn sites. She spoke as if her tongue was several sizes too big for her mouth. She had the funny eyes, but she wasn't a total munter. Best of all, her clothes were okay. Not cheap stuff. And the biscuits and things in the bag were market leader brands, not supermarket's own value label.

He stood up, looking at her. He could tell she was weighing him up, taking in the expensive new threads the Big Man had sorted for him. The new haircut, which he was secretly thrilled with. He had just the right touch of expensive aftershave to be intriguing rather than overpowering.

'Do you live round here? At least let me carry your shopping back home for you, by way of an apology for being so clumsy.'

'Yes, I have a flat.' When she mentioned the address, he had to make a conscious effort not to react. He could have hit the jackpot first time out with this one, with a bit of luck. He could hardly believe it. 'Do you share with flatmates?'

'No, I live by myself. I can carry my shopping by myself. But do you want to come and have a cup of coffee?'

'I'd love that, thank you. But I insist on carrying the bag. I'm new round here. I've only just moved here, so it's lovely to

meet someone. A friendly face. What's your name?'

'Robyn,' she told him.

'That's a pretty name.' He stopped walking, put the shopping bag in his left hand and held out his right one to shake hers. 'It's nice to meet you, Robyn. My name's Data.'

The End

Made in the USA
San Bernardino, CA
16 January 2020